CLUB X
ZOMBIE IN THE FRIDGE

S.P. SOMTOW

DIPLODOCUS PRESS
2023

Club X • Zombie in the Fridge
© 2023 by Somtow Sucharitkul

This novel originally appeared as Episodes 26 through 77 of a
serial in Amazon Vella.

ISBN Paperback Edition: 978-1940999-84-5

To Income, Title, Zen, Bingo,
Thala & Japan
the real-life members of Club X
What a wild year we had!

ZOMBIE IN THE FRIDGE

1

Prelude: The Cardinal's Report

To His Excellency, the Supreme Secretariat of the Crystal Pathway Project

Blessings and Greetings.

I am the supervising officer of the Seventeenth Arondîssement of the Transdimensional Map and it is my pleasure to report to you the current situation with regard to some interesting developments in our sector, in particular with a certain species on a world rather quaintly known, in their native parlance, as "the world." As if there could be only one!

In this world I've established an observation center in a corner of a world-wide religious structure (one of many on this planet) and my main task is now to nurture the project and push it through its next stage. My "secret identity" — to borrow an expression from their popular literature — is a major religious leader — indeed, a 'prince of the church". I wear red robes and, in public, I have to remember to keep my head on at all times, even though my head prefers to be stored in a subzero replenishing chamber.

Compassion is essential; after all, one possible consequence is the destruction of this entire fork in the Crystal Pathway, and the demise of a million worlds — yet what is that demise, really? For in the prime dimension, it will be as though those world had never existed. One cannot pity that which has never existed.

Let me, therefore, speak of more positive things.

Our human counterpart, whom I have partially let in on our secrets, has been seeking out the ones we need ... the Crystal Pathfinders.

It is they who can navigate the spaces between the worlds, who can die from possibility to possibility.

To this end, working out of a neglected office in a remote corner of their world, disguised as a religious mission, we have managed to bring together four possible candidates. Any one them could be the one we seek.

They have some inkling of being special. But no idea of just how special they *could* be. And this is wise, because surely the wrong candidate would be driven mad by such responsibility.

We have tested them — intellectually, through the use of puzzles that they need to solve — and emotionally — though being of tender years they tested themselves as much as we did. We do not interfere in their curious desires, their loves, their petty quarrels, because we have not really studied enough about this species to know how important such emotions are. We will leave them to their strange little passions and hope that they survive them and reach maturity.

Recently, I made a visit to the nursery where they are being housed — known as a "boarding school" — run by a legitimate arm of the religious institution to which our own department has been clandestinely attached.

I did a bit of shock therapy, dismantling my human soma in their presence, and otherwise projecting an extreme alienness whilst the rest of the humans were temporarily placed in time stasis. They took it well. None went mad, and their putative ringleader even found a clever way to tell the story while disguising it as fiction.

I should like to present a brief summary of the four juveniles under consideration.

First, there is the one called "Kim". He is a bundle of neuroses. He changes his hair color from time to time; it may be some kind of mating ritual. He is always trying to solve puzzles, especially the one known as Rubik. He has emerged as their leader. It seems like a strange choice. Kim's unusual ability is in putting the pieces together. His mind holds trillions of possibilities open ... like those cube puzzles he loves to solve ... and he sees a pathway through to the desired solution ... that is why he is a candidate for Crystal Pathfinder.

Second, there is the one named "Fluke." I made some errors during first contact. I may unwittingly have introduced a bit of trauma into his mind, but should he make the grade, I daresay we can fix it. He is a musician, and he is a polymath. He knows extraordinary things, whether it's the history of a tarot card or the meaning of "porphyria." His memory is eidetic, especially when it comes to music. He rarely speaks but he exudes charisma.

The one named "Polo" is of some interest. Like the other three, this one possesses a penis, but often acts in a manner that resembles the opposite gender; this I find a little hard to grasp; one rarely finds a world where fewer than seven genders is the norm, and I myself take great delight changing during the mating season. This species is stuck in a binary physicality, but mentally, they do break free of the chains of biology. Polo's ability to be fluid in this is what has also given him the talent to walk the Crystal Pathway. His talent is extraordinary — he could almost be one of us.

And then there is the one named "Danger." Danger doesn't live in the real world. He has one foot on the pathway even without thinking. He walks the pathway and doesn't even know it exists. He has the most natural talent, but I would say that he is in the most danger ... he could lose his soul, if such there be, even before he has discovered it.

Perhaps I should mention the one named "Donut." This one, oddly, doesn't actually have a penis, though it seems to be a requirement of their "school." She has managed to infiltrate the group and though she hasn't walked the pathway on her own steam, she has contrived to be present on numerous occasions when the others did it, so was carried along by the tide of the other's abilities. However, who knows what may emerge in her case? In their world, there was a great composer — an organizer of sound-patterns — who was, in fact, blind. Thus it is that we can never take any of these creatures for granted. We cannot always be smug in our cultural and technological superiority.

That, in sum, is who the membership of this "Club X" comprises. Will we discover the *one*? Or will we discovered *several* ones? Perhaps that is to much to hope for. But here is the truth: this obscure corner of the countryside in a third world country, contains, tucked in a closet in an old wing of a school, a transdimensional nexus so powerful that it *must* be mapped, and most importantly, *controlled*. A nexus is inherently unstable. We must know all there is to know ... before it slips away.

As I submit this report, the "Christmas holidays" are ending. The fledgling pathfinders are returning to the school and I will file this report and step out of the way ... it is, after all, *their* story, and I am but a facilitator.

I flit from mind to mind. The stronger their connection to the pathway, the easier it is for me to see their thoughts. But sometimes the view is blurred ... we can only relay the story in bits and pieces, leaping from mind to mind ... such is the fragmentary nature of consciousness in this species. I imagine the humans find it equally hard to find the continuous thread of thought in the minds of their cats and dogs.

It is, it would appear, time for the next stage in the children's rites of passage. We call this *mindfulness of mortality* ... the idea that death is but a doorway, another way to enter the Crystal Pathway, albeit a method that cannot easily be reversed. It is time to bring forth the zombies! Let's have a bit of fun, shall we?

We'll start inside the mind of the boy-girl Polo. I am focusing on Polo now....

Focusing....

2

Where We Keep Our Zombies

Polo

This is pretty weird but I'm actually sitting in a train with Sister Evangeline. Just the two of us. Just two happy travelling companions, girls together. Girls with a little extra, I guess you'd say. We're going north, to some kind of secret nun hideout. Sister Evangeline has been assigned to take me to a special meeting with the Cardinal, but *I* take this trip as a way to delve into a few more of the nun's dark secrets. She's the most interesting nun you could ever imagine.

Yeah, so I asked her, over a shared plate of fried rice, "How can you live this way? Aren't you actually living a lie? Shouldn't they have excommunicated you by now, or defrocked you, or whatever it is they do to naughty nuns?"

"Come now," said Sister Evangeline. "The church is compassionate about human frailties. They don't push us out into the cold. Rather, they ... find a place for us somewhere."

"Compassion?" I said. "Or is it sweeping things under the rug?"

"This fried rice is a real feature of the Thai railways," said Sister Evangeline. "It's quite famous, you know, has been for half a century. You should eat up."

"Bit spicy for me," I said, noting that Sister Evangeline was munching contentedly on a *prikhinu*, a tiny and lethal pepper which can easily burn a hole in your throat if you're not careful.

"My dear boy — or are we a girl today?" said Sister Evangeline, "spice is, literally, the *spice* of life. You haven't lived until you've chomped down on some spicy little ... oh! I shouldn't talk this way, should I? You're a mere child."

"And you're a *nun*."

"I must seem ridiculous to you," she said, "but God does have a purpose for me." She looked out the window. The rice fields reeled by. Now and then, a water buffalo or an elephant wandered by, or else we saw a clump of stilted huts. "Though I haven't figured out what that purpose is, yet. Have you?"

The train rattled. The sky was a clear bright blue, the rice fields emerald. I didn't know why I was on this journey at all, but then again, I had nothing better to do. The school vacation wasn't quite over yet and home could be excruciating, especially the dress-up high society parties where perfumed aunties fawned over me.

And Sister Evangeline was very interesting. She was eccentric of course — St. Cecilia's isn't just *any* school, it's almost kind of like Hogwarts in the weirdo teacher department, except the school is a shiny, modern thing of glass and chrome where you don't expect any dark secrets, let alone vampires, flying nuns, and aliens with removable heads.

I really agreed to this trip because I was looking forward to the train ride. Not the fields or the buffalo. But I was hoping she'd tell me more about her time in New York. About her ambition to be a singer before her vocation dragged her in another direction. About what it was like to be a Catholic nun studying psychiatry. About how she managed to conceal the fact that she still had a penis.

"Why don't you just ask?" she said.

"What? You read my mind?"

"Ha, no, but there's a little bit of me in you."

"I think I resent that."

Sister Evangeline finished her rice. The she got up and left the cubicle, and I drifted off. When I woke up she was staring into the night, and she smelled of tobacco. I thought I saw tears in her eyes and wondered if I should be trying to help.

She was pretty interesting, for a nun.

I drifted off and didn't wake up until we pulled into the station, a one-platform blip called Baan Kraduk — *Village of Bones*.

After an interminable and bumpy taxi ride, we arrived at an unpretentious boarding house on the grounds of a rundown church. The town was more or less a ghost town. Not even a 7-11, I mean not *one* ... the tiniest hamlet in Thailand has a few of those! ... and basically a single intersection.

The church had a wrought-iron fence painted white, but the paint was peeling in parts. To my surprise, the gate had the logo of St. Cecilia's — our school — even though this was an overnight train journey away. Nuns of our school's order walked by without saying a word. An old woman in traditional hill tribe costume ushered us into the sitting room and, as soon as we sat down, a bell rang and we had to go up and enter the inner sanctum.

Cardinal Crank had his head on, and was sitting at a desk. There was a sofa by the door, and an armchair near his desk. Oddly enough, he didn't have a computer.

"Sister," he said, looking up, "sit down over there and I will summon you if I need you. I wish to speak to the boy alone. Don't bother to kiss the ring. Take notes, if you like."

"Yes, Your Eminence," said Sister, curiously humble, and sort of slithered to the sofa which was completely in shadow.

The Cardinal motioned me to the armchair by the desk. He said to me, "I am speaking to all of you individually because I need to file a report."

"To the aliens?"

"That's such a fuzzy word, Polo. Ideally, in the universe, we should never feel we are among aliens."

"So ... the interview. You want to know how I do it. How I can switch so quickly, so convincingly, from boy to girl. Without makeup or magic tricks. What the transition is like."

"Actually, Polo, we don't need to know that. We already know how that works ... it's *you* who don't have it entirely under control yet ... but we will teach you. Train you. If you wish, and only if you wish. We're not brainwashing you, this isn't some kind of suicide bombing madrassa training ... it's about ..."

"Brainwashers never believe they're brainwashing people."

"This interview is about ... life and death. How do you feel about it?"

"What do you mean?"

"Is death the end? Or is it a doorway. And if it's a doorway, is that doorway one-way?"

"I guess I don't think about those things. I'm a teen."

"Would you prefer that the doorway be one way?"

"Maybe," I said. Now, I don't know why, but I was starting to get upset. Something inside me, like a big hard lump I'd been trying to swallow for years. Something that had always been there but I was so used to it, I didn't even realize I was in pain.

"And if the doorway swung both ways ... would you be willing to step through? ... always knowing you could come back at any time."

"But that would mean there is no death."

"Perhaps it would," said the Cardinal. "Now my question is ... has someone close to you ever died?"

That got to me.

There were things I hadn't thought about in ... I don't know, ten years. Suddenly, my gorge rose. I thought, for sure I am going to vomit on the cardinal. *Control yourself!* An inner voice. Oddly enough, it had the slightly Indian accented tones of the guru in my dreams.

"I had a twin sister," I said. "She died when we were seven."

And I was deluged with a welter of images. We were fraternal twins of course but we still looked alike and we loved to dress as each other. Suddenly I remembered beating my fists on the little coffin. The sun was bright in the temple and there were hundreds of people in chairs in an open courtyard all dressed in black. In the distance, monks were droning.

I remembered screaming. I remembered being dragged away.

I remembered the look on my parents' faces. Not "poor kid" but more like ... "how embarrassing." Dodo and I had our own maid. She took me away and I sat in a small air conditioned pavilion nearby and bawled and I missed the false cremation ... but once most people had left, and it was just close family, the maid brought me back out for the real cremation.

"You look pale," said the Cardinal.

"I'm fine."

"No. Now, to my left, there is a door to an inner room. You probably thought it was my private bathroom, but actually it's a storeroom and a pantry. Run along inside, dear, and you will find a very large refrigerator. Get yourself a bottle of our fine, ice-cold spring water — it's from wells on the grounds of our very first mission in the Swiss Alps. Pour yourself a glass and get one for Sister Evangeline as well..."

I got up.

"Be careful though," I heard him say as I started to go around the back of his desk. "That's where we keep our zombies."

I giggled. Nervously.

Well, all right. I crept behind the Cardinal, walked under a huge crucifix that dominated the wall behind him, and went into the little room. It was freezing in there. The refrigerator was indeed, huge, almost taking up one narrowish wall. It had a wooden door. In fact, it looked as much like a closet door as a fridge. When I touched the handle, a coldness seeped through me and I almost let go.

This is ridiculous, I thought. What the hell, I'm just getting a glass of water.

I opened the refrigerator door.

The light was blue.

I knew that light. Pale blue light always means something weird is about to happen. There was a smell, too, like a rice field after lightning. Unseen energy. I opened the door wider. I didn't know if should scream in advance or wait until I saw whatever horror they kept in there.

But the fridge held nothing but bottles of spring water. Rows and rows of bottles. I laughed again, relieved. I grabbed a bottle.

Then something grabbed *me!*

I yanked my hand out. The bottle went flying and smashed on the floor. Something was clutching my wrist. A hand. A *severed* hand, and it was wriggling, and I couldn't shake it off. It was going to cut off my circulation! So, I admit, I screamed.

I mean *scream queen* screamed.

I was flailing around trying to dislodge the hand which just wouldn't let go, it was squeezing my wrist harder and harder and I think I tripped over the shards of water battle and I went barreling backwards into —

Sister Evangeline's arms.

And there was Cardinal Crank, peering down at me. He touched the hand and stroked it and said, "There, there, off you go." The hand detached itself from me and scampered back to the fridge. The door was still open and it let itself in.

"Calm down," said the Cardinal. "I did warn you."

He swung the door of the fridge open all the way and I saw them now. Hands, fingers, a foot ... even an eyeball, swivelling on a stalk. "Just the body parts, mind you," said the Cardinal. "Whole zombies are kept in a much bigger facility, of course. Well, strictly speaking they are not *zombies*, as that's a very specialised subcategory. That would be the Haitian religion, which is only nominally Catholic."

"And you, Cardinal, are *you* 'nominally' Catholic?"

He started laughing. "Such a wit, my dear," he said.

"I think she's going to vomit," Sister Evangeline said.

"You'd better take her back," he said.

Sister took me by the hand and opened the door of the pantry and pushed me through to the Cardinal's office.

Except it wasn't the Cardinal's office.

It was a place I had never seen before ... but I knew where I was. Well, it depends on what you mean by the word "where."

I guess the shock of being attacked by a zombie hand must have thrown my equilibrium a bit out of whack. I had become unmoored from the real world. And now —

I was walking down a glittering corridor. A *crystal* corridor. The walls were studded with brilliant excrescences that sparkled like gobs of cubic zirconia.

Ahead, there was a spider on the wall. Well, at least that was a lucky omen.

Except that I was walking really fast and according to the rules of perspective, that spider had to be at least the size of a standard poodle.

Shit! I had propelled myself into the Crystal Pathway and that meant I could be anywhere in the entire universe.

I wondered if my cell phone would still work....

3

Don't Shoot the Piano

Kim

During the school break, my relationship with Fluke evolved. I mean, there were times when it was the same as, you know, before all that happened. I used to be bothered when he would just sit there, or play the piano or some other instrument and be in his own world, and I would sit in another corner and solve the latest Rubik's and we wouldn't speak for hours. But now, after our new round of adventures, I came to realize that those moments doing nothing were some of the happiest times of my life.

My parents decided to take Fluke with us on our New Year break. We didn't go to some big fancy ball-dropping festival, but we did spend the week in a sleepy town somewhere in Europe. You know, where my father always disappears to anyway, on business; he joined us from Vienna.

My parents got a two-room suite and they took the master bedroom, so we sort of hung out in the living area and would fall asleep right on the comfy couch, after a hard day of sitting around doing nothing and barely speaking. Sometimes we woke up with our arms wrapped around each other, sometimes I would open my eyes to find his feet in my face.

There were, of course, things we didn't talk about. But it was not *that night* when we thought we had killed the man in black. There was a new thing we couldn't talk about, and that's because neither of us remembered it too clearly, maybe as a blur, or a dream … the night we thought we were going to have "another go" … but I guess we were too exhausted. What happened? If I couldn't remember … it must have been nothing.

As far as each other … we are still all innocence. As for girls? There are parts of Fluke's life that are still closed to me, but he once said he had a girlfriend in New Zealand.

It was idyllic, except…

Well, there was this piano store in the small town. In an alley, between our hotel and our favorite restaurant, which was an Italian one even though we were actually in Germany (I think.) And every day, on our way back from carbonara and pizza, he would stop in the window and look longingly at a piano. It wasn't a Steinway or anything. In fact I'd never even heard of the brand.

So … the third day I catch him standing there again.

"If you like it so much, why don't you go in and play it?" I said.

"I will."

So he just walks into the shop and asks if he can play the piano — in German, if you please! — and he sits down and starts tossing off a fugue. And pretty soon several people have gathered around, both inside and outside. They were rapt. Almost as though they were in church. No amount of puzzle-solving would ever get me that kind of response. It's something to do with *emotion*, and I'm not good at reading that.

The piano has a tinkly, *small* sound — I realize it's not actually a piano but a piano-like instrument, something old. It's smaller even than an upright, but it doesn't pluck like a harpsichord. It's either an antique, or a decent copy of one.

When Fluke plays any instrument, but especially the piano, he lights up the whole room.

I make movies. I win awards. I can't light up a closet, let alone a concert hall.

I reached in my pocket for the icosahedron Rubik I always carry nowadays. The others are just too easy. I started moving it around blind, not even bothering to take it out of my pocket. I can see the colors in my mind's eye anyway.

The crowd was gathering and the fugue was crescendoing. I watched the gleam in their eyes. But Fluke's didn't gleam, you know, he said it all in sound. When you looked at his face he didn't seem to be there, even … he was in another place.   And I wasn't there with him.

"Don't *do* that all the time!" I whispered.   Well, more like *shouted* in a whispering kind of way.

He ignored me.   Just went on playing.   And it was exquisite.   And the customers were transfixed.

I'm not sure why I was getting so furious, but I have learned not to blurt things out quite so often, so I just kept it to myself, until I felt like I was going to explode.

Actually I stalked back to the hotel by myself.   When I got back to the suite, I was even more amazed.   My parents were both there — which *never* happens — and there was a chocolate cake on the coffee table with seventeen candles.   They even had some champagne on ice.

"Whose birthday is it?" I started to say, but —

I'd *forgotten*.   It was *Fluke's* birthday.   "Just kidding," I said.   "Of course I knew."   How could I not know?   His birthday is just the day before mine!   Then, suddenly, I remembered something —

We were around five years old. Fluke's birthday party was at our house.   My parents gave him a new violin.   A hundred year old half-size French violin, they told him.

What did I get?

Some piece of paper.

That was twelve years ago, so I don't think I was supposed to have any hard feelings about it.   I smiled, a little wanly, and went to help my mother put out the cake plates.   The cake was shaped like a keyboard, with little slabs of dark chocolate and white chocolate as the keys.   I couldn't help noticing that the keys were wrong … there was a black note in between every white note instead of skipping at E and B … and for some reason that made me more furious than anything else.   There were exactly seventeen notes.

One for each year.   Such simplistic crap.

My dad … as all of you know since you've been following my life … never appears at all, but he always seems to be around for my birthday.   Normally I love to see him.   Not because of the unending sequence of new cameras, sponsoring my little movies, and unusual Rubik's cubes he brings me from all over the world, but because I'm a lot like him.   My mental condition must be genetic.

So if I say, "I could eat a horse," Dad says, "No, you couldn't."

If he says "I can't, I'm tied up at the office," I say "What kind of knots?"

And so today, I say, "I wish Fluke would stop playing the piano all the time," and my Dad says, "He only plays about four hours a day."

My mother joined us from the inner room.

She lit the candles and my Dad switched off the lights.

And at that moment, Fluke walked in the door. He was just glowing. He didn't even notice that the lights were out and there was a chocolate cake on the coffee table!

Flushed with excitement, he cried out, "Uncle, there's an original Krummheimer in that piano store in the town square!"

"Not any more," said my Dad.

As we sang *Happy Birthday* to my best friend, the door of the suite was thrown open and something was being wheeled in. The lights came back on and two personnel from the piano store where removing a floral cover from —

It was the piano thing from the shop in the town square!

"You bought him the Krummheimer for his birthday?"

"Uncle, this is incredible," Fluke said. "No one in Thailand has ever owned a real live fortepiano."

My mother said, "Now you have to understand, we're actually going to "lend" it to St. Cecilia's. But we will do that it your name. It will be *your* fortepiano, on loan for the duration of your time there, so you'll be able to do all the early music you want with the authentic sound. Of course when you're famous you'll be able to have many old these instruments and you might make the gift to St. Cecilia's permanent...."

Fluke didn't even bother to have a slice of cake. He was already playing. It was beautiful.

Frustration just exploded in me and I just left everyone and went into the bedroom. I sat at the edge of my parents' bed and sulked.

"Are you jealous?" my mother said.

I didn't answer her.

She said, "The last time you sulked like this was when we gave Fluke a violin, twelve years ago."

"And I got a piece of paper."

"Where is that piece of paper now?

"I don't know. In the trash."

She sat down beside me and took an envelope from her bedside table. She put her arm around me. "We retrieved it."

She put the envelope in my hand.

"We've been holding it for you for the last twelve years. But now that you made a movie with your classmates for so little money and it won awards, your father and I think it's time you got to do something big. So open it now."

I opened the envelope. I took out the paper. It was dated twelve years ago and it was a receipt for the purchase of five bitcoin at the cost of 25 baht per bitcoin, in my name.

"But —" I said. "Those are worth over a million baht now! Maybe even two million baht each!"

"Yes, son," she said. "You can make even get a real film crew for that. Or some top Thai actor. Or some really cheap washed-up Hollywood one for a one-day cameo. And I've arranged for you to be able to access it whenever you need it. Call your father's secretary and she'll help you. But don't blow it all. You only get one shot. Who knows, if you wait twelve *more* years, you'll have enough for some epic fantasy series."

I was flabbergasted. Getting this piece of paper had been a major trauma of my kindergarten years. Now I realized my parents had thought very carefully about what to give me and what lesson I should learn twelve years later.

"Now," my Mom said, "you're probably wondering what your present will be this year."

"I am."

"But your birthday's not until tomorrow, so today you should be happy for your best friend." She swabbed at my face with a tissue and I realized I'd been crying. "He's probably waiting for you to go out and give him a hug."

That night, I'm lying on the couch and it's almost midnight, and Fluke is still playing. And talking to me while he is playing, which is confusing; I'm not really sure how he can do that.

He's saying to me, "Did you know this piece was actually composed because some rich guy needed music to put him to sleep every night? It's supposed to work as like a musical sleeping pill."

"It's not working."

"Hey, tomorrow's a big day. Before midnight you and I will be on a plane back to Thailand, and within 24 hours we'll be in Weird World again ... with all the vampires, aliens, and magic nuns you can imagine. Plus we'll be sharing a room again. Maybe the nuns will let us push the beds together."

"That'll be the day."

"Okay! It's midnight! What do you want for your birthday?"

"Um ... nothing. I'm sorry I ruined your big moment."

"You gotta want *something.*"

"No, seriously, I'm good."

"Okay — I'll give you a kiss."

"What — no!"

He stopped playing. He came over to the couch, spread out his arm, and he kind of tensed his neck and took aim.

I panicked. I dodged and my head banged against the coffee table. I yelped.

"Shit! A concussion?"

"No," I gasped. "But I've got chocolate cake all over my face, and a candle up one nostril."

"Ok. I get it that there's an undercurrent to our relationship that makes you nervous. I suggest a compromise. I'll lick the cake off your face."

"I'll have to shower afterwards, get your filthy sputum off my cheeks."

"We can do that, too."

4

Donut for Breakfast

Danger

When the holidays come, my friends all go away. Some go to Phuket or Chiangmai, to their country houses. Some go to the French Riviera or Gstaad. Some go to Disneyland. Some even choose to chill on their Bangkok estates. I stay at school and spend time with my mother, the cook.

She only has to cook for the nuns, for Father Vichai, and for a few odd stragglers who get stuck in school during vacation, so it's actually the time she does her best work.

She excels at simple, basic Thai dishes like chopped chicken fried in basil over rice or sweet green curry, but the nuns come from all different countries so she has an international repertoire, too. Buddhist monks have to eat whatever is put in their begging bowl, but these Catholics can eat three meals a day, and they can drink, too. In fact, apart from their funny costumes, they are much more secular than our monks. As you know, they sing and dance. And they love a glass of wine sometimes. And....

Breakfast, for instance. When I'm not in school, my mother has me deliver the food over to the convent in a trolley, so I know the menu by heart.

Father Vichai only has coffee. Sister Evangeline has rice porridge with pork. Sister Edward likes patongos dipped in condensed milk. Sister Euphemia likes her toast burnt, and covered with a double layer of raspberry jam. The other nuns are of lower status and eat whatever they're served. Today, as it happens, it's doughnuts.

The thing is, my mother does it all by hand, from kneading the dough to cutting the doughnuts so they're not perfectly round but all slightly different ovals. Her doughnuts drive Kim crazy.

She puts in a pinch of cinnamon and nutmeg and doesn't use too much sugar. She has to get up at five a.m. to do this because it takes an hour and a half for the dough to rise.

It's good bonding time. I sit in the kitchen and she kneads dough or whatever, and we don't talk. Sometimes the staff walk past and they call me "khun noo" which is kind of embarrassing because I'm hardly a "high society" kid. In fact if I get less than perfect A's I'm liable to be sent back to a government school and have to give up my nice blue private school shorts.

So this morning, around six, I'm sitting in the school kitchen and my mother is making doughnuts … and who should pop in but Donut.

"Hi," she said.

"You're management," I said. "You shouldn't fraternize with the help."

"I'm a school vacation orphan, too, like you."

"Come and lick this dough," my mother said.

"Thank you, Khun Tui," she said. Rather precious of her to refer to the cook as "khun" but maybe Donut was just trying to act egalitarian. She took a lick of the wooden spoon. "Stunning!" she said. Then she shared it with me.

Donut was actually pretty nice, really, I guess. Despite her being with the Club most of last term, I never got completely used to her. And she would get in the way of all our relationships. She was always complicating things. Maybe that's just something they do. Girls I mean.

My mother went to the larder in the back to get more yeast and Donut squeezed in beside me at the kitchen table. She looked intently into my eyes. "I really wanted to talk to you," she said. "About Polo."

"Polo?"

"I had a dream last night … it was disturbing … do you think you could …."

Donut pulled a silk-wrapped deck of cards out of her blouse. "I just got this from Club X," she said. "I know you don't really need it but … maybe it will help you focus."

"What was your dream?"

"Well … I mean … part of it was a bit private, but…."

"You had a *sexy dream* about *Polo?*" I didn't know whether to be annoyed or jealous. "Did he come to you as a boy or a girl?"

"Um ... both. That was the cool part. The uncool part was that he turned into a zombie."

Nervously, I gobbled down one of the nuns' doughnuts. "I've been uneasy since getting his text," I said. "Where he said he was running off with his new BFF, Sister Evangeline, to see Cardinal Crark. But he'd be back in time for the first day of school."

"Which isn't until Monday, and it's only Saturday ... but the nightmare...."

"What exactly was the nightmare? You can skip the x-rated parts, I suppose," I added, because, as I say, Donut still made me nervous.

She said, "He put his arms around me. He said, 'I'm lost.' Then he became very cold. I mean, *cold*. It was like I was with a corpse. He was moving, but he was dead at the same time. Look, read the cards."

"Okay, okay."

I unwrapped the deck. I was getting dizzy. Was it because she'd kept the cards inside her blouse, close to ... I couldn't helping noticing ... a little bit of cleavage? The cards actually felt hot. I almost dropped them. Then as I started shuffling, my mind started whirling, as it does when I'm about to get a vision....

"I don't need to read them." But I started to lay them out anyway.

The Moon. Illusion. Desolation.

I closed my eyes. I saw —

Polo hurrying down a hallway... sort of a school hallway but ... glistening, covered in crystals, suffused with cold blue light.

The Fool. The start of a journey with an unknown destination. Not looking as you step off a cliff. I saw —

A crystal mountain. A ledge. And Polo running straight towards it, blindfolded.

"He's in danger," I said.

"Duh, yeah," she said. "What are we going to do about it?"

At that moment, my mother came back from the larder. 'Good morning, Donut! Playing a card game with Danger, are we? But he's got a job to do. Be a dear and take the nuns' breakfasts over to the convent building."

"I'll help him," Donut said quickly, and I gathered up the cards and wrapped them and stuffed them in my pocket. I got all the food into the trolley and we went out the back door where there was a path leading to the nuns' quarters, through some thick trees.

We walked quickly; breakfast was running late. I was aching to talk about Polo, but before we knew it we were in the nuns' sitting room and having to serve them their toast, porridge, and whatnot. The unease I'd felt when Donut told me about the dream had only grown when I saw the first two cards, and now it was really gnawing away at the base of my skull.

The sitting room was a spartan place, with non-matching chairs and a lone crucifix looking down on the nuns. Sister Euphemia was holding court, seeming pretty lucid for a nun with Alzheimers. At least she was fully clothed this time! "Ah yes, the stigmata!" she was saying. "I felt really blessed. And it didn't hurt one bit. Floating in the air was fun, too, though I got a nasty bump when I hit the ceiling."

"Breakfast, Sister?" I said, giving her her burnt toast. "I've already put on two layers of jam. Is it enough?"

"Such sweet children," she said, patting me on the head. I ignored it because foreigners don't realize how insulting that is.

Donut patted her back, causing the Thai nuns to look daggers at her for her impertinence.

Sister Euphemia said, "Be a dear, will you, and bring us some milk from the pantry?"

A chance to resume our conversation! "I'll go with her," I said.

The pantry was behind the sitting room and we went in and closed the door.

There was a tray with some glasses, and a pitcher, but the pitcher was empty so Donut went to the fridge. "Don't!" I said, sensing danger.

"Don't? It's just a refrigerator."

She opened the door.

A cold blue light came streaming out. The light sparkled with crystal dust. An alien music, high-pitched, thrummed.

Two hands … purple from cold … reached out and grabbed Donut's wrists. "Polo!" she gasped. She squealed.

"I told you not to open the fridge!" I shrieked.

Too late. She had been pulled inside and the door slammed shut. No glittering blue light. Nothing.

I stood there with my mouth open.

I don't know how long I was standing there, but eventually Sister Euphemia came in.

"Where's the principal's daughter?" she said.

I pointed at the refrigerator, looking, I know, like an idiot. "Donut — she got pulled into the —"

Sister Euphemia said, "What nonsense are we talking about?" She opened the fridge. I looked inside and there were some apples as well as a large plastic container of milk. She took it out and poured it into the pitcher, and shut the fridge.

"Come on, Danger," she said. I picked up the tray of glasses. "I wish you children would stop playing hide and seek all the time. Come and give the Sisters their milk, and I don't want to hear any more nonsense about a Crystal Pathway."

But I never mentioned any Crystal Pathway, I thought.

I hurried back to the school building as quickly as I could, the pushcart clattering over the uneven flagstones. My mother looked up from her cooking and asked me if I was okay.

"I'm not," I said. I reached for my phone and started texting. Kim and Fluke had to come back to school early. We had to find our friends and that meant we had to go back through the closet again. Without a map.

I couldn't go in there alone.

I needed Kim, because he was the one who could always put pieces together and find the pattern. I needed Fluke, because he knows so much about everything. And they needed me ... because I live with one foot already on the Pathway.

Frantic, I texted with one hand while devouring my mother's awesome doughnuts from the other. The message wasn't getting through.

They must be on the plane right now, I thought.

I was going to have a sleepless night.

And nightmares.

5

A Message from Danger

Fluke

We got Danger's message when we were waiting for our luggage at the airport. Suvarnabhumi is an architectural marvel that doesn't make sense. You can't find a toilet when you need it and the doors aren't numbered the same inside as they are outside. But it's home.

Our phones both went off at the same time. Kim's was a standard ring, mine is a Bach prelude. We both looked at the same time and our luggage sailed right by on the conveyor belt.

Come back to school NOW! the text said. *Polo vanished down the Pathway!*

"What do we do?" I said to Kim.

"We're supposed to go back to my house first, pack our school stuff, then leave on Sunday," he said. "But I supposed I can tell the driver there's a change of plans."

"Won't you parents be pissed?"

"I'll handle it," I said.

We had to wait for the luggage to come all the way around again — at this airport, that is not a short wait because that conveyor circles for *ever* — then we drag our stuff out to where Vichit, Kim's driver, is waiting. Vichit is standing close to the exit and pushes both our luggage trolleys, one with each hand, expertly navigating through the crowd like an inner voice of a Bach fugue.

We get into the car, a white Fortuner, a surprisingly bourgeois car considering how much money Kim's parents have. It's already evening.

"Vichit," Kim said, "drive us straight to school."

"Your parents told me to —"

Kim slipped a crisp thousand-baht note over to the front seat. "It's an emergency," he said. "You can bring us our things tomorrow. C'mon, they'll never notice. They're in Europe, for God's sake. Just do it."

He waved another thousand.

"Money is power," Kim said, laughing.

Vichit sighed and kept driving. I knew he would do what Kim wanted. It wasn't the money, really. Kim was pretty spoiled. His family, the household staff — even the teachers, especially since he managed to get Cardinal Crank down to present an award. I couldn't fault Kim's parents, though, because the spoiled me, too. I love his mother. His dad is rarely there, but he does pick up the check.

Well. Okay. We drove on.

My friendship with Kim has many sides. His parents don't know how complicated it is. They didn't mean to cause a problem by giving me that fortepiano, but somehow, there *was* a problem. Kim doesn't believe that people love him. I guess that is the problem.

I'm different. Everyone loves me. They don't say anything, but I feel it. My whole life, I have been floating on an ocean of love, and maybe I don't appreciate it. I back away from it because it's overwhelming. Kim yearns for it, not seeing that it's already there. It's one of the ways we fill each other's empty spaces.

His tantrum over the fortepiano took even me by surprise. We're growing up, and our feelings are hard to tame. If he gets all emotional this term, maybe it's my turn to be the quiet one.

"Kim?"

He was already asleep. In one hand, there was a Rubik's cube.

On the back of the front seat, I started fingering a fugue with one hand. My other hand joined it. The four parts wove silently in and out. It's fugue that connects the dots in the cosmos and music that gives it meaning. I alone could hear the music now. My fingers moved, swift as a cat.

The driver took the expressway, avoiding Bangkok completely. We missed the sweeping spectacle of Bangkok at night. We passed through ghostly rice fields, lit only by a half-moon.

We said nothing. There was a warm feeling just being together.

The terrain grew hillier. We passed through a densely wooded patch before coming to the gates of St. Cecilia's.

When we arrived, the school wasn't even open for registration. Sister Edward's desk wouldn't open up until morning. Luckily, we hadn't returned our keys at the end of last term. It was past midnight. We skipped the lobby completely and went round the back to the old building. We tried to find Danger first, texted him a few times. Knocked on his door. Listened. No one insider. Not even snoring.

"He's asleep in his mother's quarters," Kim said. "He hates to sleep in school alone. We'll see him tomorrow. Let's do some scouting on our own."

"Sister Evangeline knows something," I said.

"What do we do, bust in on her cell? She'll scream rape!"

"Nah," I said. "She's modern."

"And we can reach the convent how?"

"Through the closet," I said. "Polo taught me that!"

"Hare-brained," Kim said. "Anyway, we can't get through the closet door on our own. We all have to do it together."

We opened up our room, threw in our luggage, then went up the back staircase to Club X.

Kim said, "You'll see, there are some changes. I'm not spending all the bitcoin loot on making a movie when our club needs improvements. I called in a few of them from Europe. I'm hoping one of them has arrived. We really need it."

But when I opened the door, I didn't notice at first. It was just as dark and lived-in as before. The old sofa might have been dusted. Maybe those old busts had been polished a little.

"In the shadow. Near the closet."

I squinted.

"Turn on the light?" I did. The lights were new. Brighter. Not sure I approved.

So, what else was new? A paint job. That was nice, but hardly something we couldn't live without. Then I looked over to the corner he indicated.

Oh! We had a refrigerator! A tall, shiny, full-sized fridge!

And, standing in front of the fridge, pulling at the handle with all her might, so fierce in concentration that she hadn't even noticed us come in — was Sister Evangeline!

She saw us and gave a little scream.

"What are you doing in Club X?" Kim said.

"What are you doing in school? No one is due until tomorrow."

"We got an urgent note from Danger. He said something's happened to Polo. And you know something," I said. "Or you wouldn't be trying to break into students' fridges."

"Well, help me," Sister Evangeline said. "I can't even get it open."

"Why do you want to open the fridge?" Kim said.

"Well, it makes no sense, but I thought *Polo* might be —"

"Don't be silly," I said. "Polo's not in the fridge. Especially not *this* one. Kim just had it delivered."

She went back to yanking at the handle. "He — might — be!" she said, grunting. "Haven't you kids learned *anything* about this place yet? *Anything* can be true here." She pulled so hard she flew backwards and banged into the wall.

Kim said, "You'll never get it open. Here."

He walked over to fridge and touched the handle with the tip of his index finger and the door immediately swung open. "It's the same technology they used in iPhones before face recognition," Kim said. "I keyed to the fingerprints of all our members. We don't want strangers stealing our stash of chocolate."

We looked inside.

A fine blue mist came from inside. There were some Diet Cokes. And a chocolate cake with both our names on it. Danger must have been up here earlier.

But there were no gender-dysphoric schoolboys on the shelves.

And yet —

Sister Evangeline was pointing and screaming. I told you! I told you!

A hand suddenly reached out of the fridge! It held a Coke can and was wildly shaking it! "No! Don't shake it!" I screamed. Suddenly, the hand popped the can, spraying us with sugar-free fizz. Then it flailed around for a moment, before pulling the fridge door shut.

"We didn't see that," I said. I went to the door and used my finger the way Kim had used it and it opened again.

Nothing. Not even stains from an exploding Coke can.

"Told you." Sister Evangeline abruptly turned, opened the closet door, and slammed it shut. She had taken the short cut to the convent. Through the Crystal Pathway.

"After her!" Kim said, and now it was our turn to pull on a doorknob. Pulled and pulled. It was one of the most uncooperative doors I had ever met.

"It's a door from a badly-written novel," I said ruefully. "It only opens when the plot demands it."

"We need Danger," Kim said,

"No. We need ... *us*. I mean, the quality of being *us*." Together, we *could* open it. Even without Danger. We just needed to pool our power. That's why Kim and I were always together ... because the two of us were a bigger force than just two people. We filled each other's gaps.

"Kim," I said.

I put my right hand on the door. He put his left over mine. I felt electricity. Blue light tingled, leaping from his fingers to mine. We were like like voices in a fugue, one chasing the other.

Blue light played over our hands.

I thought of Polo, lost in the labyrinth.

I looked into Kim's eyes. *Is this love?* I thought. His eyes were fierce and wild. I gathered my inner strength and tried to meld with his. There were sparks. There was blue fire, bone-chilling.

The door slowly creaked open.

Kim said, "There's nothing in here but a coffin."

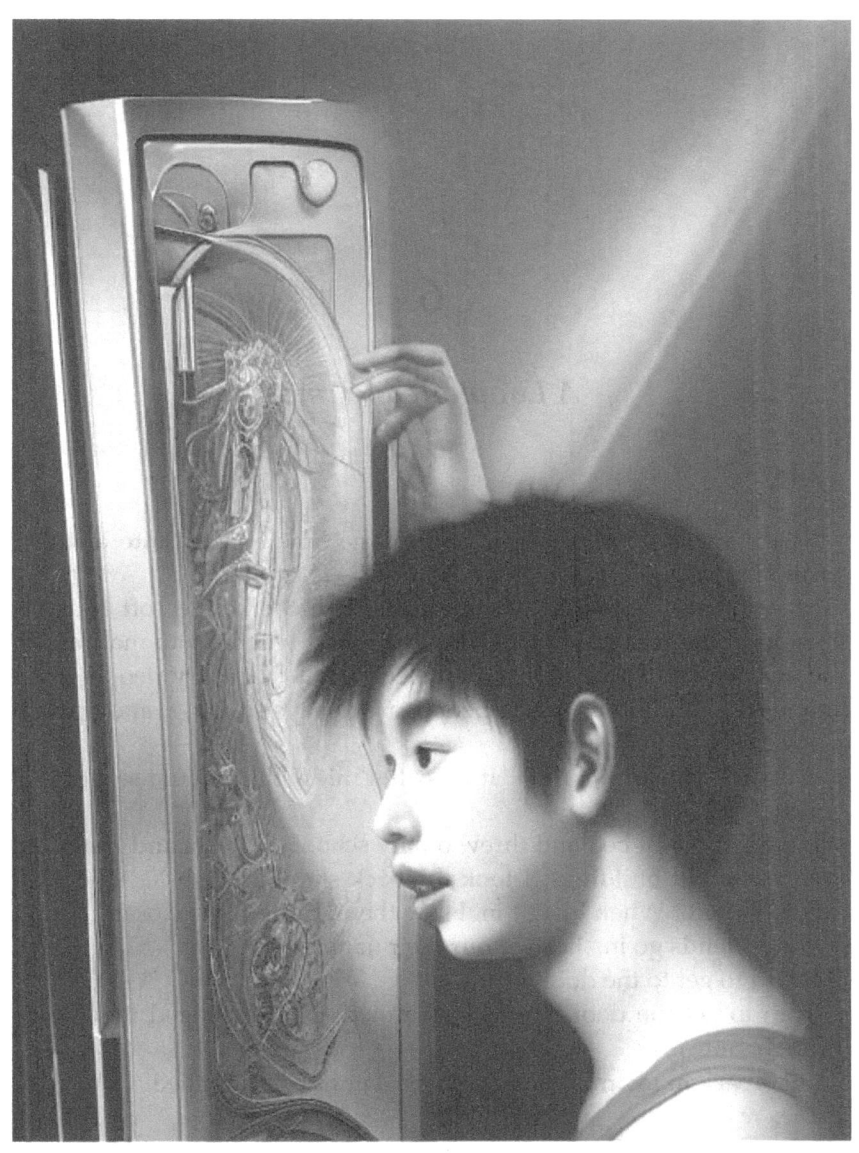

6

A Loophole in Time

Danger

I did have a sleepless night, and by the time I jerked into a sitting position I realized I was probably too late.

My mother's quarters at St. Cecilia's are not like the soft beds we sleep in in the residence hall. The bed is just wood — no mattress — and a woven plastic mat. And an electric fan. Country people don't care for air conditioning; rich people are always freezing, and putting on sweaters, even in summer.

It wasn't hard to wake up. It was after midnight. I could sense it.

They're here!

I jumped out of bed and threw on my school uniform, and I sneaked over to the old building. I took the back stairs to Club X. The door was unlocked. When I went in, I saw the light from the closet ... and I saw my friends go in. I called our their names —

I tried to get to the door —

I ran to get the door before it slammed and I managed to squeeze through, but ...

I was back in my mother's quarters. I jumped out of bed.

They're here!

I threw on my school uniform and sneaked over to the old building. I took the back stairs to Club X and ...

This happened already.

I jumped out of bed and threw on my school uniform —

Stop!

I forced myself to slow down.

Time itself slowed down.

I moved across the floor of Club X in a weird, swimming, slow-motion way. I was speaking but the words were all slowed down too, and deep, rumbling.

I was in a loop. I was waking up in my mother's quarters again. Running up to Club X again.

Squeezing into the door and — *whap!* — back to the beginning of the loop. And it was getting slower and slower and slower....

Slow down. Think.

Polo was down the rabbithole. Fluke and Kim managed to push through to the Crystal Pathway. Who else was there who could help? Who else had access? Dr. Strange? But school wasn't even open yet, and anyway, Dr. Strange wasn't coming back this term.

If time was in a loop, where was the loophole? Who had another key?

I was slingshotting back from the closet door to my mother's place again. I had to resist … resist …

And now time was slowing down even further. Each step I took toward the door was like I was stuck on a high-gravity planet.

The faster I tried to get to the door, the longer it was taking.

I needed to think in a counterclockwise way …

I jerked up into a sitting position *again*. Maybe the hundredth time. But this time I was figuring it out. It was harder and harder to travel along the path toward the door … I was meeting more and more resistance taking the timeflow in the right direction … what about reversing it? … so I just twisted myself around and ran as hard as I could *against* the stream. And that was *easy*. In a split second — I don't know how I did it — I was in the garden of the principal's residence. Just popped out and back in again, the way warping must feel. Yeah. I warped. And again! And the door opened _

"Donut!" I shouted.

She came out of the door — walking backwards. I caught up with her, held on to her as hard as I could. I couldn't understand a word she was saying because her speech was winding backwards as well. I sort of pushed against her hard, my arms around her as she backed right into me, and I could feel time itself *rattling*, as if it didn't know which way to go. I stood like that, I don't for how long, making the timestream slow to a halt, then stop, then slowly … agonizingly …

reverse itself.

"Let go," she said, "I gotta go back in."

"Go in where? Last time I saw you you vanished into a fridge in the nunnery."

"Well, yeah, obviously, that's one of the ways *in.*"

"Into what?"

"The Pathway. You know. I was looking for Polo. Then you came and got me out. Good thing, too. I was losing my way. Let's find that refrigerator and go back in again."

"No," I said. "Come with me." I kept pulling and time righted itself. "Are we in the same universe now?"

"What are you talking about?"

"Listen. You know that Polo vanished down the Crystal Path. I felt it. I sent a message to Fluke and Kim and they came back to school early — and now *they're* gone too. When I try to follow, I'm stuck in a time loop. I managed to get out of it by thinking myself backwards which means I've altered time."

"Ooh, Butterfly Effect," Donut said.

"Well, it's done now," I thought.

"Maybe when we go back to school tomorrow, we'll discover that the nuns have all become dinosaurs?"

"How could we tell the difference?"

She laughed.   Then she said, "I think the best way to find the entrance is to walk in the opposite direction. The universe is curved. We'll get there eventually."

"Yeah, after about a jillion years."

"No. We can get to the Pathway through the convent. Come, I'll show you."

She showed me how to sneak into the basement of the convent — "That's what I showed Polo before," she said — and we tiptoed past where the nuns were gathered for some late night chanting and went down into a place full of nun clothes. *This is where we switch from Wonderland to Narnia,* I thought, as we waded through stacks of fabric and found our way to a corridor in lined with familiar striations of crystal. We turned a corner — and stumbled on, almost tripped over —

A coffin.

And who should be banging on the coffin but Sister Evangeline? She was in a state. She was kneeling over the coffin, pummeling it with her fists and singing opera. When she saw us she gurgled to a stop in mid-warble.

"Good, you're here," she said. "Help me wake him up."

"Who?" I said.

"You know very well," she said. "He's the only one who can help sort this out."

"It's true," I said to Donut. "Dr. Strange knows more than anyone except the Cardinal."

"He might not even be in there," she said.

"He is," said Sister Evangeline. "I buried him myself."

I stood up and looked around. There were crystals in the walls, but they were embedded in huge gray stones, like a mediaeval castle. Wilted tapestries hung from the walls, with illustrations of forlorn knights and bored-looking distressed damsels. There was a tatty throne on a dais. There was even a stone with a sword stuck in it. All the trappings of high fantasy — but soiled and threadbare. Light filtered in from a high, arched window.

I said, "I think I know how to summon Dr. Strange."

I whispered in Donut's ear and she laughed. She whispered in Sister Evangeline's. The nun chuckled.

We all took a deep breath and chorused, at the top of our lungs: "Good morning, teacher!"

We heard a muffled sound coming from inside the coffin. "Good morning, children. And how are you?"

"Fine, thank you? And you?"

"Fine, thank you!"

"Very good." But before he could tell us to sit down, we all screamed, "Sit up!"

The lid of the coffin flew off and indeed, Dr. Strange sat up. His eyes were bloodshot, and he roared like a movie monster. His fangs glinted.

I panicked. I hid behind Sister's habit.

He cackled. Then he reached into his mouth and pulled out a set of plastic fangs, the kind in Halloween costumes, and he got out of the coffin.

"Can I help you?" he said.

35

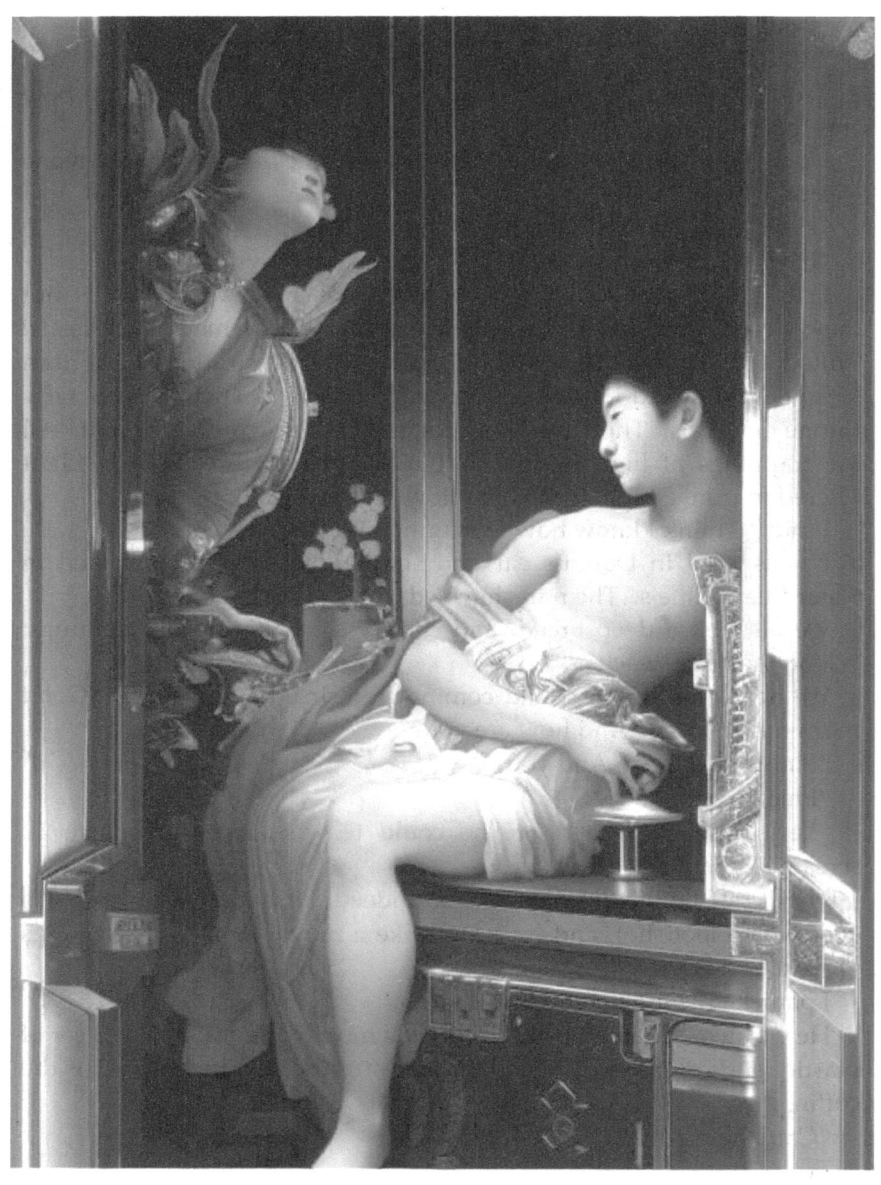

7

Coffins 'R' Us

Kim

There was a coffin, and suddenly Danger and Donut and Sister Evangeline were there, too, and they were banging on it and hollering. I ran toward them and collided smack dab into a wall of — *nothing!*

Suddenly, the coffin was all by itself and everyone was gone.

And I saw them running towards the coffin from the shadows ... then pounding on the coffin and screaming — and then they vanished again!

I tried again. I held Fluke's hand we tried to crash the barrier together.

Nothing! The whole scene repeated itself again. And again.

We were stuck in a loop!

We could see them. I'm not sure they could see us.

Considering the barrier was made of *nothing*, it sure hurt!

After about a dozen more loops, I realized that this was not the way to make it work. I resisted and could feel the loop *give* a little. I fought harder. And *harder!* We jerked free and I had one foot in the door. One foot in the real world, one foot in the pathway between dimensions. Fluke was behind me, in the real world.

"Put something in the door to keep it ajar," I said. I could see Fluke floundering around inside Club X, looking for something to wedge into the doorway. He found something — a bust of Brahms.

Then with all my might I threw myself in the doorway, trying to stop the force from dragging me back into the loop. As I lay on the floor I could feel half my body being pulled into the loop.

"Plant yourself by the doorway inside Club X and hold on tight!" I said as he pushed the bust the doorway, planted himself firmly against the edge and pulled me out.

Brahms held. The way between worlds was still ajar.

I went into the club and sat down with Fluke.

I said, "This is like when you're solving a puzzle and you're stuck on one move, and you keep doing it again and again even knowing that it doesn't work."

Fluke said, "Or like trying to write in the last voice of a fugue, you've gone every way you can except backwards."

"Wait a minute," I gasped.

"Backwards," he said. "Retrograde. Sometimes the only way the tune will fit the fugue is if we play it backwards. Kim, get Brahms out of the doorway."

"No! We barely got it open!"

"Trust me!"

I eased the bust out and planted it back on the shelf.

"Now," Fluke said, "we're going to start walking backwards."

The closet door — dimensional gateway groaned shut. I felt a sense of hopelessness, as though the people I was close to were imprisoned in some other world and I would never reach them again.

"The emptiness," Fluke said. "That's part of how it operates."

"*It?*" I said.

Fluke said, "There's a something out there that doesn't want us to know the answers. Danger knows best. I feel it too. You don't, of course, so take it on faith."

"I don't do faith," I said.

"Step back."

Do you know how when you're solving a puzzle, and it's *so* hard at first because only one or two pieces have fallen into place? That's how it felt to walk backwards, with the power of time's forward motion dragging you into the future. But suddenly it was faster.

We were walking backwards through time as well as space. I felt myself shrinking into a baby, shrinking down the evolutionary ladder … we were two mice scampering across a field, no, lumbering brontosauruses, tiny paramecia, proto-viruses, then ….

We were ourselves again. Backing right into a coffin in the middle of a crossroads in the Crytal Pathway.

Looking backward, the door to Club X was ajar. The bust of Brahms was still holding it open. I don't know how that happened since I distinctly remembered putting it back on its shelf.

Across from us, on the other side of the coffin, were Sister Evangeline, Danger, and Donut. They were pounding on the coffin with their fists.

I said, "You should stop. He's not gonna come out."

"But he has to," said Sister Evangeline. "Polo disappeared on my watch, and only Dr. Strange knows how all this transdimensional gateway stuff works!"

"Your watch?" I said. "Do you have one?"

"Why?" Sister asked.

"Because, Sister Evangeline, Dr. Strange won't come out until sundown."

Sister Evangeline tugged at what looked like a rosary ... but was in fact an old-fashioned watch on a chain. A watch with hands. "Don't ask," she said, handing it to me.

I held the watch in the palm of my hand. The watch was a watch with hands. But I couldn't see the hands ... just a blur. I showed it to Fluke.

"The hands are going around so fast you can't see them," he said.

"Why is that?" Donut said.

"Because," Fluke said, "we are *outside time.*"

"So it's every time in the universe, all at the same time?" I said, thinking that this was my worst nightmare — I hate chaos.

"Saying it's every time at the same time is a bit like saying it's every color in the same color ... you just get white ... no color at all," Fluke said. "We need to somehow ... focus it, like a prism. This is Danger's department."

"Danger, take the watch. Do your thing."

"What time is sunset in Thailand today?" I asked.

"6:28," Fluke said.

"The human google speaks," I said.

"I can't do this alone," Danger said.

So that's how we ended up with the five of us, reaching across the coffin, our arms like a five-pointed star, with Sister Evangeline's pocket watch in the middle ... all of us trying to *drag* the time to 6:28.

"It feels like trying to snag Moby Dick on a fishing pole," Fluke said.

"Who's Moby?" I said.

"I've heard of Dick," said Donut.

"Quiet," Danger said. "Help me focus."

We used all our collective mind power to pull at the hands. It was like lassoing a dinosaur. We pulled and pulled and —

Got it!

The watch stood at 6:28 exactly. The coffin started to rattle. Someone was trying to get out! There was a rhythmic rattling sound, as though something was bouncing back and forth against the lid. It crescendoed. More like a pile driver now.

"It's not opening," Donut said. And then they all looked at *me*. Even Sister Evangeline.

"He's trying to get out ..." Danger said. "I can feel him straining against the — the —"

"Crossroads," I said, realizing it only as I was saying it. "Vampires are buried at crossroads so they'll get confused and not be able to come out at night."

Danger said, "You do know everything about vampires."

"Except I don't believe they're real."

"Porphyria," Fluke said.

"Come on," I said. "Let's push the coffin out of the X."

We got around to the left side and gave it a push. It didn't move. "Needs a concerted effort," I said. It might have weighed a ton, but there were five of us. We counted to three and shoved with all our might and it moved ... just an inch out of alignment with the X ... and all at once the lid slid to the crystal floor.

Dr. Strange stepped out of the coffin. He was looking pretty decrepit, and he started to dust himself off, sending noxious clouds up our noses. "Thank you for releasing me," he said. "You don't know what it's like, being stuck in a box for centuries. Time seems to stand still!"

"Apparently it *did* stand still, Dr. Strange," Sister Evangeline said.

Dr. Strange perched himself on one end of the coffin. He looked at us. He seemed a lot older, and somehow, even paler than last year.

"I didn't expect you to be back so soon," Fluke said.

"It's not him," Danger said.

I looked into Dr. Strange's eyes and I could sense what Danger felt. The eyes were bloodshot, sunken. The skin was so pale it glowed. He was leaner. And when Dr. Strange looked at us, he had an unnerving gaze. As if we were a platter of juicy steaks.

"Don't be frightened," he said. "You rescued me. I wouldn't *ever* drink the blood of someone I owed a favor too."

That wasn't reassuring.

"But before we go our separate ways," Dr. Strange went on, "it would be an honour to know your names."

"Are you kidding, Dr. Strange? You know us. You're our English teacher."

"Ah!" he said. "My brother! The one with porphyria!" He did a movie maniac cackle. "My renegade brother," he continued, "decided to remain mortal. We have a certain sibling … rivalry, you might say. He fantasizes about being me, and at times, I him as well … there is no way I could become human, but for him there is always the chance to cross over … he is academically far more advanced than I, of course. I, you see, am merely *Mr.* Strange. I have no doctorate. I am Mr. Theodore Strange, and I am eternally grateful for your assistance in having released me from my captivity."

"Makes no sense," I said. "If you're a vampire, and immortal, and *Dr. Leopold* is human — how come you look the same age?"

"Who knows?" said Mr. *Theodore* Strange. "I think he catches up by spending time on the pathway, where time does not move as in your world. I am pleased to make your acquaintance."

"Well," I said, "unless you can help us, we'll have to be on our way. Your mortal twin is the supervisor of our club and he can help us find our missing friend. But you don't know us."

"I can indeed help you, but first you must help *me*. Now that I've emerged from the tomb, I'll need to take care of certain needs …"

"No way," said Donut. "We're not giving any blood."

"Oh, we don't skulk around biting the necks of nubile maidens any more," he said. "I just need access to the real world. Perhaps somewhere close to a blood bank. And a job — I'd love a job. Perhaps I could have my brother's old job, seeing as you say he is not around any more?"

Sister Evangeline said, "Well, after a celeb TV English teacher, why not a vampire?"

"I can teach English, Romanian, Hungarian, Middle High German, and Late Antiquity Latin and Greek," he said. "Anything my brother can teach, I can teach more of. He's probably already taught you kids about Sir Gawain and the Green Knight who chopped off his own head. Sir Gawain was a personal friend of mine. I had the Green Knight for breakfast."

"Come," said Sister Evangeline. "I'll get you a meeting with the

41

ZOMBIE IN THE FRIDGE

school board."

"But first," said Mr. Theodore Strange, "I must help our friends." He pushed the coffin lid all the way off — easy for him with his superhuman strength. "Look in the coffin. You'll find what you need."

And to our amazement, he went off with Sister Evangeline, down the pathway, in the direction that, I was sure, led to the vestry and through that to the nuns' private chapel.

Arm in arm.

8

A Ball of Yarn

Fluke

We knelt down. The inside of the coffin was clammy and murky. It was also full of junk. There were books. An hourglass. A rolling pin. A map in some ancient language.

"Keep that," Kim said to me. "It might be a map of the Crystal Pathway. You're the only one who could probably figure out what language it is in."

I glanced at it. The letters were sort of Greek, but ... "Coptic," I said. My Egyptian was rusty; I'd need a night to figure out how to read this map. Worse than Coptic, actually. The main headings were Coptic, but there was all sorts of text in demotic, too, which is far worse.

"So that's it?" Donut said. "We can find Polo using this map in a dead language?"

Kim said, "The map for clues; Danger's intuition for meaning; Donut's — ah — well, we might need to infiltrate another convent."

"Yeah," Donut said. "Maybe Polo's being held captive by an all-women gang."

We laughed, but Kim said, "What's so funny? That's the plot of *Bram Stoker's Burial of the Rats* by Roger Corman."

I fumbled around inside and my hands encountered something slightly fuzzy. "Wait," I said, "there's something else." I tugged at it. It came out all in one soft lump. I tossed it over to Kim.

"What are we supposed to do," he said, "knit our way to the

43

solution?"

It was a ball of yarn.

So there we were, sitting around in the improved Club X. At least you could get a drink from the new fridge, and at least it was less dusty and musty than last year. But we had decided to keep the pictures, even the funky fake *Mona Lisa*. And now, the lights didn't go off at 10 pm. Polo had bribed Uncle Sert to reconnect us to the main switchboard without passing through the timer.

Donut said, "Time loops — how can we beat time loops?"

"We can beat them," Danger said, "by working backwards —"

"Until we find the 'node' where the timeloop splits off," I said, thinking aloud. "Like using a stiff hairbrush to untangle bad hair."

"But," Kim said, "even if we fight off these random loops ... we don't where Polo is ... and we don't have a map to *Polo*, just a map."

"Worse," Donut said, "We don't know *when* he is."

"That means," Kim said decisively, "it's not a good idea to panic. He could be stuck in the past, or he could be stranded in tomorrow. And if he is one of these loops, he'll just keep going and round until, as Fluke says, we untangle time. Which means, we can take a night and try to gather our thoughts, and bust Polo out in the morning."

"Not in the morning," said Danger. "We have school. First day!"

Kim sat down in the "president's chair" and looked at us all. "Ideas?" he said.

"Well," Donut said, "there's one really important thing. Before you guys arrived, we had already managed to get the coffin open, and it Dr. Strange sat up and sat 'Can I help you?'"

"And he had fake plastic fangs that he shoved into his mouth," Danger said. "And then somehow time looped back and you guys showed up and —"

I said, "We saw someone who *was* Dr. Strange but *not quite* Dr. Strange. And Sister Evangeline offered him a job!"

Kim said, "This closet isn't just a nexus between worlds, then." He looked at all of us, like a light bulb had gone off in his head. "It's just worlds that exist. It's *possible* worlds as well. There are other Dr. Stranges."

"And other Kims," I said. "I could trade you in for a better model. One that thinks before he speaks."

"Why? I'm a truthsayer," Kim said.

"There's a Danger who knows who to control his powers," Danger said.

"There's a Donut with a dick," Kim said.

"Shut up," Donut said.

This was a not a night where I was going to get any sleep. I was surfing the net for hours, trying to see a connection between balls of yarn, Egyptian maps, and alternate worlds. Kim, on the other hand, fell into a deep sleep. It is quite aggravating sometimes. He can turn himself off, like a robot, and then back on again.

I made some progress with the map, Egyptian hieratic isn't designed to be easy to read. It's kind of a shorthand adaptation of hieratic, which in turn is a simplified form of hieroglyphics. But hieroglypics aren't that bad if you're into crosswords and rebuses. Vultures, owls, reeds and zigzag lines of water … are all perfectly identifiable. But in demotic one squiggle is much like another.

The map was like a kind of map of a public transportation network, showing lines in various colors and circles that seemed to be "junctions" or places where you go get off one line and onto another. But it was way more complicated even than the spaghetti mess of Bangkok's subway, skytrain, and bus lines. What words I could read in the text didn't seem to make much sense. They were all, names from different mythologies. They were goddesses or heroines of ancient stories. Like Proserpina … Savitri … Ariadne. What did they have in common?

And why was there an image of a river running underneath the maze, guarded by a three-headed dog? Was that Cerberus? Was the Crystal Pathway actually the underworld — the land of the dead? On the other side of the river was a stylized image of Anubis — another dog-god. Dog-god — mirrors inside of mirrors!

I fell asleep, my eyes glazing over, slouched over my laptop. The ball of yarn lay on the desk, next to Kim's Rubik's cubes.

All day, from breakfast to tea-time, we couldn't talk about anything else. I shared my findings, such as they were, and Kim kept saying, "it's all connected, somehow. It's one of those mega-puzzles. I'm just missing one piece."

We weren't surprised to learn that the whole school schedule had been reshuffled and that there was a class at sundown. But it wasn't English. English was being taught by one of the sisters and I've found such an interesting subject to be so boring.

Our curiosity was pretty piqued, however, to learn that *Mr* Strange would be taking a class called "Social Studies." What could someone who spent centuries at a time lying around in a box possibly know about "social" anything? It got even stranger once my friends and I got to Dr. Strange's old classroom, which was now redecorated to look like a gothic castle … complete with a coffin next to the teacher's desk. Sister Evangeline was there, and we were convening a little before sundown.

"Quick, sit down," she said. "I need to talk to all of you before the lesson begins."

We quickly sat down. Me, Kim, Danger, and Donut at the front of the class, as usual, since no one wanted to take the seats. Sister Evangeline looked at the coffin. She seemed worried. She cleared her throat and started talking. "As you know, children, Dr. Strange is on sabbatical. It's a great privilege to have the world-famous actor, his brother Mr. Theodore Strange come and teach at St Cecilia's for a while. However, Mr. Strange is preparing for a the second season of a TV series, *Nosferatu in the Bronx*, in which he plays a vampire. Shooting begins in three months, but Mr. Strange is what is known as a 'method' actor, and therefore he has to inhabit the very essence of his character at all times."

There was a loud rat-tat-tat on the coffin lid, and a muffled, "Let me out! I got my cloak stuck in the breathing holes!" Sister Evangeline pulled and I guess Mr. Strange pushed from the inside, and our new edition of our English teacher pulled himself out. Imperiously, he said to Sister Evangeline, "I can take it from here."

There was a crucifix on the desk, and another on the wall. This is, after all, a Catholic school.

Sister said, "He's a bit eccentric. But do not be afraid. He's not a real vampire. He just plays one on TV."

"I thought *Dr.* Strange was one," said Pueng Pang from the back of the class.

"Yeah," said his sidekick Tommy, "He put Sister Edward into a mirror, too."

Donut turned. "Shut up," she said. "That never happened. That was just in Kim's movie."

Mr. Strange tapped his desk. "How life imitates art," he said. "Or is it the other way round?" To Kim, he said, "I very much enjoyed your film — I saw it at the Oldenburg film festival. Although my brother can't act his way out of a paper bag. He can't even play himself."

Kim started to protest but Mr. Strange put a finger to his lips. "All will be revealed in the fullness of time," he said. "But today, let's talk about … *mythology*. In particular, about Theseus and the minotaur, whom he battled at the heart of a labyrinth that was designed by —"

"Daedalus," I said. "Ask something harder."

"Heavens," Mr. Strange said. "We have a polymath in the house!"

Kim whispered to me, "I think this Mr. Strange is going to be as useful as the other one. I think he's trying to drop us a clue."

"I heard that," said Theodore Strange. "Vampires have very acute hearing. We're practically bats, you know."

"So is he, or isn't he?" Kim whispered.

I said, "Let's listen. The other Strange would always mix secret messages to us when he was teaching."

Sure enough, Mr. Strange asked a question with direct relevance to my research last night. "Has anyone heard of Ariadne?" he said.

I knew the answer, of course. "She was the daughter of King Minos. When Theseus was in the labyrinth, trying to slay the monstrous minotaur, she helped him find a way out. She gave him —"

I looked at Kim, who looked at me. I don't know if he knew the story, but he got the clue.

"A ball of yarn!" I said.

Mr Strange did one of those vampiric evil cackles, as impressive as any I'd seen in a movie. "And what did Ariadne get for her pains? Theseus abandoned her on the next desert island — so anxious was he to get back his normal life back home in Athens. Lucky for her, the God Bacchus was passing by and needed a bit of loving, so he descended and carried her up to the heavens … and *ravished* her!"

I wasn't listening. I remembered now, how a ball of yarn could be used when you are lost in a labyrinth. We needed the map, and the yarn. We had everything we needed. I whispered to Kim, "Let's get the club together at midnight. We can find Polo. And anyone else. Maybe even the real Dr. Strange!"

9

Into the Labyrinth

Kim

We were in Club X together — minus one — and it looked like I was being made to be in charge again. I don't really mind. I know patterns. I know movies — and I know how to tell a story. And I can tell you, whether it's *Lord of the Rings* or a Stephen King blockbuster, what has to happen is that the group has to *split up*. In fact, someone usually says "Let's split up," and that person might as well be me.

So first, I got Fluke to tell us the myth of the labyrinth.

This is what he said:

Theseus was an ancient Greek hero, the son of King Aegeus. He volunteered to be sent to Crete as part of an annual tribute of youths who would be sacrificed to the Minotaur, a monstrous half-man, half-bull, who lived in an unsolveable labyrinth built by Daedalus.

The daughter of King Minos of Crete, Ariadne, helped Theseus to escape by giving him a ball of yarn. As long as he held on to one end of it, he could find his way back out of the labyrinth after slaying the minotaur. Ariadne didn't have too happy a fate, however. Theseus dumped her on the nearest island on his way back to Athens. As Mr. Strange told us, Ariadne was fortunate that a passing God was able to sweep her up into the sky.

"Oh," Donut said, "Ariadne's like me. Even though I like Fluke, he never even looks at me."

"Well, if you're waiting for someone to sweep you up into the sky," I said, "it's not me."

I looked at the yarn. I looked at the map. I looked at my friends. I

48

took charge.

"So," I said, "this is the deal. We need the map. We need the yarn. But neither of those things will tell us where Polo is. We need someone with ... some of kind of *secret sense*, who can sniff Polo out like a bloodhound. And we need someone to *stay behind*, because someone's gotta watch the other end of the ball of yarn. Someone's got to keep that thread anchored in the real world. Which means, yeah, we have to split up."

Fluke said, "I know you want to lead the search party. But you're the general of the army. You should be in the bunker with your finger on the red button."

"So," I said, "Fluke and I will stay."

"I have to read the map," Fluke said.

Danger said, "And I'm the one with the secret sense. I'm more close to Polo than anyone. If anyone can find his psychic scent across a million universes ... it's me."

"I guess this means I am staying here ... with Donut," I said.

Even though I hated the solution, I knew it was the right one. The Club worked best in pairs. Polo being missing had upset the normal way that we would always split up. I wasn't happy to be stuck with Donut. Not because she was a girl ... at least, I didn't *think* that was the reason. It was more because I still resented her little crush on Fluke.

Even though that was all over now, and she was officially one of the guys. Even so, she made things complicated.

I don't think a twenty-sided puzzle is complicated, but I do think a five-way relationship can be....

First things first. "Is this a rescue mission?" I said. "If so, do we know if Polo *wants* to be rescued? Is he just on some kind of journey of self-discovery? You know he was having all these visions about 'becoming true to himself' and all that."

"He would have let us know," Donut said.

"Yeah, right," Fluke said. "And how exactly?"

"Through me," Danger said. "And my secret sense is not telling me smooth sailing, it's saying *red alert*."

This is what I did.

I tied one end of the yarn around my wrist. Double-knotted. Unbreakable.

I tied the other end around Fluke's wrist.

Why Fluke?

I told myself … Danger would barrel on ahead, heedless of constraints, because he would only listen to his inner urges. Fluke would reflect, look at all the facts, and probably avoid breaking the connection. I tried to tell myself that this was logical. But of course, it wasn't, and when things aren't logical, I go crazy.

Fluke raided the Club X fridge, and stuffed his pocket with chocolate bars.

Brahms was still wedged in the doorway.

Fluke said, "Don't think that the map's going to have a little moving dot marked 'Polo'. This is reality, not *Harry Potter.*"

I said, "That's why you and Danger work together."

Donut said, "Since time and space meant different things in the world inside the closet, they might be gone for a year and come back in five minutes."

"Don't I know it!" I said. "That's why *your* job — as the daughter of the principal, with the most access to admin, will have to help me hold the fort. If they do *not* come back in five minutes, you're going to become a Miss Propaganda, spinning stories and excuses so they don't start calling Fluke's parents. Danger just has a mother, and we see her every day — she works in the kitchen — we'll have to find another way to deal with her. As for Polo's parents … they probably won't even notice. Where are they, the Riviera? Maldives? Gstaad?"

"Yeah," said Danger. "He's your classic millionaire latchkey kid."

"Let's go," Fluke said. He grabbed Danger by the arm and walked toward the door.

"Wait!" I said.

Then I realized that there was no point in waiting. I went and sat down in the "president's chair" and I watched my best friend and favorite psychic vanish through the open door, making sure that Brahms was still stuck in place on the floor. They just rushed in. They didn't even say goodbye. Well, they were in a hurry. I can't blame them. And yet —

The ball of yarn started to unwind.

And unwind.

And unwind. Faster and faster!

And then it went taut.

So, deep inside, I had this weird kind of an aching feeling. Not pain, but loss. The way you might feel when someone dies. Like they're in another world, one you will never be able to reach. Yet I still had the thread.

"They're gone," I whispered.

Donut looked at me. "Just you and me, then," she said.

"Yes, I —"

Donut said, "I know you've always had something against me. I wish we could figure it out. Maybe, since no one else will be around for a while, we could … go on a date? I mean, my father could drive us. There's a nice Palazzo Ciocolatto at the bottom of the hill."

That was the last thing I wanted to think about.

I said, "Donut, how long is that ball of yarn?"

"Beats me."

"I'll tell you. It was probably about 200 grams … so it's about two hundred meters. How far is it from Club X to my room? It's a few flights of stairs. I could probably get there in under 30 meters. To the main building where the classes are? Maybe 100 meters.   How far will Fluke have to travel to find Polo? No way of knowing. The short answer is, maybe I can make it to most of my classes, but we're not going on any date. No way. Look at the yarn. It's already fully stretched. I probably can't even get out of this room."

"Don't worry," Donut said. "I'll fetch your food from the refectory and spoonfeed you."

"The fuck," I said.

I tried moving my arm and already I felt like I shouldn't be leaving the chair. Perhaps I'd just sit there until they came back, and Donut would have to bring my meals and tell outrageous lies to the school authorities (which they'd believe because after all, she was the daughter of Dr. Prachaya.)

I felt a tug on the yarn.

"Oh no," I said. "They're going out of range."

Then it snapped!

"Shit!" I said. "We've lost contact!"

But was it broken?

The yarn ran for about a foot and then seemed to end it mid-air. But it didn't fall to the floor. I could still feel it pulling.

"No you haven't lost contact at all," Donut said.   "It's feeding through a tiny hole into … some other place. But it's still tight. Don't you feel something?"

I tugged. The yarn tugged back.

I shook my wrist. The yarn wiggled back.

Maybe we could even use it to communicate. Like, you know, the tin-can-and-string telephone.

I was still connected to Fluke! I was going to look like an idiot, walking around with a piece of string six inches long sticking out my arm, but even if were separated by dimensions, we were still just two hundred meters apart.

This was no ordinary ball of yarn. As Fluke and Danger went into the labyrinth, further than the two hundred meters the yarn would stretch, the yarn had made a little yarn-sized wormhole, ensuring that no matter how far we were separated, we would still be connected by the same two hundred meters. This wasn't yarn ... it was hyperyarn.

Perhaps we could knit a hypersweater — then we'd be able to walk the Crystal Pathway without a doorway!

There was a downside, though. I wasn't about to tell Donut. But she figured it out all by herself, demonstrating that she did have the intellectual acumen of a Club X member.

"So we *can* go on a date, after all," she said.

10

Down Another Rabbit Hole

Polo

Yes.

A door opened and I was inside some kind of refrigerator and through it all I could see part of the nuns' sitting room. I called out to Donut. I could see Sister Evangeline hovering in the distance.

"Pull me out," I said. "I'm stuck."

I clutched her arms and I think she pulled, but somehow I pulled harder and she kind of half walked, half tumbled into the fridge, sort of landed right on top of me, and I fell backward and she fell too....

... and we were falling!

Down some kind of shaft, or well, or chute ... or rabbit hole!

Donut screamed.

"Grab my hand," I said.

Donut was flailing but I managed to grip her hand tightly. Around us, the world was whirling. We could see clocks and hourglasses. Ancient temples whizzed by. We kept falling. Around us were windows into other worlds. We were in a kind of chute or well. There were windows and doorways but they went by too fast for to grab the doorknobs.

She was panicking but I was starting to get how this place worked. I started to concentrated on falling upwards. I anchored my eye line on a glittering pyramid and tried to hold my gaze. Some kind of sacred procession was moving slowly in the foreground.

As I did that, I found myself falling more and more slowly. I was almost floating in place. And as I watched the pyramid, it changed. Sandstorms raged. The brilliant limestone casing was decaying. The perfect lines of the pyramid became crooked and uneven. The sands were desolate. No colorful processions. As I hovered in front of the pyramids, high priests and pharaohs gave way to bedouin warriors sweeping by on camels, and then to Ottoman janissaries ... and, as we slowed down further, to modern times ... the pyramids still splendid in the sunlight, but now swarming with tourists and touts.

By sheer concentration, I seemed to have got us to some kind of level ground. Our feet sank into sand.

The rabbit hole sort of melted into a bright Saharan sky. We were in a kind of tourist trap of some kind, with a few souvenir stands, a place for cold drinks, and a sign advertising camel rides, "cash only." The pyramids were there too, in the distance. But everything outside the little enclave was in a kind of soft focus. It was as if we weren't quite *in* that world yet ... as if where we stood was like a sort of service island in a network of highways ... a place between universes. When I looked at the ground, it was sandy, but when I dug into the stand with one foot I could see crystal beneath.

"What are we doing here?" Donut said.

"Um ... I think somehow I picked it. Like you pick a floor in an elevator." I pointed to the crystal. "Anyway, we're not quite *here* yet. We're in some kind of waystation."

"But it looks like we're in *Egypt!*" She was obviously in some kind of state of shock.

"C'mon, sister," I said. "We've been in other universes. We can handle Egypt."

"Yeah, but I don't see a doorway we can take back to school."

"We'll handle it!" I said again.

"Ok," she said, "but let's get a drink first. I am so dying of thirst."

"Why are you so panicked?" I said.

"Panicked? Am panicked? No, I'm not panicked, I'm just *I'm so freaked out!*"

We sat down at the little drink stand. The chairs were wobbly stools. There were just three tables, shaded by umbrellas, and a lonely-looking palm tree. A fridge stood under the palm tree, but it didn't even seem to be plugged in.

"Cash only," said the boy who served us. A little Arab boy with one of these head things they wear and a flowing white robe. He really reminded me of someone....

Donut started to panic again but I put a finger to my lips.

"It's so hot here and so dry," Donut said. "I'm so parched. .."

I looked in my pockets and found some change: a crumpled hundred-baht note and a few coins. I showed them to the boy and he nodded. He didn't seem to mind that we weren't paying in Egyptian money, which made it even more clear that we weren't yet off the Crystal Pathway.

"What can I get you?" the boy said.

"Back to school," Donut said.

"Sure, sis," said the boy, and he did a funny kind of a blink, and Donut vanished in a shower of blue sparks. None of the other people hanging around there seemed to notice.

Though when I looked at the next table, I saw nice European couple being served, and as soon as they spoke to their waiter, they too vanished.

"What if I just wanted a drink?" I said.

"Help yourself from the fridge there," said the boy. "No charge."

I got myself a soda and popped the cap and started drink greedily. The liquid was hot — surprise! That's what you get for not plugging in the fridge. But Donut had been right. It was *really* hot and I was just about as thirsty as you could get. Yet the more I drank, the thirstier I felt. I thought if I ate something, it would probably slake my thirst. I wandered back to the fridge and took out a cup of ice cream, which was, of course, completely slushy and gross … and I was right. It hit the spot perfectly. I started to feel much more relaxed. What was *in* the ice cream?

Then again, what did I expect? Backwards was forwards here.

"If the drinks and snacks are free," I said to the boy, 'what's the money for? Why does Thai money work here anyway?"

"Toll," said the boy.

Boom! He looked exactly like Boom. What a pest!

"So you sent Donut back?"

"It's what she wanted."

"What do *I* want?"

"You asked for a drink. You don't get two wishes."

"But this place … it's like a junction? Where you can get off one world and take a doorway into another?"

"Yes! we pop up whenever there's a quorum of people needing to be moved. The past, the future, this world and the next — we keep the portals running. Boom, boom, boom, one world after another!"

"I want to go where Donut went."

"Sorry. You don't get two wishes. Rules."

"But I don't want to be in Egypt."

"If you didn't, you wouldn't have asked for a drink. You'd have given me coordinates."

"But I didn't know—"

"Not an excuse! Sorry!"

"Oh, c'mon, Boom."

"Who's Boom?"

Well. I am not used to not getting my own way, let's be frank. I wanted to ask the boy more, but he wasn't interested; he was already serving at a different table. As I watched, he responded to one lady's request by spinning a live Persian cat out of thin air and dropping it onto the table. The cat leaped onto the lady's shoulder and started licking her neck.

"Hey, come back and give me directions!"

"You're on your own," he shouted back. "That's the whole point of this place. The direction that you choose is the direction that is right for you. If you didn't ask for a location, then that's not where you're meant to be going."

Well, I told myself, *I'm in Egypt. At least I'm not on some other planet. I don't need any dimension-hopping pathway to get home. I'll get that camel guy to take me to the nearest real city, call a Grab or a Uber or whatever they have here to the airport, and get on the next flight back to Bangkok.*

There's a reason my Dad always makes me carry one of his credit cards.

11

Out of Egypt - Business Class

Polo

Perhaps my father would not even notice the blip in his credit card bill, but I decided that this was definitely going to be a "whole hog" kind of journey.

The camel ride made me seasick, but I suppose that's why they're called ships of the desert. It was brief, thankfully, and I soon arrived at some kind of civilization: well, it had a Starbucks and a McDonalds, anyway. I had a phone and a credit card. Egypt had been a world power for over a thousand years, so naturally, they had Uber.

I got to the airport easily enough. Not having a passport on me was a bit trickier, but going to the Thai airways counter and tearfully talking about being abducted by thugs trying to get a ransom from my father (or were they trafficking me to a sheikh? I remember getting my stories mixed up a bit) and how I had hitchhiked after fleeing from Somali pirates ... you get the idea. I got someone from the embassy to come up and give me an emergency passport. My story was so complicated that I got lost a few times myself, but luckily I am a good weeper, and my dad is a name that, once dropped, can be used to sweep the floor.

I picked a few items in the gift shop as well. Ever since impersonating a nun last year, I'd been fantasizing about going full Islamic — so much mystery, so much concealed sexuality! I could totally out-nun the sisters, and maybe claim I'd had a conversion in Egypt ... *that* would cause a ruckus indeed! So I bought one of those black veiled outfits you see in movies set in the Middle East. I didn't put it on right then and there, but I sure was going to surprise the X's when I got back!

You know I'm good at causing commotion but, unless it's my own commotion, I find these things quite boring really, so let's just skip the chaos at the airport, my screams and protests, the security guards, and all that ... and segue right into the relaxing, comfortable, business class in-flight lounge on this massive two-storey plane. It wasn't a bad arrangement, though of course, it's nowhere near as nice as first. I had been tempted but I just didn't want my dad to notice the credit card bump too much.

I seemed to be the only one in my class and this was one of those middle eastern airlines where business class is grander than other people's first. There wasn't a set mealtime — you could order food whenever you wanted off a menu — and some guy with a French accent and chef's hat actually stood around talking about the food before serving it.

It takes almost a whole night to get to Bangkok. Luckily, the plane had internet. I tried to reach my friends but for some reason, some server was down somewhere. In fact, service was so spotty that I ended up watching the news. It was surprisingly interesting. I hadn't realized that in the U.S. state of Alabama, there was a new law criminalizing marriages between people of the opposite gender. In fact I had to look at the item twice, it almost seemed like an April fool's joke. Only it wasn't April.

One of the items on the menu was a raw sheep's eyeball, but I didn't order it.

Instead, I lay back in comfort and reflected on how I was going to deal with Donut for ditching me in Egypt, and how I was going to terrorize the nuns on my return.

I woke up after a few hours. The plane was moving smoothly. There was no one in Business Class at all. I couldn't sleep so I decided to try the inflight lounge.

The lounge! The sight of the night sky through the windows, the leather armchairs, the vast selection of alcoholic drinks that I knew would be served with no questions asked ... perhaps a cocktail or two we finally allow me to get some sleep.

Then the bartender behind the counter turned around and... I *knew* him!

"My son," said the guru from my vision in the temple, so long ago ... the one who told me I could follow my own path. "You are surprised to see me."

"Hell yes! You're not real. Which means ..."

"Quite right. None of this is real."

"I'm not on my way to school?"

"Oh yes, you are."

"But not really."

"Oh yes."

"But none of this is real?"

"What, my son, is reality? Know that you are going where your destiny intends, and that you will grow in wisdom and devotion as a result of your journey. Whether this is the material world is ultimately immaterial."

I looked at him. I studied his face very carefully. Definitely, it was him. The shaggy hair, the Brahmin robes, and the Indian accent were unmistakable.

I said to the guru, "But I've only seen you in my dreams before."

"Merrily, merrily, merrily, merrily," he sang, "Life is just a dream."

"If this is just a dream," I said, "I'll take a Long Island Ice Tea."

Kim

So ... Fluke and Danger went into the labyrinth, and I went on a date with Donut. It was not as bad as I thought it would be, because I learned a lot more about, got a much better sense of, who she was ... and what she thought about my friends. And I was the first to find out more about Polo, because Donut said she had last seen her in Egypt.

The chocolate place, a couple of kilometers past the private road, was pretty good. I hadn't even known it existed. It was decorated in full American classic kitsch, with vinyl sofas and carved eagles, and a big portrait of Elvis Presley ... I think that's who it was.

I ordered a dark chocolate brownie, a dark chocolate hot drink, and two dark chocolate truffles. I like my food the way I like my Rubik's — with the colors properly sorted out.

Donut had something crazy — it had cream and strawberries and kiwi and two different sauces on top of a chocolate cake that had been drenched in some kind of rum, or something. We are totally incompatible. Imagine living with her!

"I do feel bad," she said, "about leaving Polo behind. But I couldn't help it! The kid asked me what I wanted, and I said 'to go home' and poof! The kid looked like my little brother, too. That's the weird part."

"Kid?"

"Yeah. We were in Egypt. Little Arab kid, robes and headgear."

"Egypt, Earth? I mean not Egypt in some alternate universe?"

"How should I know? Like I go to Egypt all the time, with my Dad's schoolteacher's pay. It was Egypt, you know, pyramids, sphinx, all that stuff."

"I'm relieved, then," I said. I wasn't that relieved, but Polo was very good at dealing with being in the wrong place at the wrong time. "Polo can get back to Thailand on his own. He has credit cards. He's the most resourceful kid I know plus he has the most resources!"

"So we can call off the search?" Donut said. "Pity, I wanted to have you to myself for a few days."

I felt a little tug — the piece of yarn that was wound around my wrist and which disappeared into a black hole somewhere a few inches away — I was still linked to Fluke. This made me feel kind of guilty, talking to Donut. It's complicated!

And so, we had only just started on all the chocolate, and I had already found out everything I needed to know from Donut. It was going to be an awkward evening.

Especially since the next thing she said was ... "You, and Fluke ... I mean ... I've always wanted to ask, but I never had the nerve ... are you like, a couple?"

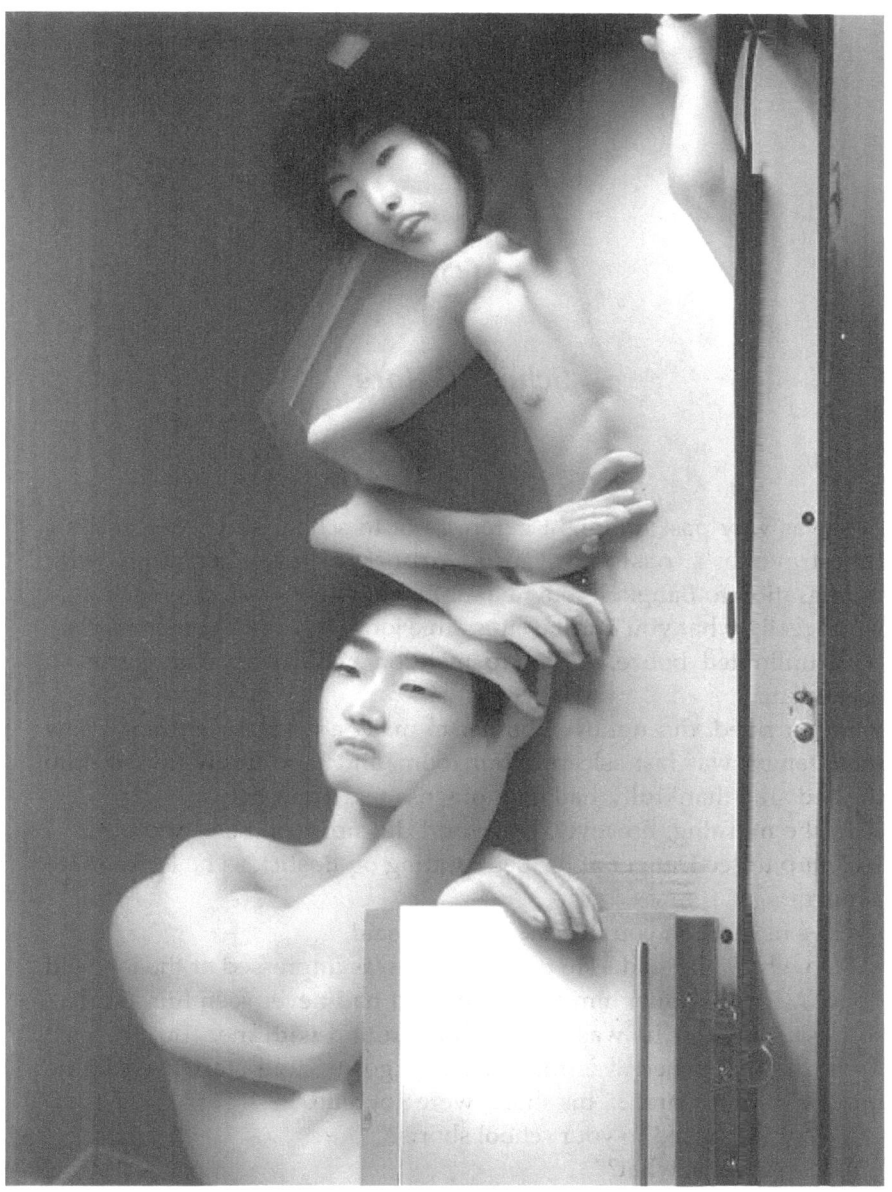

12

School Colors

Polo

It was way past midnight before I got to school and — from some time-traveller's oasis to Cairo Airport to an altercation with immigration to Bangkok to a taxi all the way to Khao Yai — well, that is not really what you'd call a stress-free journey, even in business class with unlimited booze. (Not to mention encounters with gurus in dreamland.)

So I arrived, did not even bother to make a dramatic entrance, saw that Danger was fast asleep in our room, and I too threw myself onto the bed and, thankfully, had no more insane dreams.

In the morning, however, my world did not look nearly so clear. I woke up to see Danger at his bed, putting on lipstick as he looked into a mirror.

"I've never seen you do that before," I said.

"Do what?" he said. He turned and I was impressed at the job he'd done ... I had known him all my life and had never seen him do that, so I assumed that he was just kidding around with me. But the next thing that happened was this. Danger got up and started changing into his uniform, and ... his shorts were not blue.

"What happened to your school shorts?"

"I don't know, what?"

"Color's off." More than off. Everyone in Thailand knows that school shorts only come in certain colors: khaki for government schools, black or blue or red for some pre-schools ... Danger's shorts were quite, quite lavender. He'd have had to have spilled a ton of bleach or dye into the washing machine. Thinking about it, he probably didn't even *have* a washing machine at home.

"Looks okay to me," Danger said.

It was even more bewildering when I opened my drawer and saw that my school shorts were lavender, too. Perhaps going through the Crystal Pathway had screwed up the vision centers in my brain or something. But all the other colors seemed ok. I went to the window and looked out. The sky was still blue.

Maybe they changed the school uniform while I was away. That must be it.

"Hurry up," Danger said. "We already missed breakfast. We're barely going to make it to the first class of the day...."

... which happened to be Biology, a subject I don't remember ever signing up for, but it looked to be quite fun, as there was already an anatomically detailed chart of the female body hanging on the wall.

Now, Danger's body language as we walked to class was not like the Danger I knew. He swayed, he minced a little. If anything, it looked like he was trying to be *me!* As if anyone could be me.

And yeah, everyone in the class was wearing lavender shorts.

I saw Tommy and Pueng Pang. Normally they would be aggressively beating up some smaller kid, but they were actually sitting around in a strange lovey-dovey kind of way, and both were made up — not in an exaggerated way but quite tastefully. In the back of the class, I saw Kim and Fluke ... they had matching lavender ribbons in their hair. And matching lavender lipstick. In fact, they were clearly a couple, making eyes at each other in a way that would not have happened last term ... unless ...

I waved to Kim and he waved back. I went over to where he and Fluke were sitting.

"What's with the makeup?" I asked them.

"What makeup?" said Fluke.

"*This* makeup I said," sticking my finger in his face. "Boy you sure laid it on with a trowel. You need help from a *real* girl."

"Which would be you?" said Kim.

"Of course," I said, and pulled my lipstick out of my shorts.

"Put that away before they catch you!" Fluke said in a panic.

"Catch me? What are you talking about?"

"Everyone has to present as the opposite gender. It's a school rule.

It's some kind of wokeness thing. It's the law, now that we have a *kathoey* as prime minister."

"Well, even if all this is true, I've got a dick," I said. "I'm entitled to lipstick."

"Not according to your gender ID," Danger said.

"What are you talking about?"

Kim said, "You're zoning out again, Polo. You blank out and you seem to be coming back from somewhere far away … and you don't remember things."

I reached into my shorts and pulled out a card I had never seen before. I looked pretty good in the photo. Under Gender Registration, the card said: "identifies as female." I looked pretty. I must have had a ton of hormone treatments. The picture even looked like I had tits. I felt my chest. Holy shit! I *did!*

"Wait," I said. "I *choose* my gender when I want, if I want, and whenever it suits me," I said. "And I *do* have a penis."

"Not since the law was changed," said Kim.

I felt down there.

I had no dick!

I was *not* home! I was stuck in some nightmare parallel universe! But I never planned to cut it off — the whole point of being me is have the best of both worlds!

I was about to scream but at the moment there was a ruckus. "Sister Edward is coming! Get to our seats!" Everyone sat down and this wasn't like our real school, either, I mean, they sat down with machine-like precision and there was one collective *splat* as their bottoms hit their seats. None of the freewheeling randomness of my real class.

I looked at Kim and Fluke and Danger. Underneath the makeup, I felt they were still the people I knew. I had to reach down to their essences somehow … was there even a Club X here?

At that moment, Sister Edward entered the classroom.

She was wearing a black clerical suit with a priest's collar.

Wasn't this the kind of thing nuns used to get burned at the stake for? Had I somehow landed in a reality where gender was legislated with totalitarian efficiency?

"Good morning, Sister," the class chanted.

Sister Edward said, "Now, children, let's talk about the differences between differential and integral calculus…." She looked at me and winked.

I freaked. I started screaming.

"Someone fetch the school psychologist!" I heard someone shout.

"No! Not the school psychologist!" I screamed and screamed and I guess I passed out.

When I woke up again, I was in a room I knew well. It was Sister Evangeline's office. I recognized the pink couch and the psychedelic painting of a thousand faces that looked down from her wall. This was the very room where Sister had told me her dark secret last term. Or wasn't her secret "dark" anymore?

I was lying on the couch. Sister Evangeline was sitting in her chair. Like Sister Edward, she was dressed as a man.

When she saw that I was coming to, she went to the window and drew the shades.

"I know," she said softly.

"How did I lose my penis?" I said. "I *like* my penis! I'm not a girl or a boy. I'm *me.* I can be whoever I want, whenever I want.

"I'm in the wrong world, aren't I?"

"We're all in the wrong world," she said, "people like you and me. And sometimes we wish so hard for a world that's *right,* and yet when we arrive at that world, it's not as *right* as we had hoped."

"But where's *your* Polo?"

"Wandering the Pathway," said Sister Evangeline.

"How do I get back? I have to find my way home!"

Sister Evangeline shook her head. "There's a reason you came here. Once in a while, the thread of our lives becomes tangled, and we can't go forward in time until we untangle it."

"What should I do?"

"I imagine your friends are looking for you. You won't be able to go back, you know, not until you've solved the riddle of why you are here in the first place. When the cosmos is wounded, it finds a way to heal itself. However unpleasant it may seem, you're here because you're *meant* to be here. Perhaps if you relax, try to fit in, try to learn more … you can solve the dilemmas of many … not yourself alone.'

Suddenly I had a realization. I just *knew.* "You're lost too," I said. "You're *our* Sister Evangeline, aren't you?"

"You know I can't answer that," she said. "To tell you would tangle up the twisted skein of possible worlds even more. The less you know, the better." Of course, "I can't answer that" was all the answer I needed.

"But you knew very well I'm not going to sit around waiting to be rescued. No one takes away my penis without my permission. I'm going to speak out. I'm going to change things around here. That's the way I am."

"Perhaps," said Sister Evangeline, "that's the reason *you* were brought into this reality."

13

Dangerous Donuts

Donut

Since I am the only student in the whole school who gets to sleep at home, you'd think I'd feel privileged. Maybe I'd be bragging about getting to eat real food instead of the junk they serve in school, for instance, but St. Cecilia's isn't a normal school. At home I get rice porridge with pork for breakfast, but in school they have a whole buffet, like a hotel.

Sure, I get a more comfortable — and bigger bed — but who do I have to share it with?

And what's a lot worse than *not* having a roommate who can share secrets and diss people and gossip about boys, there's the person I *have* to share breakfast with every morning — my dad, because he is also my school principal.

And this morning, he was bearing down on me over our pork and porridge, which he took with enormous spoonfuls of garlic deep-fried in lard. I don't know why we don't get the catering from the school kitchen — the nuns get it, after all. I think my dad is just punishing himself because I was kicked out of so many schools — he thinks it's because my mother's not around to control me, and that he himself is doing a bad job and so he has to overcompensate — by making my breakfast every morning. Which sucks.

My dad is probably a great, progressive educator, but he can't cook.

And I love to bitch about his cooking, which is what I was doing. "How can this pork taste so *not* moist, when it's actually floating in rice broth? It's like, against the laws of physics or something."

"Where did you go last night?" he said.

"I went out."

"Obviously, since you weren't home."

"I went to the chocolate place."

"Who with?"

"Father, I don't have to tell you where I am all the time, I'm a big girl."

"With a boy. Who?"

"Why? Will he get detention?"

"What kind of father do you think I am?"

"A nosy one," I said.

"Enough of this, young lady," he said. "I don't want you hanging around with those boys any more than is necessary. I have to protect you, you know. You're all I have. And you're always getting into trouble."

"What will you do, Father? Expel me?"

He sighed. I felt sorry for him them. I decided to tell him where I had been after all. "I went to the chocolate restaurant. With Kim." Defiantly, I added, "He's very nice."

"Indeed. A touch of Asperger's, but he is very intelligent. You could do a lot worse than hanging out with him." Amazingly, this connection seemed to have my dad's approval.

"It's no good, dad," I said. "He doesn't see me at all. I think he's in love with someone else. I tried to ask him, but he just looked away and changed the subject. That means he doesn't want to hurt my feelings, right?" Someone else, indeed ... he and I liked the same guy. But Fluke was oblivious to me, and too stuck inside a Bach fugue to "like" anyone, even his best friend. "He definitely doesn't."

"Maybe not. But if he actually *knew* he would just blurt it out. He wouldn't avoid hurting your feelings. That's the profile for people like him."

"So you think I have a chance with him?" I said.

"I don't think you should have a chance with *anyone!* I wish your mother were here."

"Tomorrow's the anniversary of her death, Father." I was surprised I remembered and he didn't.

"Yes. We'll go to the temple in the morning." He had a distant look and I realized I would never truly understand his sadness. My mother and I never clicked ... she was a good mother, maybe, but I was always closer to my father, even though he is annoying as shit. He obviously loves me. Okay, smothers, sometimes.

My mother died a long time ago. I wish I could feel more sad. Maybe, some day, I will. I think my family explains everything about why I am this way. I suppose I should have a talk with Sister Evangeline. I mean, a *real* talk.

Kim hadn't answered my question, so that made things kind of awkward between us. I avoided him all through Sister Edward's algebra class. But one of my problems is that when I have to know things, I *have* to know. I obsess.

I didn't have any more classes with Kim that day but I knew I would see him in the evening because, inevitably, we were going to be sitting and watching and waiting for something to come out of the closet. And we would have to have time together again. And he was going to be more edgy, because I'd probed into his private feelings.

Kim sat on his special chair. He was looking at his hand. The yarn, wound round his wrist and tightly tied, sprang up and was standing up straight in the air.

"Is something wrong?" i said. "Is the yarn pulling?"

"Yes. I'm still connected to Fluke," he said. "Even though I sleep alone, it's like he's always there. Attached to me."

"Do you mind sleeping alone?" I asked him.

"In a way." He started nervously playing with his 20-sided puzzle.

"Did you ever kiss Fluke?"

He didn't answer. Why was I being so aggressive? I think I was somehow put into this mood by the conversation I'd had with my Dad.

"In a way," he said. "But it might not have really happened. It might have been in ... another reality." His eyes were far away.

I had this wild thought. "Could I sneak into your room at night? I mean ... just to be close to Fluke. I won't bother you."

Kim didn't answer.

"Can I kiss you?" I said. "I mean, just to be close to Fluke."

"You're obviously not going to take no for an answer." He dropped his puzzle on the floor.

I put my hand on his hand. I ran my finger up the taut yarn. I wondered if I could tease the opening bigger, somehow, slip my finger into the other world ... once, in another school, a teacher told us about the Dutch and how they reclaimed land from the sea .. and how a small boy saved the country by plugging a hole in the dike with his finger ... I wondered if I could ...

The yarn trembled. It began alternately tightening and loosening. It felt kind of exciting.

Kim's eyes were closed. "Get it over with," he said. He half-heartedly puckered.

Here goes, I thought.

I sort of got ready ... I mean, I wound myself up like a spring and prepared to get sprung on Kim's lips. I then sort of jumped onto his lap zeroed in for the bull's eye.

At that moment, there was a pounding from inside the closet. I gasped and sank back onto the big couch. The pounding became insistent. We could hear voices. Kim looked at the door and his eyes widened.

The pounding went on and on and —

Stopped. Dead.

Total silence.

Kim and I looked at each other. But we had no time to breathe a sigh of relief because at that moment, the door of our brand-new fridge swung open and out came —

"Polo!" I whispered.

"A zombie!" Kim rasped.

It was a hand, anyway. A withered, rotting hand that could once have been a teenage boy. It was clawing at the air. Something was trying to get out.

"Shut the fridge!" I said.

"What if it's one of our friends?"

The hand was flailing now. Then it clutched the side of the fridge and something came shambling out, in a shower of half-empty soda cans and half-eaten sandwiches.

"Polo!" I said. I got up to give him a hug.

"That's *not* Polo," said Kim.

I could see why he said it. The piece of yarn was really taut, practically trying to drag Kim in through the infinitesimal hole in spacetime. Our friends were still in there looking for the *real* Polo.

We both stared at the person standing in front of the fridge and now slamming the door shut.

It was Polo ... and not Polo.

Right away, we could see that he had bright red shorts on. That was impossible because in Thailand, bright red shorts are only worn in elementary school.

Second, Kim wasn't far off when he called him a zombie His face and arms were ashen and covered with sores. One eyeball looked like it was about to pop out of a socket. The flesh was definitely decaying. The room stank like a garbage dump. If this was Polo, it wasn't the Polo we knew and loved ... my new best friend. It was something dark, terrifying, and ... incredibly smelly.

When the creature spoke, its voice was deep, wheezing, like something from a low-budget horror movie. The kind Kim loved so much.

"Kill me," Polo said. "Please. Kill me."

14

Brain Candy

Kim

"That's ridiculous," I said. "We're not going to kill you."

"You'll regret it," Polo-in-the-red-shorts rasped.

"You're our friend," I said.

"Until I eat your brain," Polo said.

"You'll have to gouge it out first," said Donut. "And we won't stay still for you to do that."

"Yeah," I said. "If you're anything like the zombies I'm used to, you'd be sluggish and easy to outrun."

"Hmm," Donut said. "But he talks. That's not like the ones in movies."

"I just had brains for lunch," Polo said. "It'll wear off soon and then I'll be more like the kind of zombie you can handle."

"I think we can keep him docile without killing him," said Donut. "We just have to give him enough brain to keep him coasting along but not so active that he'll run around ripping off people's heads."

"They don't have to be human brains, right?" I asked Polo.

"Well … once you've had human, nothing else tastes the same. All those memories, those traumas, those delicious sex scenes … they all taste great. If I go back to sheep and cows, it's all bland."

The conversation ended abruptly, because Donut whacked Polo on the head with a bust of Mozart. "Help me restrain him," she said.

"What did you do that for?"

"I want to hold on to my brain for a few more days."

"But he's out cold," I said. "Why do we have to restrain him?"

"Because he'll come to, and he'll want lunch."

Donut went over to one of the cabinets in the room and pulled open a drawer. She pulled out a pair of handcuffs. "Where did those come from?" I said.

"I put them there," Donut said. "I was planning to use them on Fluke, actually. You know, if I could ever get him alone. Kinky, huh?"

The picture that formed in my mind was ... very bizarre.

She clapped the cuffs on Polo and said, "Help me drag him to the chair."

"No, no, not my chair."

"The sofa, then."

We half-dragged, half-carried him. As we plopped him down, his left ear tore off and landed on the rug. Panicking, I picked it up and tried to stick it back on. Fluke told me a bible story about sticking an ear on someone once, but it didn't work for me.

"I've got superglue in the drawer ... with the cuff links." Donut crossed climbed over Polo to reach the cabinet behind the couch.

"And you were going to use superglue on Fluke ... how, exactly?"

She just gave me a mysterious smile.

"What else is in there?" I leaned over to look. I got a quick before she slammed the drawer shut: some makeup, a rosary, more handcuffs, and a couple of condoms. "Condoms? What exactly have you been planning?"

"You never know."

Polo stirred. "Do you think we should gag him?" Donut said.

She reached into that drawer and pulled out ... a gag. She slid it over Polo's mouth. Polo grunted. He writhed wildly for a few seconds, then slumped back again.

Donut hit him on the head with Mozart again.

"You'll kill him!" I said.

"He's already dead," Donut said. "Well. Undead."

"You're right," I said. I picked up Brahms and gave him a clout on the side Mozart hadn't pummeled yet. Polo was immobile again. I quickly glued his ear back on.

"Now, we need to figure out if there's a cure," Donut said.

"There's no cure," I said. "I've seen every zombie movie there is. All you can do is blow their heads off."

"But this is *Polo!* We can't do that."

"Well ... he's not exactly *our* Polo."

"But on some level, he is. Because when he came out of the fridge, he didn't try to eat us. He tried to protect us. Even if it meant we had to kill *him*. He *is* our Polo," she said softly. Kim, *do* something."

"I know all about horror movies," I said, "but I never met a real zombie."

"We need to talk to someone who knows *everything* about *everything*."

"Fluke's not here."

"Can't you call him … on that string?"

"If I attached it to a tin can, and if he *just* happened to have a tin can on the other end, and *if* sound waves could travel between dimensions…."

"How about if we talked to Mr. Strange?"

"We don't even *know* him. We hardly even knew *Dr.* Strange."

"But he's the only one we know who has walked the Crystal Pathway."

"We'll ask him after class," I said. "But meanwhile, we have to find some brains."

We found ourselves sneaking into the school kitchen. Though it was after midnight, there was a light on. Luckily for us, it was Danger's mother, who sometimes stayed way past her bedtime to chop vegetables or stir a simmering hot pot.

"Oh," she said, happy to see us. "Feeling peckish?"

She opened a larder and pulled out a tray of egg tarts. "These are for the nuns' breakfast. Just don't tell anyone."

"Great!" I said. Her egg tarts are amazing, and these were still warm. A little touch of nutmeg, not too sweet, really flaky crust. You want to just scarf the whole thing and yet you also want to savor it and the minute it's in your mouth you have to decide — scarf or savor — I almost forgot why we were there.

But after two tarts, I finally said, "Auntie, do you have brains?"

"Brains? That's an odd request. I've never had a teenager want to eat brains."

Donut and I looked each other. "I — I have this *craving*," she blurted out. "It's irrational, I know, but I have to have brains now."

Danger's mother stared at her. "You're not — you're not — pregnant, are you?"

I said, "Of course not. she has condoms in the drawer."

Danger's mother looked like she was about to blow a gasket. "The drawer? Does your father now you two are ... sexually ..."

Donut said, "Oh no, it's nothing like that. We just need the brains —"

"To feed a zombie," I said.

"Damn Aspergers!" Donut said. "You did it again! The first thing that comes into your head —" I had put my foot in it. Frying pan to fire! Me and my big mouth!

Danger's mother looked from me to Donut, then back to me. Suddenly, she burst out laughing — a rich, fruity laugh. What we all loved about her the most. "You had me going for a while!" she said. "You're just making another movie, aren't you? What are the brains for — a special effect?"

I was about to say no — because I have a hard time not telling the truth — but Donut nodded enthusiastically. Auntie chuckled. "You're in luck. That French priest who is visiting Father Vichai absolutely can't live without my *'cervelles de veau au beurre noisette et capres.'*"

"Sir *what?*" I said.

"I didn't know you could speak French, Auntie."

" I don't speak French, my dear. But I *do* speak *food!*" She went to the fridge and pulled out a bowl. "I bought too much anyway," she said. "Father Boucher's getting on in years, his appetite isn't what it used to be. If this batch isn't a movie prop, it'll just go to waste."

I looked at the bowl. It looked disgusting. It was a brain all right. Small, but definitely a brain, full of convoluted gray matter. Chilled. I was sure Polo would find it very appetising.

Polo had come to, and was straining against the cuffs. It was now after lights out, but his face was lit by candlelight and we were nonplussed to see that Mr. Strange was already there. Mr. Strange and Polo were having a kind of conversation. Rather, Mr. Strange was talking, and Red-shorts Polo was grunting and moaning.

"You wanted to see me, didn't you?" said Mr. Theodore Strange, looking up at us when we arrived. He was sipping blood from a plastic bag, the kind they use to give blood transfusions He must have found a blood bank nearby. "I did indeed," he said. "One that allows after-hours withdrawals."

"Are you a telepath?" I said.

He laughed. "I have very acute hearing. My senses are, shall we say, *attenuated.*"

Polo was straining now. I put the bowl in front of him.

His voice was barely a whisper. "Uncuff me," he said. "Or you'll have to feed me."

"I don't have a spoon," I said.

"Use your fingers."

"What, and let you bite them off?"

"Open the drawer," said Donut. "Under the handcuffs, there's a silver spoon. In case of vampires."

Mr. Strange seemed bit nervous. "I'm allergic to silver," he said. "I'd better sit farther off." He moved to the piano bench.

I ungagged Polo and started feeding him the brains with a spoon.

"That feels so much better," he said, and he started to sound a lot more human. "If you can keep feeding me brains, I'll be able to talk normally and I won't go chasing people down."

"So … what were you doing in the fridge? How did you get here? *Why* are you here? And what can we do to fix … what you've become?"

He nibbled delicately on a spoonful of brain.

"It's not just me," he said. "It's the whole school. Maybe the whole world. We don't know much since the internet went down. Thanks for gluing on my ear, by the way. I've lost the ear three times already. I came through the fridge to get help."

"There's no cure for being a zombie," I said.

"That," said Mr. Strange, "is the reason you need to consult me. You would find out that zombies are not some Hollywood invention but a genuine feature of the vodun religion on Haiti, where African deities are blended with Christian saints. The creation of the 'zombi' is a common ritual in that culture and subject to perfectly non-supernatural rules."

"So we're talking science, not magic?" I said. This was interesting. I love logic. I hate stuff that doesn't add up.

"Yes," said Mr. Strange, patting Polo on the head. "To make a zombi, you introduce a substance called the 'coup poudre' into the bloodstream. It's made from the internal organs if the puffer fish. Yes, the same *fugu* that the Japanese eat as a delicacy which has a tiny chance of making you drop dead. The victim falls into a death-like state, is buried for three days, and then dug up again. He then is given datura, a kind of schizophrenia-inducing herb, which disorients him. And then, you see, he believes himself to be a zombie. It's quite interesting, actually. From the Kikongo word 'nzambi' you know."

"So he's not actually dead at all? What about eating brains?"

"Your friend seems to have all the signs of the Haitian ritual, but because of his cultural indocrination, he's behaving like someone who has seen *Return of the Living Dead* instead of an average Haitian villager."

"So you can be brought back? Can you do it?"

"Hardly. Your friend needs science, whereas I ... I actually *am* undead, beyond the limitations of the human world — I don't have anything to do with science. Your friend needs two things ... first, a psychologist, to help bring his mind out of the mess it's in ..."

"Oh! Sister Evangeline!" both I and Donut said at the same time.

"And then, to actually treat the physical condition cause by the *coup poudre* and the datura .... someone who can brew the antidote. A *houngan.*"

"What's that?" I said.

"Oh. A Haitian vodun priest ... in layman's parlance, a witch doctor."

15

Too Many Polos

Polo

"Anyway, sister," I said to Sister Evangeline, "we have to fight this. We can *not* let people dictate our gender roles to us. I haven't even picked my own gender yet — but I'm certainly not gonna let a school administration pick it for me."

"It's tough." said Sister Evangeline. "You have no idea."

"How did you end up here?"

"I think maybe I will show you, not just tell you," she said.

Sister Evangeline took me from her office through a back stair that I did not remember from my real school. We popped out of a side door and to my amazement, there was a motorcycle parked there. I mean, not some little toy scooter but like, a *Ninja*, which cost, I don't know, over a million baht. Two helmets lay on the seat and she handed me one. "Hop on, little sister," she said.

"I'm impressed."

Did Sister Evangeline have a motorbike in my world? A Ninja?

"Yes," she said, almost as if she had just read my mind. "But I kept it hidden. I only used it on rare occasions. We take vows of poverty, you know. But it was useful when they wanted to send me to get supplies for the convent, so I kept it. As long as I didn't flaunt it only used it in ways to benefit our community."

That was it.

Down a little pathway and then out through the main driveway that led out of the school to — well normally I'd say *freedom*, but I was still in an alien reality. We both were.

Sister Evangeline took us down the skinny country road. Not surprisingly, she drove like a demon. We went all the way to the nearby village and past it, turned uphill, screeched up some hair-raising hairpins and then Sister brought us to a tiny church.

"There's a church here in the hills? But there's no Catholics in this part of Thailand."

"True, but this is where all seventeen of them worship."

"What about the chapel at St. Cecilia's?"

"That's a private chapel. This is the parish church. Father Vichai and Father Meechai take turns here."

"But I don't think you brought me here for a tour of the Jesuits' failure to put Siam in their column a hundred years ago, Sister."

She laughed. "I wanted to show you something."

We walked through the gate and around to the side where the hill sloped downward. There was a small graveyard there. A stone angel stood guard. There were not many graves, but there was one, near the back, that seemed new.

"This grave," said Sister, "is just outside the church grounds. You see where the grass stops being evenly trimmed, and grows wild?"

I followed her. The marker was simple. But someone had left flowers.

"Oh! *Someone* cares," I said.

"I left those flowers myself," said Sister Evangeline. "I don't want her to feel alone in there."

And then I saw the name on the headstone....

Sister Evangeline, it read, *to our perpetual sorrow. Greatly missed by her devoted students.*

"This is your grave?" I said. "But you're standing right here."

"Shall we dig it up? Maybe it's empty."

"This is the reason there aren't *two* of you in this world? One of you is dead? And buried in unconsecrated ground, which means you must be —"

"Yes. I told you it is tough to fight back. In this world, Lavender Evangeline couldn't handle it. In this world, she — I — committed suicide. I'm told it was quite spectacular. Quite bloody. It's really uncalled for, considering I am supposed to be a trained psychologist, and I help other people not to do what I do. As Father Vichai would say, 'Physician, heal thyself.' *Not.*"

"So you're dead."

"I am."

"But you came back ... how did they handle that?"

"I'm not sure, really. My being here must violate a hundred different laws of physics. But for now, it looks like reality is temporarily broken, and it doesn't mend itself right away. There's a window — we can fix it."

I sat for a while on the knoll, contemplating the grave of the person I was with.

Meanwhile, the nun who was in the grave was walking around, unable to sit still. She was nervous. I don't think she was that comfortable dressed as a man. It was probably triggering a lot of painful memories, like being picked on as a child.

I was a lot more calm than she was. Maybe the Sister Evangeline in this world had given up. But I wasn't going to.

The first thing that occurred to me was this. Was it possible to have two of the same person in one universe, or would some kind of spacetime paradox get triggered? Obviously, there was only one Sister Evangeline here, because the one that belonged here was dead.

So where was the other Polo?

Dead, too?

I did not want to ask Sister Evangeline. Well, I was scared to ask her. If she knew something and wasn't telling me, that would be scary. If she didn't know, that was even more scary.

But that night, I kind of got a clue when Danger and I were lying in our beds. And Danger was the one who hinted at it. I thought he was fast asleep. I couldn't though. The moonlight streamed in through the window, and the longer I was in this world, the more little differences I was spotting. Even the sounds in the night were different.

"Polo," he murmured.

He climbed out of bed and got into mine. He was shaking all over. Diffidently, I held on to him. "Did you have one of your visions?"

"I dreamed I was at your funeral."

"But I'm not dead."

"In my dream you were. It was really vivid. We were in a temple. You were in a white coffin and they lifting up the lid so they could hammer it down. And then ... when I looked at your face, just before the lid slammed down, your eyes opened ... and you were about to scream...."

I sat up. Danger was shaking. It seemed natural for me to comfort him. He reached for me and I found myself kissing him. It was pleasant. I mean, Danger had kind of an electric glow to him. I don't mean that, metaphorically, sparks flew. I mean there were actual bolts of blue mini-lightning dancing on his lips and I was getting these mild electric shocks. It wasn't unpleasant. Just, well, weird.

He said to me, "Do you want to do it?"

"Do what?"

"You know. Like the other night."

So, the real Lavender Polo was a *lot* more different than I thought. Maybe even wilder than me. I wasn't sure I was ready to assume his identity completely. "I ... um, I have a headache," I said, reaching for an excuse I'd seen in movies.

"Oh," he said, sounding rather disappointed.

"Listen, Danger. I'm just piecing things together right now. It's as if I woke up in a different universe from the one I fell asleep in. But your visions ... they often are about the future, right? You often see things *before* they happen. So your dream could be a warning."

"Still scary. I don't want you die, especially since we started, um, fooling around."

"So maybe I'm not dead."

"What? You're obviously not dead. I mean, you're talking to me."

"Wait. Listen. Do you know about the Crystal Pathway?"

"I've dreamed about it."

"Have you ever heard of Club X?"

"Yeah, of course. We're all members. It's a club for studying the X chromosome. We went on a field trip to a biolab in Bangkok once."

"Ok. I'm going to start telling you things, and you need to believe me. First, I'm not the only Polo. I come from another reality. *Your* Polo, maybe, is alive, but we can't have more than one Polo in the same universe at the same time, so reality needs to fix it, just like it did with Sister Evangeline, by killing one off. There's only a tiny window to save *your* Polo or one of us is going to snuff it."

"Are you crazy?"

"Danger ... you *know* I'm telling the truth. I'm your best friend ... in *every* universe."

He thought about this for some time and then he said, "What you're saying ... I've seen bits of it in other visions ... but it never made sense. But what can we do?"

"I can't let me die."

"Now *that* does not make sense."

"At first I wanted to stay here and fight this weird gender thing that seems to be affecting your universe. But that's probably a job for Lavender Polo. I'm *Blue* Polo, you know. Where I come from, in school, we wear blue shorts. And we can pick our own gender. We need to get to the Crystal Pathway, find Lavender, and I need to change places with him and get back to my own universe."

"Where's the Crystal Pathway?"

"In Club X."

"Sister Eunice's biology lab?"

"No ... no ... the Old Building ... you mean you don't even have a proper Club X headquarters here?"

"Yeah, we meet in the biology lab."

"Okay. The room I'm talking about is probably still there, maybe never opened in a century. I'll take you there. Now. We have to deal with it now."

Because I couldn't get Sister Evangeline's tomb out of my mind —

"Now?"

"Yeah, now! You want the nightmare to go away, don't you?"

"I guess."

"Get dressed."

"But they turn out the lights at the Old Building after 10 pm."

"We'll use the flashlights on our cell phones."

"What's a cell phone?"

That was the last straw. This alternate universe was the pits.

16

A Head of Time

Polo

"You don't know what a cell phone is? The thing you use to watch web series, chat with your friends, send voice messages —"

"Oh, you mean my *handy!*" Danger went to the bedside table and pulled a cell phone out of the drawer. "You call this a cell phone? Some new rich people's slang?"

So things have different names in this universe. I'd have to prepare myself for vocab chaos! Lavender World probably has all sorts of language traps. I've got to keep my mouth shut and listen. The more I was in this world, the more insecure I felt.

But at least they had cell phones, after all. *I shouldn't have panicked.*

I turned on the light, got completely out of bed, and started to tell Danger about my world. Where boys were boys, girls were girls, and where Polo is Polo, because Polo just *is.*

"It sounds like heaven," Danger said, "and it makes where we are now feel like one of those dystopian sci-fi movies."

I told Danger to wipe off the traces of makeup, and not to tuck his shirt in so neatly. "Trust me. Where we're going you'll blend in better."

"Where *are* we going?"

"Trust me. No. Trust your own visions."

The good news is that Club X was in the same place in this world. Thank God Kim had keys made for all of us last term. And thank

God my key worked.

The door opened with a familiar creak. I started to feel more at home.

Once inside, I saw all the familiar things. The Egyptian gods. The Indonesian masks. The busts of composers. The tarot cards, wrapped in a piece of silk. Yes, this was all stuff I was used to.

"Where are we?" Danger said.

I touched his shoulder and I could feel him getting cold. Like he does when he has visions.

"Are you okay?"

"I feel like … I'm wavering in and out of existence. Like sometimes I'm not here."

I held onto his arm. "You're solid," I said.

"I don't feel solid."

I waved my cell phone flashlight around the room. The pink sofa, the old piano. All familiar, all comforting. "This is Club X," I said, "where I come from. This is where the four of us hang out. Five now, since Donut showed up."

"Who's Donut?"

"Really," I said. "That would take some explaining. Can't you just pluck all this info from my head?"

"That's kind of creepy. But I do it sometimes. It gives me an awful headache afterwards and I feel dirty."

"Donut's a girl."

"A girl-boy? Or a boy-girl? I don't think we ever had any girl-girls here."

If this had not happened in his world, I was never going to be able to explain it.

And then there was this …

The door to the closet was ajar. "It's open!" I said.

"What?"

"The door to the Crystal Pathway."

The doorway was shimmering with a cold blue light. We didn't even need the light from our cellphones anymore. The whole room was lit with the eerie illumination. The Egyptian Gods on the shelf seemed almost alive. There was a low thrum. The door was active. It sensed us. It had been left open for a reason.

"Do you trust me?" I said.

"I don't know."

"Do you trust yourself?"

"Maybe."

"Isn't your inner voice telling you that you must straight through, into the vortex, screw the risks?"

"Actually my inner voice is telling me that I'm in danger of snuffing out of existence — like a candle."

I said, "Through there … there's answers."

Danger said, "What if the answers contradict the answers I already know?"

I didn't know what to say.

"Look," he said, "you're so different since I last night. I know you were gone for a little while — you told me your parents were sending you to some meditation retreat to clean out your brain — but I didn't think your brain *could* be cleaned, I mean, you're *Polo,* right?"

So the meditation center was true here as well. But it hadn't worked out in quite the same way. Or had it?

I was starting to realized that we were not just displaced in terms of space — in a different universe than before — but also in *time.* This was probably why he didn't know who Donut was. This is why he hadn't entered *our* Club X before … maybe he hadn't met Dr. Strange yet, hadn't been told about our true purpose … in fact … did he look a little bit younger than *my* Danger?

"Don't you know Dr. Strange?"

"Yes, of course. Sister Dr. Eunice Strange, she's the supervisor of Club X."

One bombshell after another! I didn't care. This guy was still my friend, too. I wanted to show Danger there was a better way to live than the weird autocracy of the Lavender World. I didn't believe he would just pop out of existence immediately if Blue Danger came. How long had the two Evangeline's coexisted? Was the grave actually empty? I was scared, too, but I don't like to be told what to do. I took Danger by the hand and half pushed, half pulled him to the door.

Before we got there, though, the door swung open.

I saw Danger in the door. "I've found him!" he was saying over his shoulder. I could hear Fluke muttering behind, somewhere behind Danger. "The map doesn't say it's the right world…"

Danger had one foot over the threshold. He was about to step in. It was Blue Danger — *my* Danger! He was so happy to see me that he was just about to run in and give me a hug. He hadn't even seen the person I was with —

I had been holding Lavender Danger's arm and he basically popped out of existence. I realized what had happened. It was the two-Polo paradox!

"Throw the door wide open," I cried out, "and stay behind it. Don't step into this universe!"

As soon as he stepped back, Lavender Danger came back. "What happened? I kind of blacked out. The whole world stopped and I was just inside a big *nothing*." He looked at his blue twin on the other side of the door. "It's true," he whispered.

"I've seen you in my dreams," said Blue Danger.

"Me too."

"I always hoped there was another person just like me."

"He's not," I said, "*just* like you." A twinge of jealousy, perhaps. Danger is my best friend. Well ... they *both* were. Wouldn't it suck if your best friend suddenly cloned himself, and they liked each other more than they liked you? But I realized I'd have to deal with it for now, and if we could solve all these mysteries, we would eventually end up with everyone in the right universe, and all the universes *fixed*.

So I prodded Lavender Danger into stepping toward the doorway. "I told you we have to go through. The two of you can't coexist in the same world, but in the Crystal Pathway, the rules are different."

"Yeah," Fluke said from beyond the door. "It's kind of an *in between*."

I pushed Lavender Danger a little harder.

We both stepped into the closet.

And all at once, were in the throneroom. I knew this room from our adventures last term. We had almost lost Danger in that throneroom because he'd become seized by megalomania and started acting out about his insecurities with being the only poor kid in our group. He was like this all-powerful emperor ordering people's heads chopped off and meaning a general shit. He had learned a major life lesson in that throneroom. But Lavender had not.

But he was definitely feeling the power.

Blue Danger — my *original* danger — was all over me, he was so happy to see me. And when I turned to look at Lavender, I could tell that *he* was experiencing a whole lot of mixed emotions.

I think the moment had come a little too soon in Lavender Danger's timeline, because suddenly his face became all contorted. He marched up to the throne in the middle of the room. He clambered up. Knights, nuns and courtiers appeared and started kowtowing.

Lavender was huffing and puffing as he sat down. Some lackey handed him a scepter and put a crown on his head. "It's true, isn't it? I have unlimited power here."

"Yeah, you do, but —" Blue Danger began.

"Can I execute people?"

"Um —" I said.

"Okay then. This universe isn't big enough for two Dangers!" He snapped his fingers. Guards ran in and seized *my* Darger.

"Of with his head!" said Lavender Danger.

"On the contrary," said Blue Danger, wriggling free from the guards. "What a fucking usurper! Off with *his* head!"

17

S.O.S.

Danger

So here we were in *my* throneroom, and some dude who looked just like me was trying to get people's heads chopped off. That was the bad news, but the good news was that we found Polo. But before we could celebrate, I had to deal with the other me.

"Tie up the other me," I said to the guards. They grabbed Purple-Pants and threw him onto the throne — *my* throne! — and trussed him up with ropes. "Is he secure?"

"Yes, Lord Danger."

"Hey!" Other Me shouted. "Untie me and tie up the other one!"

The guards began loping over in my direction.

"No you don't!" I said. I used all the mental tricks I'd learned over the past year to *force* the guards to obey me. A halo of blue light gushed from my hands as I pushed against the empty air.

The guards went back to the throne and one of them held an axe over Purple-Pants.

Other Me flung a bolt of blue flame at me, but it sputtered went out.

I threw one back at him. Big, with a sci-fi spaceship *whoosh* as it pierced the air.

"How'd you do that?" he said. "Aren't we the *same?*"

Fluke looked up from the map. "This Polo is *our* Polo all right," he said. "Can we just pick him up and go? We can get back to the real world now. I want to get back to Kim, he's worried sick, I'm sure."

"What?" said Purple-Pants. "And leave me here?"

"You're obviously not the real me," I said. "I've spent the whole of the last school year discovering how to unlock my powers. I've been walking the Crystal Pathway all this time, getting stronger. That's why the guards listen to me, not you. This whole Kingdom of Danger came out of my imagination. Each time I came here, it became more real. You're just a shadow version of me. So stay here and rot and leave the real world to the real people."

"Wait, Danger," Polo said. "His world is real too. Their Club X is in Sister Eunice's lab and they haven't discovered the Crystal Pathway yet, so obviously he hasn't come into his full power yet. But he's just as real as you are. And I brought him here to get our help."

"Our mission was to save you," I said. "Isn't that right, Fluke?"

"Yeah," Fluke said. "And we've been wandering in here for days, Crystal Pathway time."

"We haven't even popped out for anything to eat, let alone sleeping or taking a piss. Who knows how much time has transpired in the real world," I said.

Purple-Pants struggled against the restraints.

Polo looked from me to the other Danger. Then he said ... "Our mission isn't over yet."

"After all we've been through?" I said. "Maybe we should bring you up to date."

Fluke

Seeing the two Dangers hurling superpower bolts at each other was disturbing. I mean, the other Danger wasn't *our* Danger but he had all the same quirks and mannerisms and even the same tendency to get a bit over the top if he was given just a little bit of power. I felt queasy about tying him up and just leaving him.

Danger said, "Tell Polo everything we've been through."

I told Polo about our adventures but to tell the truth they had not amount to that much. Just going from corridor to corridor, following the map, nothing to eat our drink, and none of the doors opening. Danger seemed to know where we were going, though. It had been a kind of circle, or maybe a spiral, since we were ending up in a place we'd already been to ... Danger's own fantasy kingdom.

To be honest, it hadn't been an adventure at all. Just me and Danger getting more and more confused, and every time my bit of yarn yanked at my wrist, I missed being back in school and able to confide in Kim. I missed his curt way of talking. Kim always spoke the truth without thinking. Danger was a bundle of bewilderment.

"Calm down a bit," I said to Danger … I mean Blue Danger. Lavender Danger wasn't talking, just trying to zap at the ropes with some kind of psychic energy beam. "If our friends also exist in other versions in other worlds, we at least should allow them to coexist."

"Sure," Danger said after a while. "Okay, Purple-Pants, get up and walk." He clapped his hands and the ropes fell off Lavender Danger. Lavender got off the throne and looked up at his counterpart sulkily.

I said, "Are we the real world? Did the other worlds branch off from us? Or are we some kind of weird offshoot ourselves?"

Polo said, "Listen. Lavender Danger needs our help. I brought him into the closet so we could help him, not tie him to a chair."

Polo then told us about how at the Lavender school world, gender seemed to have gone haywire. "No one is allowed to be themselves," he told us. "They're trapped in these fake identities. I want to go back and fight them! But I can't. In there world, there can only be one of each person at a time. Maybe that's true of all worlds. Did you know our Sister Evangeline is trapped in Lavender World? In *their* world, Evangeline committed suicide and she's buried in an unconsecrated grave just outside some church. It's like she's standing at the doorway looking at redemption, and she can't get in. I wish I could help our Evangeline … and bring her home."

"If there can't be two of anyone in that world," I said, "how come *you* were there?"

Lavender Danger said, "A few days, Polo went somewhere. I thought he was ill, or something. Then … *you* showed up."

"The other Polo is dead?" I said.

"Or lost," Polo said. "Lost somewhere in *here.*"

"Or the rules don't apply to you," Danger said. "Why not? Rules never apply to you."

It was at that moment that something yanked at my piece of yarn. *Hard.* So hard I lost my balance and sort of flew through the air a bit. Polo steadied me.

The yarn was pulsating, jerking.

"Kim's trying to signal me," I said.

Three short yanks. Three long yanks …

Danger said … "The yanks. They mean something They're regular."

"It's morse code."

It came again. S.O.S. S.O.S.

"Something's wrong, I said."

"Can you send a message back?" Danger said.

"I'm trying." I waited for a lull and pulled on the yarn myself. W.H.A.T? I messaged.

More letters came. "What's it say?" Polo asked.

"It can't be," I said. "It's like, Z.O.M. —"

"Zombies?" said Lavender Danger.

"Shut your face. You're not even really one of us."

"But we had to do a whole project on Morse code with Sister Eunice," Lavender said. "That's exactly what it says, Z.O.M.B.I.E.S."

"That's the dumbest thing I ever heard," said our Danger.

"No, it's not," said Polo. "There was something ... in the fridge up in the St Cecilia headquarters in Chiengmai. When I took the train up north to see Cardinal Crank. There were ... things in the fridge. Quivering body parts. And the Cardinal mentioned zombies ... in a special facility, somewhere."

"Looks like another mystery for Club X," I said, sighing. "Let's get back."

"C'mon, guys! Don't leave me behind!" said Lavender Danger.

18

Too Many Worlds

Polo

"Look, we're going to have to leave him behind," I said. "The only place that can definitely contain more than one version of each person is *inside* the Crystal pathway. Once we step back out, it's one Polo, one Danger. one Kim, all that."

"We can't keep me, I mean *him*, tied up like that, though," said Danger — *my* Danger. "I couldn't live with myself if I left myself to rot."

"I'll cooperate," said Lavender Danger.

"Getting rid of you would be convenient," I said. "Blue Danger and I could then operate freely in your universe. And we could bring down the establishment, wreak havoc, and have a wild bring-your-own-gender party."

"I'd love to have met Sister Strange, too!" Fluke said. "What a trip!"

"Yeah, yeah. I met the other Sister Evangeline. That was wild, too. But the thing is, you came to the Crystal Pathway to find me. You found me. One mission at a time. Take me back and *then* we'll sort out the zombies."

"What about me?" said Lavender Danger. "I gotta eat."

"I have an idea about that,"Fluke said. "Who's good at Morse code?"

"Me," Lavender said.

"See?" said Blue Danger. "One way or another, you need us both."

Fluke said to Lavender Danger, "See this little bit of yarn that sticks up from my wrist and seems to disappear into a whole somewhere? Purple-pants, you're gonna yank on the string, ever so carefully, and the message you need to send is "BRAHMS."

"What will that do?" said Lavender.

"It will get us home," I said. I knew that Fluke would know the answer.

And I really wanted to get home. The Lavender world was intriguing, but I didn't want to live there. I wondered how Evangeline could choose to live in a different reality like that. I wondered how Lavender Evangeline was feeling when she killed himself.

Donut

This wasn't exactly a subspace relay, but there was some kind of communication going on. The string was dancing in the air. Red Polo, gorged from a surfeit of *cervelles,* was asleep, snoring and farting and dripping slime, still cuffed to a chair. *Mr.* Strange was off already, said he had a dawn curfew.

"This message was definitely from Fluke," Kim said to me. "Look — see? It says *Brahms,*" he went on. "The first message just said WHAT? — it could have been anyone. But only Fluke would pause in mid-adventure to carry no a discussion about classical music."

"That's it?" I said. "Brahms?" Honestly, I wasn't even sure who Brahms was. Sometimes these boys made me feel like I didn't know anything.

"So move the puzzle pieces around in your mind," I said. "You'll figure it out."

"He sent this message because it refers to something only I would know." He went to the sideboard, where all the composers' busts were. He took one out. Bronze. Looked like it weighed a ton. "In case you're wondering," he said, "*this* is Brahms. Catch!"

He didn't actually throw it, but it was an armful.

"It won't break," he said, "it's solid bronze."

"More likely to break *me,*" I said.

He went to the closet door, put his hand against it. "Come closer," he said. "Kneel down by the door. When I give the signal, shove the Brahms in so the door can't close."

I watched him. His hand glowed felt the familiar tingle of opening my mind's eye to be receptive to other realities, other possibilities. I heard the latch pop and pushed the door open. Then I wedged

Brahms very carefully inside the doorway.

"He wanted you to stick a composer in the door?" I said. "What was that about?"

"Brahms solved our dilemma once before," he said. "He knew I would remember."

"He's coming back."

Another message was coming through. I could see the string dancing wildly in the air.

"Shit," Kim said.

"What?"

"A.V.O.I.D. D.U.P.L.I.C.A.T.E.S."

"Avoid duplicates?"

"We already have *one* duplicate here. We have a Polo in red shorts. But if *our* Polo comes back...."

"Maybe it solves our problem. Maybe the Red one goes back to his own world."

Red Polo stirred. "Brains," he murmured.

I said to Kim: "If Fluke comes back ... we won't be able to on another date, will we?"

"Shut up. We weren't on a date."

"Well, we were alone together. And you almost kissed me."

"Who knows? We were interrupted by a zombie."

Fluke

We're communicating, I thought. "Let's get back and regroup."

"Lavender?" said Blue Danger.

I made a decision. "We'll let him come with us," I said. "In his own way, he's our friend."

"We have to be careful," Polo said. "When I landed in Purple World, I didn't just switch to an alternate timeline. I think I stepped into an earlier place. Lavender Danger doesn't know who Donut is, for example."

Our Danger said, "I'm not going leave myself behind. I mean ... would you?"

I thought to myself. Our lives are like a sonata. The different people in our lives are like *themes.* When a sonata starts, we introduce each theme, and we tell a little piece of each person's story. That's the *exposition.* And then we get to a midpoint. That's when we're ready to set out on our journey. Then comes the *development section.* It's like a quest, and all the themes, they shift, they play in different keys, they start relating to each other differently. We travel far and wide and sometimes it seems that we are lost.

But I'm not like the others. Kim is closest to me, and yet, in some way, so opposite. His universe is a mechanistic one. It's a giant puzzle and he's the one to put each piece in its rightful place.

I'm not like that. In the end, you see — the others will never really understand — in the end, I believe there is a God.

And therefore, the quest, even at the point of no return, when all seems lost, I believe the quest is taking us somewhere, to a place where we will once again be home — home, but changed, wiser, more compassionate. This is what Bach teaches me, you see. It teaches me that you always find the way home. No matter how wild the journey.

Danger released his Lavender alter ego from the throne. I looked at the map, but I also followed Danger's instinct. We made a left and we were at one end of a long corridor. How long, I don't know. It was so long it ended it a point. There were doors on either side. The doors were all identical. We kept trudging on. I don't know how many doors we passed. A million. There was no sense of time, either.

I looked at the map.

We kept walking. They were all the same. We were on a kind of multiverse treadmill, and opening the wrong door was not an option.

"This is like a branching-off spot," I said. "One of these doors is the door to our world. But which?"

The map just showed thousands of lines, all converging into a single spot. And that spot was *us*.

"How much further?" Polo said.

"Danger," I said.

"What?" they both answered.

"Pool your superpowers."

"Okay." I heard it in stereo.

"What is the *one* doorway that has a bust of Brahms wedging it open?"

"We're standing right in front of it, you idiot," said my Danger.

In fact, *every* door had Brahms wedging it open.

I had a huge, and terrifying thought. If a new universe branches off at *every single fork*, whether it's a human decision to turn left or right, or a subatomic particle deciding whether *to be or not to be*, what guarantee did we have of *ever* returning to the same reality that we left? And how would we even know the difference?

Reality, I suddenly understood, *is fuzzy.*

Which flew against everything I wanted to believe in.

I picked a door at random. I peeked through the crack that Brahms had created.

"Kim?" I whispered. But my eyes were closed. For a moment, I didn't dare open them.

19

Too Many Dangers

Kim

My eyes were still closed but I felt something warm and a little bit wet on my lips. It was, I have to admit, a nice feeling. But right in front of Donut? Was that really him? I opened my eyes and found myself grinning like an idiot.

Without turning around, I could also feel that Donut was feeling uneasy, like we'd be caught in the act ... of what, though? Cheating? It wasn't like that.

"Thanks for making it back," I said.

The yarn was connected all the way, now, and all in the real universe. With our free hands, we untied it. "Free at last," Fluke said, laughing.

I looked at the door. Polo was stepping over Brahms. But the minute he crossed the threshold, his leg vanished. I mean, he was just stepping into nothing.

"It's the Two-Polo Paradox," Fluke said. "Who's that, dribbling slime all over the sofa?"

"That's Red Polo," I said. "He's a zombie."

Polo stepped back. He was all there again. As long as he stayed behind the door.

Behind Polo, I could see, not one, but *two* Dangers. The other Danger was wearing lavender shorts and had makeup, so that meant that we were dealing with at least *three* timelines.

Fluke, reading my mind, said, "Yeah, I know. Makes your head spin. But it can't be worse than a twenty-sided Rubik."

"Please don't send me away," said Red Polo.

That's when our Polo noticed him. "Why is it always me?" he said. "No matter what universe I'm in, I get to be the outsider. This sucks."

"Being you isn't as bad as being me," said Red Polo.

"At least you're not always on the wrong side of the gender divide," Polo said.

"So? I'm on the wrong side of the alive-and-dead divide," said Red Polo.

"At least you're sitting comfortably and getting fed," Polo said.

"I think we all need to make a plan," I said. "And it's hard to make a plan when some people can't get past the door crack."

I had to think. I was happy to see Fluke again and sure, they had accomplished their mission, I guess. They had managed to find Polo and bring him back. And we could all be together again if we just forced the zombie back into the Crystal Pathway, and pulled our Danger back into Club X and slammed the door shut, we would all be back to normal.

Everything would be in order.

But it wouldn't be the right order.

I said to Fluke, "I feel like shutting out all these other worlds. I'm having enough trouble with just *one* universe. And who knows how many more we'll have to deal with if we get involved. We could just wind the yarn back, make the clock go backward, whatever."

"But you don't *really* want that," Fluke said, understanding the part of me I did not like to acknowledge.

"No, no," said Red Polo. "If you're gonna do that, *kill* me first. You think I *like* being a zombie? I'm trapped in a nightmare and I can *never* wake up."

I could see that Fluke was feeling sorry for him. I know Donut kind of liked him, too, especially after we fed him all those brains; he was like a macabre kind of pet snake. She said, "What if we just made him go back into the fridge?"

"No, no! Not the fridge! I hate the cold."

"Just for a while, man, just till we sort it out," I said.

Fluke and I each grabbed one of the zombie's arms. He didn't really struggle much, didn't resist at all, but he was heavier than our Polo. It was like he was encumbered somehow with the weight of the earth. We steered him toward the refrigerator and Donut held it open. Fluke and I shoved.

Red Polo murmured, "Guys, I thought you *liked* me! Don't do this to me."

Fluke and I pushed hard. There was a blue shimmering light in the back of the fridge as we shoved him. Somehow, he managed to *fall through* the food ... like they were overlapping realities for a moment.

"No, please!" he said.

Donut slammed the door.

"The back of the fridge," Donut said. "It must be another way into the Crystal Pathway. I mean, how else would he fit in there?"

I sighed. There was a sad and empty feeling. I didn't want to do this to a friend, even if he *was* one of the living dead. But I felt better when our regular Polo stepped across the threshold.

"We were worried," Donut said. "Where have you been?"

"Oh, God. Egypt. Well, not *actually* Egypt, just a kind of pseudo-Egypt in the middle of the Crystal Pathway. And then ... the Lavender world ... where Sister Evangeline committed suicide, and *our* Sister Evangeline is hiding out, and ... everyone's the wrong gender?"

"You should have felt right at home, then," I said.

"You don't understand. I didn't feel at home at all. In fact, I felt like I needed to fix it."

With Red Polo in the fridge, we still had to deal with the Dangers. Both of them were pushing and shoving, each of them trying to get into the room, but since they couldn't coexist in the same universe — they were continually having their arms and legs pop in and out of thin air. It was actually pretty comical.

Fluke said, "Let's take out Brahms, and put a big chair in the door instead. It can hold the door open and Purple-pants can have a seat, while we talk this out. Just as long as he doesn't try to come in here. He can still be part of the conversation."

"But the only chair in this room that would fit the doorway —"

"Yeah," Donut said, laughing, "your official chairman's 'throne.'" Laughing, she and Fluke lugged *my chair* over to the open door. We were able to have the whole chair on the other side of the threshold, *and* keep the door wide open. I should have thought of it myself, but hey, it was *my* chair.

And Danger in lavender shorts was occupying it, while *our* Danger gingerly stepped over into Club X.

We were back to normal, except for someone from another universe watching from the doorway, and a zombie in the fridge.

Lavender Danger was fidgeting and pouting. He wasn't *naturally* a girl, the way Polo could be whenever he felt like it. He was more like an exaggerated *katoey* from some TV soap.

"Club X is in session," I said, eyeing my chair and looking for somewhere to sit. I settled on the piano stool. Fluke was there before me, and already playing some fugue or other, so I just sat on the edge. It was comforting to feel his back against mine.

I said, "We've got too many mysteries. Too many worlds We need to concentrate on one at a time."

Polo said, "This all started with zombies. Let's save the zombies first. The zombies have been leaking into our world for a while. I saw hints of it in Chiangmai."

Fluke said, "Maybe whatever weird experiment is happening in Chiangmai — maybe the Cardinal is running some kind of weird lab or whatever — and it's causing major ripples."

I said, "Dr. Strange's brother said something about having to get the antidote from Haiti."

Polo said, "Why not? I just flew in from Egypt. Business class. Haiti, no sweat. Dad's credit card seems to work in any universe."

"We need our Club counsellor," Fluke said, "We need *our* Dr. Strange. *Mister* won't do. He might suck our blood while we're sleeping."

"And our Dr. Strange is wandering around on the Pathway, in some research trip," said Polo. "Did Red Polo say anything about *his* Dr. Strange?"

"Let's not let him out of the fridge yet," I said.

"He won't come out," Polo said, "as long as I'm here. He knows he'd just disappear." Polo went over to the fridge and opened it up again.

A wailing sound came from inside. We all gathered around. All we could see were Red Polo's eyes, peering over the top of a six-pack of Coke.

"You can't come out anymore," Polo said. "I'm back."

"Can you push the brains over to the back?" said Red Polo.

"Tell us about Dr. Strange," I said. "Then I'll give you a spoonful of brains."

"Dr. Strange is way over the line," said Red. "He was the first zombie. We got him good. We jumped him and crushed his head, and buried him out in the field. That was before I ... caught it. He bit me when we were trying to restrain him."

"I guess that's not going to work."

Lavender Danger piped up from beyond the door. "I can fetch *our* Dr. Strange. I'll think of something to say."

I realized that he could be useful after all. Especially since there was no time in the Crystal Pathway, so possibly he could go and fetch *their* Dr. Strange in what would seem to us to be no time at all. "Okay," I said. "You bring him. Hurry."

"Her," said Lavender Danger. "It's *Sister* Dr. Mary Leopold Strange."

20

For a Spoonful of Brains

Polo

With Lavender Danger gone, and Red Polo trapped in the refrigerator, we were now once again the old Club X, just the five of us. I was anxious to tell the others everything I knew. And just anxious to calm them down. "I mean, I would have found my way back," I said. "As long as the Pathway still surfaced in one of the known locations. I've got the credit card."

It was the delayed reunion of Club X after the adventures of last year. And here we were, already plunging headlong into new mysteries — in parallel universes.

So much had shifted in the intervening time. It was easy to blame it on Donut. But the change had begun even before Club X existed ... when Kim and Fluke had their trauma with the cardinal, and when they awkwardly ... endearingly ... became aware of feelings for each other that got in the way of their friendship. And Danger and I were best friends, both of us outsiders, and *then* I started to experiment with my identity, and he started to discover his secret superpowers. Still, when Donut showed up, she really busted up relationships.

Kim said, "If we're going to have a proper meeting, can I have my chair back?"

"We need the closet door wedged open," Fluke said. "He could be back any minute."

"Yeah, but not my chair," Kim said. "You know I hate when things are out of order."

We ended up wedging the piano stool into the doorway instead, just so Kim could have "his" chair. He gets really nervous when something isn't in its proper place, so this multiverse stuff must have really been taking its toll on his mind.

When he sat down again, he seemed much more able to take charge.

"Prioritize," Kim said forcefully. Now he sounded like the old Kim. "Zombies first, then gender. Because zombies are life-threatening, but for the whole world to become like Polo isn't going to *kill* anyone, just make them uncomfortable."

"Very," I said. "It's the only time I *ever* felt uncomfortable in my own skin."

"Do you think we can interrogate the zombie a bit?" Donut said. "As long he stays inside the refrigerator."

"Let's try," Kim said. "Danger, go down to the school kitchen and ask your mom for some more brains."

"Actually I'm pretty sure we got the last of the brains," Donut said.

Kim said, "Ok. We'll just have to use smaller dosages."

They opened the fridge, took out the bowl of *cervelles*, and spooned out a small dollop. He thrust the spoon deep inside. Presently, we heard a revolting sucking, chewing, and burping sound.

"If you want more," said Kim, "you're going to have to answer a few more questions"

"Let *me* do the asking," I said.

"Sure," Kim said. "You probably have a lot more facts at your disposal than we do."

I looked into the fridge and saw myself. Not clearly. It was a wavery reflection, shimmering against the back, behind the orange juice and the half-eaten mango. The back of the refrigerator wasn't a solid wall. It was sort of half-liquid. My face floated in the liquid, but it was a parody.

"You look bad," I said.

"Just forgot my makeup this morning," the other me said.

I turned to Kim. "Inside that thing," I said, "It's another me all right."

"More brains?" Red Polo rasped.

"Be serious," I said.

"I'm dead serious," he said. "Pun intended."

"You are definitely *me*," I said, "just not quite as alive. I recognize your bad jokes. So tell me. How are we going to fix you up? Tell me of your world. Is it like that movies where zombies have taken over the whole universe and only Will Smith is left? Or … is St. Cecilia's an isolated outbreak?"

"Hard to say. There's like … a wall around the school."

"A wall?"

"Not a physical wall. But we can't leave. If you go to the edge, you boomerang right back into the middle of the school again."

"How many zombies?"

"A lot."

"But you're not completely gone yet. I mean, we're talking."

"It's more complicated than *Dawn of the Dead*, sis. They're not just animated lumps of flesh. Even the most rotten ones are still *somebody*."

"But where are you getting all the brains from? Did you eat Dr. Strange's brains?"

"Um … kind of."

"What was it like?"

"What the hell are you asking?" Kim said. "We don't need to know what Dr. Strange's brains tasted like."

"They were kind of spicy," said the forlorn voice from inside the fridge. "They made me sick."

"This is useless," Kim said. "Danger, *you* do something."

"Do what?" said Danger.

"I don't know," Kim said. "Pull some more information out of his mind."

Danger stepped up to the refrigerator. He closed his eyes and he concentrated hard. "I'm not getting much," he said. "There's a residual consciousness, but —"

"Residual?" I said. "He's giving as good as he gets. For every smartass remark, I get one back."

"But maybe that's just your *own* mind, being reflected back. Maybe he is a blank reflector — like a mirror. But … wait," Danger said. "Now I'm getting something."

Danger

Probing into someone's mind wasn't something I wanted to do very much. I didn't even know if a zombie *had* a mind.

I like to open bottles, boxes, doorways, stuff like that, you know, inanimate shit. Opening a mind, especially an unwilling one … I felt

105

queasy even thinking about it, but I always do what Kim asks. He's our leader, Asperger's and all. We trust him.

Nothing … then, I felt a blip of an consciousness for a second. I recognized it as the real Polo, *my* Polo … not that I've ever probed his mind, but we've shared a room for years, and I can tell the color of this thoughts.

"Feed him again," I said.

Kim scooped out another spoonful.

I concentrated hard and I tried to send my mind into the void. It was making me woozy. I was spiralling into a dark place … a *dead* place. There was a rotten stench in the air. I was burrowing into Red Polo's skull and I was coming up with a terrifying emptiness.

"Gather round," I told the others. Fluke, Kim, Donut and Polo all instinctively reached out to touch me. I could feel their love. It steadied me.

"What do you guys see?" I said,

"Nothing," Kim said. "Blackness. But wait —"

There it was! Swimming in the dark, a stray thought, flitting like a fish. There were images. Images from *before* … and I knew the others, as they held on to me, could see it too, maybe not as clearly as me, but enough to scare them shitless.

… I saw Cub X. Not this one, the one in the Red World. It was like a black and white movie. I was seeing through Red Polo's eyes but he was barely conscious now, and I just got images —

Dr. Strange, snarling, growling, leaping at Kim, tearing off Donut's arm —

"Holy shit," Donut said. "Did that really happen over there?"

— then I felt myself pick up the bust of Brahms from the shelf and bring it smashing down on Dr. Strange's head, I felt myself breaking open Dr. Strange's skull, could feel his rotten fangs grind through my hand, tearing flesh and bone, and —

Again. Again. I was reliving the scene again and again. I was trying to scream but nothing came out.

And other glimpses. Watching Kim's eyes go dead. Hearing myself whimper, "No, dude, don't turn. Please don't turn."

Lugging corpses down the stairs. Corpses that kept twitching, that wouldn't stay dead.

— Red Donut and Red Polo digging graves, out in the field, and —

In the distance, more kids. In the moonlight, their shorts looked bloodstained. Holding weapons — here a shotgun, there a baseball bat

— in the middle of the field, a pile of corpses. Little Boom was there, pouring a bottle of vodka over the heap. "Flambé the fuckers!" he was yelling.

— I could feel my lips moving. "Gotta burn them," I was saying. "Burial won't be enough." Flames leaping up in the field, bonfires everywhere.

The kids were gripping me hard. They were all seeing what I saw now. The images were getting clearer. My powers were stronger. I could see and I could transmit what I saw.

I felt consciousness leave Red Polo.

I could feel blackness … and this huge, yawning, insatiable hunger … and this despair. A whirlpool of despair and we were slowly being sucked in, like being flushed down a toilet. We were drowning. And there was like this knotted, sick heaviness curled up inside our guts.

"For God's sake, shut the fucking fridge," Fluke said.

Donut slammed it hard. The horror dissipated, but the feelings still hung in the air. We couldn't speak, we couldn't even scream

So we just all went and sat down in our familiar places, the five of us. I looked at all their faces. I knew we'd all felt the same thing.

"I don't know if those little pieces of consciousness flitting around — were him," I said. "Maybe they were just reflections from Polo's mind, bouncing around in the emptiness. The darkness is hungry. It wants our minds … our souls. Red Polo won't be content with calf brains for long."

We sat there, just bummed out, for a long moment. I think even Kim was thinking there was nothing we could do about this.

There was a pounding at the closet door.

"I've brought Sister Strange," Lavender Danger was shouting.

21

That Which We Call a Rose

Fluke

Dr. Strange came barreling into the room. Lavender Danger tried, but immediately started to vanish, so he sat down reluctantly on the piano stool.

Dr. Strange was exactly the same as *our* Dr. Strange. When Dr. Strange, it was the same drama-filled, booming voice. But ... she was a nun!

"Ah! delightful!" she said. "Now, I am Sister Mary Leopold Strange."

"Good evening, sister," we all said.

She breezed into the room.

"No need to introduce yourselves," she said. "I already know you all ... at least, I know your alter egos. My, you are very handsome as boys! Oh! There's a girl here, too. Aren't you the principal's daughter? When did *you* join the school? Perhaps your universe is a little more gender-progressive than I've been told."

"Our universe is *fine*," Polo said. "*Yours* is some kind of totalitarian dystopia."

I said, "Polo, calm down. We won't get anywhere if we act like our universe is somehow superior."

"Oh, but it is," said Sister Dr. Strange. "Let me explain. Kim, give up the throne for a moment, will you, dear?"

I know how much that irked Kim, but he got up meekly and let Sister Strange sit. Then he squeezed next to me, so it was pretty cramped on the sofa. Eventually, Danger and Polo slid onto the floor. It was awkward.

"I'm addressing my remarks to you, Fluke, because you know enough to grasp the enormity of all this post-Einsteinian quantum mechanics. But first I want you to know that this universe — the place were you have blue shorts — *is* the true world. All the others are ripples that encircle the real world, becoming more and more alien the further they get. Maybe you're not *superior,* but your world is the null point, the *sine qua non.*"

Polo said, "Why do they always have to say things that only Fluke can understand?"

I shrugged. "She's just saying that without our world, the others would not exist."

Polo said, "So if someone kills me in *this* world, I go *poof* everywhere else?"

"Not exactly," said Sister Strange. "These things are true on the quantum level, not in the macroverse."

"What she means," I said, trying to patient, "is that you might go poof in a few nearby worlds, but the farther way the ripple goes, the more it could diverge."

"Such a clever boy," said Sister Strange. "Even smarter than *our* Fluke."

"Why am I not in your world?" Donut said. "Looks like Purple-Pants over there had never heard of me."

"It's temporal lag," Sister Strange said.

"Oh!" I said. "So there's a time gap between divergences. Let me guess — at the quantum level, the lag is almost undetectable, but by the time our shorts start changing colour, we're quite a bit separated in time."

"Right again."

"And how far behind is Lavender World from ours?"

'Perhaps a year." I wondered whether the Red world was even further back. It made a kind of sense, since Lavender still has blue in it, but red doesn't.

Kim looked at me. "So ... where you come from ... Donut isn't at our school."

"No, she's in a girl's school in Bangkok."

"You should tell her father," Kim said, "that she's about to be kicked out of school again."

"No spoilers," I told Kim. "You'll end up changing the present if you go screwing up the past."

"Right," he said. "Please go on, sister."

"A few beings are *originals*," she said. "There is only *one*, no matter how many universes branch off. They're one in many, and many in one."

"Cardinal Crank," I said.

"The cardinal's not from any world," she said. "His dwelling place is *inside* the Crystal Pathway, you see. The creatures who come from *inside*, people have seen them … they call them aliens, or angels, or ghosts … it all depends on their belief system. There is a city in the heart of the Pathway. That's where you can find them. They rarely interfere in any of the worlds *outside*, but Cardinal Crank is a bit of a maverick."

I could see this was just too much information for most of us. Sister Strange didn't seem to realize we were in the middle of a crisis. In fact, she carried on in this vein for a while and though I was fascinated, I could see we were losing all the others.

Finally, Kim said, "*Our* Dr. Strange's brother, Mr. Strange, told us we have to find a *houngan* … a witch doctor. Do you have know one?"

"I might," said Sister Strange. "But first … I have a present for all of you."

She reached into a fold of her robe and pulled out … some rosaries. She handed one to each of us. Then she went to the closet door and gave one to Lavender Danger.

I said, "Sister … my friends aren't Catholic."

"Look closely."

I held the rosary up to the light. The beads were crystal … not that different, in fact, from the crystal key that Kim and I had swallowed last term. The circlet of crystal did not end in a crucifix, but in a kind of "X". X for "Club X," I said.

Sister Strange giggled. "Cute, isn't it? We disguise science as religion. Just as in some societies, we must disguise magic as science."

Both Dangers held theirs up at the same time.

"It's glowing," they both said.

"Double trouble," said Polo.

These were more than just rosaries. Mine, too, was starting to glow, perhaps drawing on the warmth of my body. I saw that the two Dangers' rosaries had different-colored auras — our Danger's like mine, a pale blue, the other Danger's a rich purple.

"This … ah, *rosary*. You can keep it in your pocket. You can wear it on your wrist, or better yet, around your neck," said Sister Strange, "though that's not really the usual place you'd put a rosary. But actually around your neck is the best location to make sure the field spreads evenly. You wouldn't want to have a hand stuck in an alternate world and not be able to yank it back."

"You mean —" I began.

The two Dangers looked at each other.

"Step into the Blue World, Lavender Danger," said Sister Strange.

Lavender Danger got off the piano stool and entered the room. Polo and Kim moved the piano stool back to the piano. I went back to my logical seat. The two Dangers kept staring at each other. Sure, Lavender was wearing a bit of lipstick, and a touch of eye shadow, but … "Wow," they both said.

The glow from the rosaries was spreading now. All of us were haloed in blue or purple light.

"I call it an A.R.G," said Sister Strange. "Deep inside the Pathway, there's a Catholic gift shop. You'll find they have all been charged to Polo's dad's credit card. The Pathway was able to store the number when Polo was buying a business class plane ticket in Cairo."

"Thanks," Polo said, a bit miffed. "What's an Aaargh?"

I knew. "Alternate Reality Generator," I said. "I just figured it out. It creates a field around you so you're in your own reality, and not part of whatever world you're in. We're all here, but we're not here."

Sister Dr. Strange said, "That which we call a rosary, by any other name …"

"Would smell as sweet," I said.

"Cardinal Crank will probably end up inviting you to the interworld Shakespeare competition," Sister Strange said.

"Except all the contestants would *be* Fluke," Kim said, laughing.

I took the last rosary from Sister Strange and I opened the refrigerator door. I hung it on the end of the spoon that we have been feeding him brains from. I poked it down there, as close to the back as I dared. A whiff of decay hit us, and everyone was holding their nose.

"Okay, my zombie friend," I said. "Put this on. You can come out now."

22

"Inside Outside"

Polo

A drum roll would have been cool. But no. Just the rattle of soda cans and a bowl of brains. We watched as Red Polo emerged. Very much the worse for wear, but he was wearing the crystal rosary around his neck. I use the word "neck" loosely because a big old chunk of vertebrae showed through. His cheek had a flap, loose, too. He was in a bad way.

"Don't make me go back there again, please," he said.

"Phew," I said. "What a stink." I put my hand over my nose.

"I can't help it, I'm a rotten human being," he said.

Okay. This Club was designed for four people. Then Donut joined, and everyone's relationship with *everyone* else went haywire.

Now there were seven of us, including duplicates, and our official club advisor had changed sex. So we were cramped and nervous and the stench sucked.

The room felt crowded, especially since Red Polo was stinking up a storm, and oozing slime over the carpet. We were all wearing those rosaries that were actually high-tech devices. So we were all glowing a bit. The people from our world had a soft blue light; Lavender Danger had a pretty purple halo, making him look fairly convincing in his makeup, and Red Polo sulked in a pool of crimson that made him look even more nightmarish. He was a ghastly parody of me and yet I recognized myself.

He looked up at Dr. Strange ... now Sister Mary Leopold Eunice

Strange. "Nobody expects the Spanish Inquisition," he said. Then he giggled, like one of those Chucky dolls.

That sounded familiar, couldn't think why. I think it was supposed to be funny, but then again, his brain was probably pretty decayed at this point.

"Can we start the interrogation, please?" Red Polo said. "I mean, it's brains for answers, right? And I'll say anything for a dollop of gray matter, you all know that."

Sister Strange sat in Kim's chair. For once, he didn't seem to object. She was like the judge, we were like the jury, and my living-dead replica was like some kind of criminal suspect.

"First question," said Sister Strange. "How did you get into this world?"

"In our school, there's like a big freezer room. They use it to store the meat for the kitchens. But they also stack up the bodies there. I mean, when they cull the zombies."

He got a spoonful of brains.

Polo painted a terrifying picture. It was a nightmare version of our school, where gangs of vigilantes roamed about, zombies ambushed the unsuspecting, and most of the kids barricaded themselves in their classrooms and foraged for food.

"When did this start?" I asked him.

"There was a video game. *Zombie High.* It's set in a Catholic boarding school for boys in the Khao Yai national park. Everyone was playing it. Then, suddenly, the school *was* the video game."

More brains.

"But," Danger said, "why would everyone start playing it?"

"It was like a virus," said Red Polo. "It was on everyone's phone, everyone's laptop, even on the school computers. You try to message someone on FB and suddenly you were playing the game."

"Outside the school," Fluke said. "Beyond that wall of force that prevents you from going off-campus. Is the world normal?"

"I don't know," Red Polo said. A blackish rheum oozed from his eyes. Icky. "It happened all at once. It started in the kitchen. "I think I'm the only one in Club X that turned, though. The others are holed up inside Dr. Prachaya's office. Dr. Prachaya is holding them off with a shotgun."

I really wanted to help. I asked Sister Strange if there was something we could do. I said to Sister Strange, "You have to do something! Mr. Strange told me that he needed two kinds of help —

scientific help from a psychologist, to see if he can recover from this trauma — *and* scientific help to reverse his condition."

"If only you'd found me earlier!" said Sister Strange. "My twin sister is right; science *and* magic could have helped him once. But the process ... well, you can see he's falling apart before our very eyes. As far as the physical self is concerned, if you could locate all the missing bits and glue them back together again...."

"Ew!" I said.

"And psychologically speaking, I'd have to talk him slowly out of believing that his is a zombie. Which is a bit of a problem. He really does believe it."

"Can't you *un*-believe it?" I said.

"You must be joking, sis!" said Red Polo. "Take a look at me!"

"The process is probably irreversible," she said. "Unless...."

Suddenly, it was like a lightbulb clicked in Kim's mind. There's this look he gets when he suddenly sees the solution of a puzzle. He knew what Sister Strange was going to say. I looked at Fluke and it seems that he might be thinking along the same lines

Kim said, "Sister, the Crystal Pathway ... temporal lag ... that's the key, isn't it?"

Fluke said. "You're right, Kim. The universes are not in sync. There's no simultaneity, Which means ..."

"Oh!" I got it too. "We have to find the door that opens up to *before* they started turning into zombies."

"Yeah," said Donut. "Maybe before that video game started leaking into the school computers?"

"That is not so easy," Sister Strange said. "The temporal displacement between universes is a fixed constant. So I've been told."

'But Sister," I said, "you know a way around that. Otherwise you wouldn't be here."

"I do," she said. "But you somehow need to get —"

"*Inside,*" Fluke said. "That place where Cardinal Crank lives. It's like a kind of control center for the Pathway, isn't?"

"Yes," said Sister Mary Leopold Eunice Strange. "You're going to have to turn the *Inside 'outside'*."

"Let's do it now," I said.

Sister Strange said, "I've signed a non-interference pact. I can advise, I can give information, and I can warn. What I can't do is lead you to my boss's headquarters and show you which buttons to push. I'd better get back to Lavender, post-haste."

Sister Strange popped out, just like that, just like her counterpart in our world tended to do. So it was just Club X and two extra-Xers.

"Well," Kim said, "We're not going to solve it without some advance planning. Time doesn't mean too much in the Pathway, so I suggest we take the night off. I'll do some research with Fluke about the *coup poudre* and the *datura* aspect of this, though I'm not sure how we could lay our hands on either of those substances. Tomorrow, same time, same place. Better bring some supplies."

"What?" I said. "A flashlight? food? a towel?"

"Whatever you think you will need. Our intuition is the best thing we've got going for us. Let's go to bed now."

Red Polo spoke up. "Where do I sleep?"

Everyone else said, at the same time ... "Not in *my* room."

23

Away in a Menage

Danger

So, stinking Red Polo followed us all the way our room. Which only had two very narrow beds in it.

"Don't worry," Lavender Danger said. "Me and Polo only need one bed." He looked at Polo. "Don't we?"

"Wait a minute!" Polo said.

I said to Polo, "No! You didn't!"

"I didn't."

"What are you talking about?" said Lavender Danger. "Of course you did. We're an item."

"We're not," said Polo.

Lavender said, "What about that time in the closet, when I showed you mine and you ..."

Polo said, "What closet?"

Lavender said, "You know, the *closet*. When you kissed me."

"No way," Polo said.

I always liked Polo. He's always been my best friend. But ... there are things I thought about that I never told him. I mean, he *is* the richest kid in the school, and I'm the poorest. That will never change. But in the *other* world ... somehow ... that *had* changed. Why? I felt a pang of envy, even though Lavender Danger looked ridiculous.

Meanwhile, Red Polo stood in the doorway, stinking up the room.

Lavender Danger said, "Tonight ... with that cool blue light glowing around you ... you look *amazing*." Lavender moved toward Polo and Polo didn't exactly shrink away. In fact, he seemed intrigued. "You're perfect," Lavender said. "You're just at the midpoint. You're all girl and you're all boy. The school preaches to us every day about respecting gender by learning to live the other role, but I know that is fucked up. I know from what you've told me that somehow our reality was tinkered with. But you ... I know that you're the only one who really fulfils what they're talking about."

He talked just like I *thought*. Which was not surprising since he was *me*. But why couldn't *I* be that me, too?

"I'm not the Polo you think I am. In fact, I still have my —"

"Even better!" said Lavender Danger. "I've already tried it without, and now I can try it *with!*"

"I don't belong in your world," Polo said. "In this world ... Danger and I haven't *done* anything. Though I know he wants to."

Lavender looked at me. "Pussy!" he said. "If I lived in your world, I'd have the guts."

"Leave Polo alone," I said. "He's mine."

"Says who?" said Lavender.

"Wow!" Polo said. "I'm being fought over."

It was true. I couldn't stand the idea of another *me* being with him, when the real me wasn't. I flung myself at myself and we actually got in quite a few punches. Then I realized that I'm not a physical person. Instead, I balled up my resentment and flung it at him.

My anger manifested as a ball of blue flame and guess what, a purple shield sprung up to reflect the rage back into myself, which made me even more pissed off.

"Bitch!" said other me, hurling a purple ball. I turned it into a hail of butterflies. "Nice trick," he said, clapping his hands and transforming the butterflies into hornets. I quickly fended off the hornets with a well-aimed volley of blue darts.

"Stupid," Polo said. "I'm trapped in a low-budget VR game." He dived between us and put one arm around each of us. "There's only one way solve this," he said. He pulled us both close. "Kiss and make up," he said.

We did. "Each other," Polo said, "not me."

Too late. The three of us fell backward onto the bed with Polo sandwiched between us, and we were all fumbling with our clothes. Something amazing was about to happen. I could sense the electricity. The purple and blue light played over the three of us, shifting, dancing.

Suddenly, a hideous whiff swept over us. It put a damper on the mood.

"What about me?" said Red Polo, unbuttoning his shirt and shambling toward the bed.

***

Fluke

We sat across from each other, each on our own bed. Kim was glowing. He was radiant, like how you would imagine a saint or an angel. I was glad to be with him again.

"You look like a pillar of light," I said.

"You look like a boy with an ARG," he said.

"You're so fucking literal-minded all the time."

"You've always known that."

We stared at each other for a long time.

Finally, Kim said, "Donut."

"Donut?"

"I had a date with her."

"Where to?"

"Chocolate Factory."

"Good for you," I said, though I didn't think it one bit. "Did you ... ah ... you know? Do anything?"

"We might have," Kim said, "but a zombie came out of the fridge and kind of interrupted us."

"We don't need other people," I said. "You can't blame a zombie."

"Maybe I blame Donut, a little bit. I mean it's not her fault, but our world was perfect with just the four of us, and she kind of screwed up *everyone's* relationship."

"You can't blame a girl, either."

"She did ask me if you and I were an item."

"What did you say?"

"I didn't answer."

"Are we?"

"In the confessional. Last term. You said it. Not me."

"And you were the one who rescued me. I still love you."

I crossed over to his side, sat beside him. I put my arm around his shoulder. He felt weird. It must be the ARG, I thought, stopping us from being in the same universe. It felt like a kind of nothingness. I hugged him then. It was an empty, a strangely desolate sensation. He hugged back. I felt only nothingness.

"We're not really here," Kim said.

"Does that mean ... if we happen to ... you know ... we're not *really* doing anything? At least, not as far as the real world is concerned." I said.

"We're both Blue," he said. "We don't need to be protected from our own world. Or from each other."

"I know. It makes no sense. But ... I can't feel you."

"Then take off the rosary."

"No. I'm afraid to."

Then, without warning, his lips were on mine. And still, I felt nothing.

***

Donut

I'm at home, the only student at St. Cecilia's who gets to sleep outside the school dormitories. Well, fifty meters outside. And tomorrow, we're going to travel to the heart of the world inside.

I've got to be *ready*, I thought.

It was stupid, but I started to pack a little bag. I didn't need clothes — time had no meaning in the Crystal Pathway, right? we never had to spend the night there, or even go to the toilet — but I was sure I was going to need some defensive stuff. A crucifix. A bulb of garlic. A silver necklace. Silver was good for a lot of different monsters, werewolves as well as vampires. And zombies? What do zombies hate?

The internet wasn't helpful. One website said, "Zombies don't like hippies and nudists ... and clowns." That was the best I could find. Plus, you have to get them in the head.

My brother, the pesky Boom, can sleep in school because he's a boy. I know that's stupid, but I guess it's how the world works.

I didn't expect him to pop over to the principal's quarters tonight, but suddenly, while I was hunched over the computer researching zombies, he did a horror movie cat-jump and scared me out of my skin.

"So, zombies hate hippies and nudists, eh!" he said, laughing.

"Shut up and go back to little boys' dorm."

"No way, sis! You're going on an adventure, and I'm not going to miss it this time."

"Bullshit! I don't go on adventures!"

"Bullshit yourself. I watched Kim's movie too, you know."

"That was a movie. It never happened."

"You can't fool me, sis. Last term it was vampires. I'm guessing zombies this year. Look. I can help, for a small tip."

He went to his room (which is a filthy mess and no one ever goes in there — not even him since he started sleeping in the school dorm) and came back with a pile of stuff. He's a real hoarder. He showed me a tie-dyed headband. A bottle of water marked "Lourdes." Most impressive was a clown mask. But not funny at all — it was one of the scary ones, little something out of a Stephen King movie.

"The website said they hated clowns, right?"

"And hippies. And nudists."

"Well, you can just take your clothes off for that. As for hippies — here are some beads as well as the headband. And look, I won't charge you for any of these important monster-fighting tools. I just want to go on the adventure, this time."

"You can't," I said. "You see this thing I'm wearing around my neck?"

"You can't wear a rosary around your neck, sister. Father Vichai says that's blasphemy."

"It's not a real rosary. It's something to protect us from infection by parallel universes."

"Infection! So your zombies are a virus, like in *28 Days Later*, not from biting and scratching like in *The Walking Dead?*"

"I don't know. Anyway, you can't go. We only have enough of these protective shields for our group."

"Oh. I'll just take a bribe, then. Let's say, five hundred baht."

24

Once Upon a Time in Khao Yai

Kim

It was time to go on a quest. An epic quest to save the universe.

Last year, we sneakily broke our vow of silence by making a movie, pretending truth was fiction. This time, I knew we'd be able to make a really *big* movie because of that little piece of paper that I'd gotten twelve years ago for my birthday. With five or ten million baht worth of BTC, I'd be able to hire people instead of doing every job myself, from director to gaffer to slating the shots.

But before making the movie, we first had to have the adventure. Every story has to come to some kind of climax and resolution, and right now we had been at that point in every quest where everyone splits up and has their own mini-adventure before being brought together for the final thrust.

I may be a social misfit, but I know how a story is supposed to be told.

I was beginning to imagine how good Danger must have felt when he ruled his own kingdom in the Crystal Pathway and was on the verge of having Polo's and Danger's heads cut off! Those were the days! For him, anyway. Not for anyone who got decapitated.

A good size for a quest party is seven. That's a number that's filled with magical meaning, a lucky number. And we had seven as well, though some of us were imperfect duplicates of each other.

We had two Dangers — blue and purple. We had two Polos — red and blue. Purple Polo had gone missing, might even be dead. And me and Donut and Fluke makes seven.

We didn't have Boom, because we only had seven of those dimensional-barrier rosary things. But Boom came to Club X that morning, because every epic also needs someone who doesn't come on the adventure but who, well, "sings the songs" — a bard. Of course, the idea of Boom as our Homer was kind of stupid, but there it is.

One thing we learned from last year ... Boom can't keep his mouth shut. Especially if he's paid.

If we didn't make it out alive, Boom would tell our story.

I explained all this to the Club, but they didn't really take me seriously.

"That's ridiculous," Fluke said. "If we don't make it out alive, and he isn't with us on the adventure, how the fuck is he going to tell our story?"

"He'll make it up," I said. "You think the Trojan War really happened just as written?"

"Poetic license," Boom said.

"You'll lose that license over this," Donut said.

"I'll call it the *Kimiad*," Boom said.

"All right, all right. Are we prepared?"

"I've got the food," both Dangers said. They had raided the kitchen at different times; Danger's mother never realized there were two of them.

"Twenty-one boxes of Mama noodles," said our Danger. "Twenty-one hard boiled eggs. And a jar of brains."

"Twenty-one Hokkaido tarts," said the other Danger. "My mother's greatest creation. Twenty one *more* boxes of Mama. Oh, and a jar of brains."

"But how will we cook the water for the noodles?" Donut said. "We're not bringing a microwave. There might not even be anywhere to plug it in."

"Don't be silly," said Boom. "Teenage boys *never* cook the noodles. They just scarf them straight from the packet."

"Gross," Donut said. "You're lucky I brought brownies."

"Do they have 7-11 in the Crystal Pathway?" Donut said.

"I've got the map," Fluke said. "I'll check."

"I don't have to bring anything," said Red Polo. "I'm dead."

"And what have *you* brought for the quest?" I asked our own Polo.

"My keen wit and powers of observation," he said, and did a sexy turn, and winked at the two Dangers. What *had* happened last night?

It looked like Polo was hiding something. "Oh, I brought my lucky compact, too. The one we caught Sister Edward in last year."

"Fair enough," I said.

"*You're* not bringing anything," Donut said to me.

"That's where you're wrong. I fished my contribution from my back pocket and threw it to Boom.

"A ball of yarn?" Boom said.

"You're going to hold on to your end of it for dear life. And if the yarn goes limp, we're probably not coming back, so you can start making up stories."

Fluke

"But what," I said, "*is* our quest?"

"What is this, Monty Python?" said Kim. "Do you want to know my favorite color, too?"

"It would help if we all had a purpose," Donut said.

Danger said, "Yeah, like find the One True Ring or find the missing Stone of Power."

Kim said, "But we know from last year that the magic isn't in stones or rings or keys. It's in ourselves."

Polo said, "I want to fix the other worlds. The zombie infestation, the gender-gone-haywire."

"Let's just have one quest at a time, or Kim's next movie will be a mess," I said. "Shall we vote?"

"There's no real question," said Danger. "Our zombie friend is stinking up the room and last night ... last night he actually tried to make out with me."

"With me, not you," said Lavender Danger.

"I vote for zombies, too," said the zombie. We all caught another whiff; he seemed to have popped a pustule or something. "I don't want to be a pariah anymore."

"You don't get a vote," Polo said. "Dead people can't vote."

"They can in America," Red Polo pointed out. "I saw it on the news."

"Well," said *our* Danger, "*I* vote to go after the zombies, too."

Polo said, "No, I wanna go and rescue my sisters from their sexual enslavement in the Lavender Universe."

"I'm with Polo," said Donut.

124

"I think I'm with Polo on this one," said Kim. "Fighting zombies is a bit too similar to fishing keys out of shit like we had to do last time."

"You made *me* fish it out," I said. "You just watched and filmed it!"

I suddenly realized that I had to cast the deciding vote.

Everyone was looking at me. Except Boom, who was trying to tie the yarn around his wrist. Usually it's Kim who makes the decisions and everyone just goes along, because he's the one who cuts straight to the chase. And he had sided with Polo.

If I agreed with him, people would just think I was automatically doing whatever he wanted. If I disagreed, people would start worrying about if our relationship was going to break up again.

I've always believed that we should know where we are going. In a Bach fugue, you know how it's going to end. It's the getting there that is the story. But maybe life isn't a perfect musical composition. Maybe *not knowing* is important as well.

And anyway, there was a better answer.

I said, "We don't choose our quest. Our quest chooses *us.*"

There it was.

So, in confusion and uncertainty, with a dubious map and a ball of yarn, after carefully wedging the bust of Brahms in the closet doorway, we set off into the labyrinth yet again.

25

French Fries from Heaven

Danger

Where to begin? We trooped through the closet door, hoping the bust would stay wedged there. Donut had the yarn around *her* wrist because after all it was her brother back in our world. There was only one way to go at first, a corridor overhung with crystal stalactites, with doors at irregular intervals on either side.

The idea was that Fluke would use the map, and I would use my instincts, and between the two of us we'd know where to go.

But it was complicated by the fact that there was another me there.

And he so like me.

He walked like me. He answered when someone called his name.

But he'd done things I'd never done, things I've fantasized about but never dared consider for real. And yet, he also never been a king, with the power to cut off the heads of his best friends.

How we travel is like this: I should go first, because I have the sixth or seventh or eighth sense, whatever, I have the psychic nose. But it's hard because Lavender keeps wanting to get ahead of me.

"Maybe you know more about Polo's dick than me," I said, "but I know the Crystal Pathway. You're just a tyro here."

"What dick?" he said.

"What do you mean, what dick?" I turned around to look at Polo.

Our Polo was way in the back, deep in quasi-conversation with Red Polo.

"Polo! Lavender says you don't have a —"

"It's complicated," Polo said. "Look, Lavender, in *this* world, I am a fully equipped male. I haven't had anything done." Polo pushed his way to the head of the line. "Not that I haven't thought about it. But then Sister Evangeline told me the story of St. Origen and it made me kind of queasy."

Unfortunately, the zombie Polo was also coming to the front, carrying his powerful stench of decay with him.

"Don't walk so fast," Fluke call out from the back. "Remember, I've got the map."

"What use is a map? This is just a corridor."

Yeah. There was just this endless corridor. Sometimes the walls glittered with crystals. Sometimes they were pitted with bullet holes. Sometimes it was peeling floral paper, sometimes marble, sometimes plain old concrete.

And doors, often marked in strange languages. Often unmarked. One door, in English, said "GENTS".

All kinds of doors.

Iron gates, dungeon doors, modern doors, glass doors, doors with curtains, doors with hippie beads, doors with padlocks.

"I've seen that door already," Lavender said. It was a door like something in a mediaeval castle, oak, with bars and a rusty antique key in the lock.

I looked. He was right. We passed that door before. Maybe more than once. Why were we both at the head of the line of adventurers? Because, apparently, we had the nose, the instinct. It was our job to correct course, if we felt something amiss.

"I think you're right," I said. "Guys, stop a sec. I think we're going in circles."

"But the path is straight," Polo said.

"Odd *you* should say that," said Lavender, blowing Polo a kiss.

Fluke

I'm the only person who knows how to read this map. And even I can barely read it. For one thing, when you open it, it's not always the same. It's more like a googlemap in the form of a scroll, showing a different part of the manysided universe depending on your own location.

For another thing, it's in Coptic, which is like crazy Greek writing but the language is Egyptian. And I don't actually speak Egyptian. Nobody does, not even Egyptologists.

The Dangers were right. The path was not straight. It was an illusion. Unrolling the map I could see this huge spiral road bang in the middle. The spiral had what looked like little hairs ... so the whole thing resembled a rolled up centipede. The little hair-like centipede legs, I thought, must be the doors, but they weren't really labeled, so I couldn't figure out where they led to.

The Dangers were up front because we figured they'd have an instinct for the right direction to go, but actually there seemed to be only one direction right now. I said to Kim, "Call a halt, we need to assess."

"Lunch break!" said Kim.

The corridor widened a little. We were in like a mini-lobby — we happened to reach it the minute Kim called lunch. The walls were like a crystal cave, with stalactites and stalagmites glistening,

Donut said, "This lobby just appeared, I mean the corridor grew *wide* just when Kim said *lunch*."

"Shit, Kim, you *changed* the world, and you're not even me," said Danger.

In fact, they *both* said it.

Then, "I have an echo," they both said.

We laughed. "Let's break out lunch," I said, "then we'll talk."

Polo started to unpack the dry Mama noodles, but the two Dangers looked at each other and laughed. Our Danger said, "Guys, don't you remember when I was King down here?"

"I only had a little taste of being king," said Lavender Danger. "You guys stopped me."

Both of them pointed up in the air, and just like that, it was raining French fries. Hot, perfectly salted, plus little paper cups materialized in our hands so we could catch them.

"Wow!" Donut said.

I was reminded of the story in the Bible where God rained down manna from heaven so the Israelites wouldn't starve while wandering in the desert. Did this mean that Danger was a god now? Well, he'd been a king last year, so maybe a promotion was in order. He was certainly a lot mellower than before. Maybe you have to experience being about to cut off all your friends' heads before you achieve wisdom.

In half an hour, we were sated, especially after the two Dangers made a stream of cream soda fountain up from the floor, only running out when our thirst was slaked. There was a quick rain of ice cream cones, as well. Bubblegum, Rum Raisin, and Rocky Road.

"If I'd known the Dangers could feed us," Polo said, "I wouldn't have made them pack all this food."

Meanwhile, Red Polo had only a jar of brains to nibble on.

At least we knew we would not starve on the Crystal Pathway. I said to the group, "Don't get rid of the food yet. Once we leave the Crystal Pathway and enter whatever world we're supposed to enter, the Dangers' powers might be a lot less godlike."

"More brains," Red Polo grunted.

A full-on, slime-dripping brain fell from the ceiling and landed in his hands. We all groaned. Red Polo started to slobber over It. Nauseating.

I unrolled the map. The spiral filled the whole page now. In fact, when I opened up the map some more, the spiral grew, too. As we finished eating, the soda fountain dried up and the uneaten fries popped out of existence. And the widened corridor began squeezing in on itself, like the garbage compactor on the Death Star.

I looked ahead. I looked behind. It actually looked the same in both directions.

"Let's try something," I said. "The whole company; about turn! March!"

"That's *my* job," Kim said, laughing.

But it wasn't funny, because even though we started going in the exact opposite direction, it felt as if we were still going the same way.

"At this rate," I said, it will take a very long time to get to the heart of the spiral, if that is even our goal."

"Show me the map," Kim said.

"But you can't read ancient Coptic," I said. "I've been trying to interpret it myself for hours. I don't think you'll be able see anything."

He leaned over my shoulder, nuzzling my neck, peering at the shifting shapes.

He put a slender finger on one of the little hairlike lines and drew with his finger, from the line, cutting across the spiral all the way to the center.

"There's a logical, step-by-step way," he said, "and then there's the Kim way. Saying the quiet part out loud, also known as cutting the crap."

Suddenly I knew what he meant. "We short-cut through," I said.

"Like a space warp."

I could see now that the hairlines could be seen as a grid that crisscrossed over the spiral. I could see it, but my sense of order wanted to visualize every step of the journey, like the separate lines of a cosmic fugue. It took Kim's mind to slice through to a solution.

Dr. Strange always said how much we complemented each other, needed each other to be whole.

"C'mon," Kim said, pulling the handle of the nearest door. Which happened to be one marked "GENTS."

"Not the toilet," I said, remembering our last experience in a toilet.

We looked through it. No toilet. Just another corridor, an identical door on the other side.

He started walking. He didn't wait for anyone. We all followed. There was another door and another and another. Every time we stepped through one, the previous one slammed shut behind us.

"This isn't working," Donut said. "We're lost."

But according to the map, it *was* working. Because the image on the map had changed from a spiral to a straight line and we were barreling forward as the map shifted to a kind of first-person view — like a video game.

Maybe we went through a hundred doors or more. All I know is that the process was speeding up and the doors were a blur now. It was almost like we were in a rollercoaster now, smashing through door after door and then we found ourselves falling out of a cloudy sky ...

26

Finding Haiti

Kim

We were on a kind of knoll. Beyond us, in every direction, there were hills. The sun was shining and a warm breeze was blowing. We had landed on grass. It was a soft landing — no one was hurt. We picked ourselves up and looked around. In the distance, a waterfall gushed. Rich tropical vegetation was everywhere, and somewhere in the distance, I could hear people murmuring in a strange language, but couldn't tell where it was coming from.

"It looks like the Crystal Pathway has set us down where we need to be," Fluke said. "Looks like Haiti."

Behind us, uphill, there was dense forest. Right around us were bushes with huge, bright flowers, red and pink. Everything was super-vivid. Almost like it had been lit by a master cinematographer.

I had seen this all before. I was sure of it.

The way the light fell over the waterfall ... the way the foliage swayed ... it was *all* totally cinematic.

"Hibiscus," Fluke said, looking at the flowers. "National flower of Haiti. We're there all right."

"Why Haiti?" Donut said.

"Duh," said Red Polo. "Haiti is Zombie Central."

"Oh, yeah," Donut said. "Now I remember what *Mr. Strange* told us. This is where real zombies come from. They might have the zombie antidote here."

"Oh right," Polo said. "We're supposed to look for some kind of witch doctor."

But I *knew* I had seen this scenery before, and I also knew I had never been to Haiti.

I walked a little further and I noticed something.

The closest hibiscus ... it wasn't moving in tandem with the view. The perspective of this place was off.

"I'm not totally sure this *is* Haiti," I said. I reached out toward the flower, and just behind it, my hand touched cloth. "This scenery isn't real. It's projected onto a —"

I ran my hand along the cloth. When I shifted the fabric, I caught flashes of neon green. "Feel just a few feet in front of you," I said to the others. "This whole Haiti thing is an illusion. We're in a small room, maybe the same size as Club X, and the whole of Haiti is like, green screen. A special effect. I *know*, dudes. I'm a filmmaker, remember?"

And then it came to me. I'd once seen an old movie about a scientist who travels to Haiti to learn the secret of zombies. It was called *The Serpent and Rainbow*.

This exact scenery was in that movie.

"It looks like the Crystal Pathway plucked this whole landscape from my memories," I said. "This is an old movie. I can barely remember the plot."

"How do we get out of this room?" Polo said.

I was already ripping away at the green screen with my bare hands.

But before I could yank the green screen down and uncover the bare room, an old black man came walking towards us. A gentleman in a tattered blue suit. Craggy face. Piercing eyes. Strangely, they were deep blue. Perfect movie casting for an ancient sage. Worn tote back slung over his shoulder, and he was stooping down to pick something from a bush, maybe herbs or something.

"Maybe he can tell us where to find a witch doctor," Donut said.

The old man found some plant he wanted, pulled out out, blew off the loose dirt, and put it in his tote. Then he made another beeline, this time for a shrub with little green berries, and he picked a few of those, as well.

"Picking weird herbs in the Haitian wilderness," said Blue Danger.

"Looks like one to me," said Lavender.

"Maybe he *is* one," Polo said.

"So now what?" I said. "We just go up to him and say, the Red

Universe is in peril, help us save it?"

The old man looked up at me. *"Bonjou, monché,"* he said. His voice was deep, resonant, kind of like Darth Vader.

"He doesn't even speak Thai," I said.

"Or English, I would think," said Polo.

"I'll handle this," said Fluke. He went up to the old man and said, *"Bonjou. Koman ou ve?"*

"Smoooth," Polo said.

"It's Haitian creole," Fluke said. "I can just about fake it from elementary French and the info I memorized from Wikipedia." To the old man, he said, *"Ou konnen yon houngan?"*

"Wi!" the old man said, and began laughing.

"Ki koté?" Fluke asked him.

We stood around being bewildered as they went on gabbing. Fluke always forgets that he knows a lot of obscure shit no one else knows. But we perked right up when the man mentioned *Dokté Etranj.*

"Shit," I said. "They're talking about Dr. Strange."

"Yes, me talk Dr. Strange. Good friend to my village."

"He speaks English!" I cried. We all turned on Fluke. "Fucking showoff."

"Of course me can English," said the witch doctor. "Have clients all over the world. Wall Street. Buckingham Palace. Had tea with Queen Elizabeth last week. Good crumpets."

"Ki koté Dokté Etranj?" Fluke asked, and even I managed to figure out that that meant "Where's Dr. Strange?"

The old man looked at all of us. "You on a quest," he said solemnly. "The little one who smells so bad … you want to save his people."

"But don't we need to get to Haiti? This isn't Haiti," I said. "It's like, a Haiti movie set. You're probably not even a real witch doctor."

"Witch doctor? We no use that word," said the old man.

"Yeah, c'mon," Polo said. "You can't call him a witch doctor. That's demeaning to his culture."

"As he say: Me prefer to be known as *houngan.*"

"And I prefer to be known as *they,*" said Polo.

"And I prefer *not* to be known as *it,*" said Red Polo.

"Ah, little friend," said the old man, patting the zombie on the head. "Carry my bag." He tossed him the tote. "And pick some more datura on way back, those plants with trumpet white flowers."

"I'm not a slave," Red Polo said, but he resentfully complied.

Fluke said, "Actually, you are. On Haiti, zombies are created to use as slaves. That's what the datura is for. It's a drug for keeping zombies in a stupefied state. He's probably going to feed you some."

"But we're not actually *in* Haiti," I said.

"Follow me," said the old man.

He sort of karate-chopped the green screen and it came crashing down to the ground. But — behind the green screen was the exact same landscape ... the waterfall, the trees ... and also hordes of people gathered, some in street clothes, others in fantastical costumes, their faces made up as skulls ... drums were pounding and some people were dancing.

"Byenvini an Ayiti!" said the old man.

A path led downhill toward the waterfall. Shit, it *still* looked like we were in the middle of that movie, *The Serpent and the Rainbow.* I wondered if we'd have to rip our way through another green screen.

We did.

The same scene now, but even more intense. We sidled through the latest rip in the fabric and now we seemed to be among real people. I could smell the sweat pouring from their bodies. In the middle of a circle of onlookers. a woman was swaying and heaving. Her eyes were rolled all the way up so they were just white. She was writhing around like a snake. I didn't think a person could contort like that.

"How fascinating," Fluke said. "She's being possessed by a loa, a voudun god. Damballah, the serpent god, by the looks of it."

"Clever boy," said the houngan.

The odd thing is that our zombie Polo was walking around with us, and no one even paid him any attention. In fact, there was another zombie in the crowd. But unlike Red Polo, he wasn't a mass of pustules, and he didn't stink. Apart from the glazed eyes and the lumbering walk, he pretty much almost passed for human. He has carrying a huge sack — twigs and leaves were poking from it. When he saw us, he joined our group. He was clearly one of our new friend's zombie slaves.

Our friend spoke to the zombie in a commanding tone and he shambled off.

"He just told him to go home and put the kettle on," said Fluke.

"Where are we going?" I said.

"Lunch," the witch doctor said. "After lunch, magic."

27

Zombie-Making 101

Polo

The dancing was incredible. I didn't want to go to lunch with some weird old guy. I could feel the music and the drums were calling to me As they started off down the path, I jumped into the middle of the dance circle.

"No — you no go in there!" the houngan shouted.

Too late, of course. The drumbeat was in my bloodstream. I started thrusting and leaping. I hurled myself into the pulsing rhythms, I was losing myself. I whirled myself dizzy.

And suddenly I seemed like I was falling and falling —

Someone was in my mind. Something slithery and slimy. Someone was taking over my limbs. My eyes were rolling into my sockets. I was blind now, and I could feel my arms and legs undulating like snakes. I had a forked tongue and it was whipping in and out of my lips. I was wound up in a ball, I was exploding outward, pouncing on prey.

I heard people shouting *Damballah Wedo! Damballah Wedo!*

I'm passing into another state of being. I'm being turned inside out. I'm sliding through tall grass. Rearing up. Striking. Sinking my jaws into —

Now now, my child! Just who do you think you're biting?

Where was I?

I was standing in some vague temple-like place, and right in front of me was the guru who had appeared in my meditation to tell me to be

136

true to my self.

So, this was pretty weird. I was still in "Haiti," flailing around like a serpent. At the same time I was in this place of incredible stillness, looking into the gentle eyes of an Indian guru.

"Who are you?" he said softly.

"I —" I wanted to say my name, but another name started form on my lips.

Damballah! the Great Serpent!

"Let go!" the guru whispered.

Was he commanding *me,* or was he talking to the Serpent God? I felt my eyelids quivering. I felt my skin peeling. I was moulting! Scales were flying off my body!

Let go! Let go, my child!

He took my hand. My spiritual hand, because out there, my body was still leaping around in the circle. He grasped it firmly and yanked me, *hard.* I felt myself fly through the air —

I landed in a heap in a clearing. My friends were looking at me. The sunlight was bright and hurt my eyes. A ways off, the celebrants were all still leaping and dancing, and the ground around us was shaking from the drumbeats.

"Me *told* you no go there," said the houngan.

He raised his hand and tore another rip in the fabric of the world.

Kim said, "Even *that* was an illusion?"

"Fucking real," Fluke said.

We stepped through another green screen.

"My home," said the houngan.

Kim

The houngan's home was nothing like you'd expect. It wasn't a hovel. In fact, it was a penthouse apartment — we'd stepped through the last green screen and apparently stepped to an upper level of a building without using an elevator. The furniture was pure IKEA. The living room opened onto a massive veranda and when we looked out we saw — yes, the view included the mountains, the waterfall, and, tiny figures far away, all those celebrants and drummers, still dancing up a storm.

We took Polo to a big sofa and made him sit. He had been dancing only one minute, then he'd suddenly shot up into the sky like a rocket and landed in the grass, and he seemed pretty dazed.

I looked around some more. One wall had a red drape; I wondered what was behind it. Something about it made my skin crawl. But the rest of the living could have been more nondescript. Some regular sofas and armchairs, a coffee table. And — oddly comforting — a portrait of Dr. Strange hung on another wall. There was a counter with barstools, too.

"Me have something for you," the houngan said to Red Polo. He pointed to the counter and behind it there were two refrigerators, a gray one and a crimson one. He opened the crimson door and it was full of identical mason jars full of brains. "Lunch," he said, grabbing a jar and chowing down. The slurping sounds were revolting.

"I guess you're used to zombies," I said.

"No 'living dead' zombies," said the houngan. "Just servant zombies."

He waved his hand and two uniformed servants entered with trays of food. They walked steadfastly and stared straight ahead, but they weren't falling to pieces like Red Polo.

"Wow," Fluke said, "you have *proper* zombies."

We all sat around — Polo was still in a daze — and were saved some kind of seafood. It was sliced and with a spicy sauce. *"Lanbi an sòs lanbi kreyol,"* said the houngan.

"Conch in creole sauce," Fluke said.

"Your zombies are great cooks," said the two Dangers. "Believe us, we know cooking."

I asked him, "What's Dr. Strange doing on your wall?"

He answered, "Dokté Etranj a great man. He help my people, help me. Many research about *zombi*. One day will be all scientific."

Fluke said, "So he was doing research here? Did he find a cure?"

Red Polo looked up from his brains.

"Already have cure," said the houngan. "These two *zombi* — they become human again next week. Just stop datura."

"Oh," Fluke said. "I read about this. It's all in *The Serpent and the Rainbow.*"

"No, it's not," I said. "I saw that movie."

"In the *book*, Kim," he said, with that superior smile he has when he thinks he's smarter than everyone else in the whole world. "The movie is fiction. The book's sort of science. Anyway ... *real* zombies ... it's a kind of punishment in a country that doesn't have much of a legal system. Village justice. They put the *coup poudre* into your bloodstream and you appear dead. Then they bury you for 3 days and when then open your coffin they give you datura, which keeps you disoriented. Because of the native belief system, the zombies and the villagers all think they are dead … and use them as slaves."

"*Ou se jeni!*" the houngan said.

"Thanks," Fluke said. Turning to us, he said smugly, "He called me a genius."

"But no believe too much books," said the houngan. "We not in real Haiti. We *inside.*"

"So your zombies are a bit more modern?" I asked him. "Proper rules and regulations?" I like order.

"Yes. This one over there … six month sentence. Shoplifting from Délimart."

"And the sad-looking one?" Donut said.

"Two weeks," said the houngan. "She insult my mother." He cackled, and we all laughed nervously, no doubt hoping we hadn't insulted him.

"Red Polo didn't do anything wrong to be made into a zombie," I said. "He was trapped in a video game."

"Zombie High?" said the houngan, shaking his head. "Ah, *wi.* That no science *zombi.* That *magic.*"

"But you know magic, right?" I said. "You can fix him."

"Maybe Dokté Etranj help. This very dark magic from *inside* of *inside.* From deepest part of *inside.* There have a *houngan macoute* — very evil, very dark magician, not like me, a *good* shaman! — he made this video game. He can fix you. But no one go there. Only dead people go there. Dead people. For experiments."

"Let me get this straight," Fluke said. "Right now, we're already *inside.* That what Sister Strange talked about when she mentioned that in the heart of Crystal Pathway there's a kind of HQ, a command center, whatever. But even *inside* has an *inside.* Right?"

"*Wi, monché,*" said the houngan.

"And the one who unleashed the viral video in the Red World — and maybe other crimes too — is at the heart of this *inside inside.* And we need to infiltrate it."

Danger said, "If someone can find a way in — but only dead people can get in."

"Not dead people," Fluke said. "*Fake* dead people — people who have been drugged with the *coup poudre.*"

Shit. This was really extreme case of "And for my next trick, I'll need a volunteer from the audience." Did I want to sign up to be unconscious in a coffin for three days? What if I woke up?

I felt Fluke's hand lightly touching mine. "Not you," he whispered. "You hate losing control."

The houngan said, "No, not you. Must be someone who be there before. *Zombi* no dead, no live. In-between. Cannot fear to lose self or lost inside *inside* forever."

"Well, none of us ever *died* before," I said.

Fluke said, "I think he means someone who has already been in some kind of transcendental *beyond* state so that they won't be unnerved if they recover consciousness sometime in the three days of limbo."

I thought of the many horror movies where people get buried alive and try to claw their way out. I shuddered and Fluke's hand in mine felt comforting.

"Don't look at me," said Red Polo. "I'm already zombified."

We didn't look at Red. Instead, we all turned to look at the sofa, where our Polo had been pretty much crashed out, recovering from being possessed by the serpent god then ending up as a human cannonball. But it seemed he had sat up and he'd been listening for a while.

"I've been in that place beyond," Polo said. "I'll go."

28

The Name of the Wizard

Polo

And that was when the houngan drew the curtain, revealing an inner room.

Which was *not* a room in a nice penthouse apart in 21st century Port-au-Prince, but a room straight out of a horror movie.

A rug with bloodstains.

A chicken coop with black roosters strutting about.

Candles everywhere. Weird-looking idols — one that looked like an egg, one with a skull-face. The walls scrawled with designs that looked like something out of a horror movie. Along one wall, coffins were stacked and other coffins leaned against the stacks. And against the far wall there was a kind of altar. There were things you could see at my school; statues of the Virgin Mary — lots of them — bottles of oils and brightly coloured potions, a coiled snake, even something that looked like a plastic Godzilla action figure, flags with weird sigils. A puffer fish, all dried up, hung on the wall. too!

"Puffer fish!" Fluke said. "How interesting!"

"Do you fear?" the houngan said to me. "No fear. Bondye, the Good God, will protect."

He took me by the hand and brought me up to the altar. The others hung back. They could all feel it. A pall. A darkness. Death was here.

"You choose nice coffin?" the houngan said.

"I'm not really going to know the difference," I said. "You say I'm going to be in a death-like trance for three days."

"Maybe this one," he said, going up to a gaudy one with gold roses that was leaning upright.

"I admit," I said, "it looks queer enough for me."

He opened the lid as though it were a door. There was a rotting corpse inside … a very old man … almost a mummy … dressed in like this Renaissance outfit. "Sorry," he said. *"okipé."*

"Occupied," Fluke said.

"No worry, I move Monsieur le Compte. Long time no bury."

"I don't like it *that* much," I said. "You pick. Really. But wait until *after* I pass out? Please?"

"Okay. Lie down in front of altar."

"What! It's got bloodstains!"

"Blood, life, breath, soul, death, infinity —" said the shaman, and as he spoke he was putting on some kind of robe made of thousands of beads; he turned to face the altar and I could see the back of the robe had one of those designs, in black beads over a bright green background. It was a design of stars linked by wavy lines.

"Fascinating," Fluke said. "That's a *vévé*, a sacred vodoun signal. I think it represents the snake god."

"I've already met him," I said. "Shit, I *was* the snake god for a few minutes!"

"Shush, shush, *ti frè,*" said the houngan. "This only hurt one second."

A knife gleamed in his hand. Not some fancy ceremonial knife, but like some kind of Swiss army knife. I felt a scream die in my throat. This scene was rapidly lurching from Vegas showgirl fancy dress party to low budget voodoo movie. "This isn't my scene," I said, regretting my bravery of just give minutes ago.

"Fluke," said the old man, *"Ede mwen."*

"He wants me to help," Fluke said. "Wow, I love this! It's a lot better than chem lab in school."

Reluctantly, I got down on the bloody rug. It actually wasn't bad. The stains were old and didn't smell. In fact they exuded a kind of feel-good vibe. I watched as the old man got out a mortar and pestle and began pounding ingredients, muttering incantations.

He went out into the living room again and opened the gray refrigerator. From the freezer compartment, he pulled out what looked like a frog. There was a blender on the counter … I looked away when he turned it on.

"Fluke," he said, "you go on, pounding paste here."

I was *really* getting scared. But Fluke was going along with it, and I trusted Fluke. He'd never do something that would cause me permanent damage ... would he?

Fluke

I wasn't that keen on putting Polo under, but if it was the only way to infiltrate the *inside*, I guess we had to. Besides, he had volunteered. He had actually met, no, *been* the snake god, too, so he was probably the only one of us equipped to dwell in the limbo of undeath for a day or two.

But when the houngan put the frozen, and maybe still living, frog into the blender, I could see that even Kim was getting chills. I knew, of course, the venom of a certain kind of frog or toad, along with the puffer fish, was among the ingredients of the *coup poudre,* but I didn't know you could actually put a frog in a blender; I thought that was just one of those school jokes.

I gritted my teeth and pounded away and presently the houngan came and poured some of the frog froth over it. Then he took the whole mixture back to the counter and put it in the microwave. Okay, I knew that magic had to adapt for the twenty-first century, but I wasn't quite ready for a "mod cons" vision of black magic.

"Fluke," he said now, "You hold Polo still."

"Kim," I said, "help me." Actually we all crowded around and Kim and I held Polo's arms while the Dangers grabbed his feet. Our zombie friend was out on the terrace, ignoring the whole thing. He had opened his second jar of brains.

Only Donut remained, and the shaman took a black chicken out of the coup and told her to hold it over Polo. Then, not batting an eyelid, he whipped out the Swiss army knife, slit its throat (it didn't even have time to squawk), grabbed hold of it and started using it to sprinkle the spurting blood all over us, treating the expiring chicken like a kind of watering-can. We were all too startled to scream. In fact, we were all pretty much frozen in place. The houngan took the chicken's corpse out to the counter and put it in the sink.

"Now," he said, "me make little incision in Polo foot, and me blow a bit of powder into bloodstream. Nobody breathe! You don't want *coup poudre* in lungs!"

143

Polo

I was, as you can imagine, kind of petrified during all this. But when the *houngan* started to slice into the sole of my foot, a kind of calm came over me. The houngan spoke softly to Fluke in a mixture of English and Kreyol and Fluke was explaining to us what was going to happen.

"After a while," he said, "Polo is going to start feeling numb. He'll drift into limbo and he will wake up *inside.* After that, he has to avoid the zombifying drugs they use to keep the zombies docile. The thing is, it's all zombies in there except for upper management. They don't move fast and they won't know he's not a zombie, so he should be able to slip around easily, find some kind of control center and turn off whatever it is that's preventing us from getting in ... whether it's a force field or electronic locking system or whatever."

I was going to be delivered to the *inside* in a horse-drawn hearse.

I was starting to regret not being able to witness the spectacle. I do love being the center of attention.

"Don't worry," Fluke said. "You might not even lose consciousness totally. You'll just be totally paralysed, that's all. It's temporary."

That was, well ... not too comforting.

"Your dosage will be lower than standard, so you'll awaken sooner than usual. There's going to be a button to open the coffin from the inside. They won't do the zombie ritual for 72 hours and by then you'll be out and we'll be in."

"You don't, um, sound that confident."

"I wish Dr. Strange were here," said Fluke.

"Maybe Dokté Etranj he inside," said the houngan. "He disappear long time now." He whispered some more to Fluke.

"Oh," Fluke said, "inside the inside, it's always night."

So maybe Dr. Strange *was* there.

Was he the villain who was doing all this to our different worlds?

At length, the houngan started to blow the powder over my feet.

It was the same sensation as when Sister Evangeline had hypnotized me last year.

I started to fade ...

"Listen," said the old man. "My name is Jacques Florissant. You need me help, you say name, me try to come."

Faintly, I said, "But you can't enter inside the *inside.*"

"Me no say me come, me say me *try.*"

29

A One-Hearse Town

Kim

It's true that the gilded coffin that had just housed a four-hundred year corpse was the one most suitable for our friend, but we opted for a plain wooden one with an open-on-the-inside button that glowed in the dark.

We laid Polo tenderly in there, and we put in a bar of chocolate, in case he was hungry when he came to. Then, we tied one end of the ball of yarn to his wrist before closing the lid. It connected to Donut, who was still connected to Boom back in our world.

As the lid slammed shut, the yarn disappeared too; now there were two little strands sticking out from around Donut's wrist. The yarn, presumable, was connected through wormholes that passed through other universes.

"Do you feel it tugging?" I asked her.

"Yeah," she said. "I really feel it; he's not dead. There's something there, a tension."

"I don't understand how any of this works," I said.

Fluke said, "It's all explainable by string theory."

"Well obviously," I said. "It's string."

"No, no I mean string theory as in physics. Like a Rubik's but in eleven dimensions."

"Oh, right," I said. Sometimes his smugness was so annoying.

Then we lifted the whole coffin and carried it to the living room.

"Now," said Jacques Florissant, "we deliver to *inside*."

He clapped his hands and more zombies showed up; perhaps coming from an inner room. They opened up the terrace and there was a magnificent coach there, with two jet-black horses and a wagon behind covered with a black cloth. The driver wore a tuxedo and his face was made up like a skull.

'Quick, quick!" said the houngan. "Only one hearse make delivery all experiment subjects!"

We loaded up the coffin in the back of hearse and we all took our seats inside; there were two facing benches and we were able to scrunch inside. Red Polo insisted on coming along, but the odour of decay was appropriate, I suppose.

I got to sit at the front end of the bench, across from the houngan, and able to see the skull-faced driver through a slit in the covering.

I said, "C'mon, Jacques. We're on a balcony."

The houngan cackled like a movie villain.

He clapped once. A whip cracked.

The horse-drawn hearse moved — straight at the railing of the terrace.

We screamed.

The railing split down the middle — and so did the sky It was all another green screen after all. We were on a dirt road. The sun was blazing and inside the black canopy we were sweltering, and Red was pretty rank.

The horses sped up from a trop to a gallop as the driver quirted them mercilessly. I flinched from the sound of the lash. "Do we have to go this fast?" I said.

"Time short," said Jacques Florissant. "This town have only one deliverer."

Once again, our houngan's words were double edged. He meant of course that there was one hearse to deliver the corpses to the *inside*, but maybe he also meant *deliverer* like someone who could deliver us from evil … a savior. I couldn't tell whether the shaman *really* couldn't speak English well, or whether his lilting, vaguely Caribbean-sounding accent was just another veil of illusion.

Through the opening I could see that we were on an epic Hollywood ride. Barrelling through markets, upsetting fruit carts, past Hindu temples and pyramids and spaceports and all kinds of things that clearly didn't belong on Haiti. It was perfectly clear that we were whizzing through the crazy world of the Crystal Pathway.

Then, up ahead, there was night.

Not a night that falls naturally.

This night bisected the sky; we were still in bright day, and halfway to the horizon was a sheet of sheer black, as impenetrable to the eye as a wall. And we were rushing right into the dark.

And just like that, night fell.

It was pitch black at first, but then we seemed to emerge from what had been thick forest into a plain. There was moonlight, and the moon was full, but its light was pale and fringed with blue. It was cold, too.

Abruptly, castle walls reared up.

There was a huge gate, guarded by zombies wearing generic old movie evil villain uniforms — you know, gestapo or KGB or whatever. When they saw the hearse, a barricade lifted and we went inside.

Now there's one thing about this night. It was *noiseless*. You didn't hear birds, or wind, or rustling foliage. It was almost like entering a vacuum. Even our horses made no noise. And that was the scariest thing about this place.

It was like, a whole city of industry inside. There were buildings with weird machines with cogs and gears, turning, zombies lifting and carrying, cranes moving containers back and forth. The avenue widened. On one side there was what looked like a night market, the kind they have in small towns in Thailand, but there were only stalls manned by zombies, no customers. On the other side was a building with a neon sign that read *Motel 666*.

Then the road ended. It led to a large door. No guards.

"Bring coffin," said Jacques.

We stepped out of the back of the hearse and carried the coffin to the door. Red Polo waited inside.

The houngan rang the doorbell. It was so loud I jumped.

We scurried back into the hearse.

As I peered through the opening, uniformed zombies opened the door and carried the gilded coffin into the building. They shuffled. Not a sound.

I watched them disappear into the darkness. I had a lump in my throat and a sense of dread. Impossible to avoid dread around here, all this gloom, all this silence.

Every horror movie has a scene where they're sitting somewhere, hugging their knees, shivering, and listening to something ... footsteps. An alien machine. A monster breathing.

There was nothing. And you know what?

I don't get scared — okay, startled, but I don't usually get scared.

Noises wouldn't have scared me.

Nothing scared me.

Donut whispered, "What happens now?"

Everyone looked at me.

"How should I know?" I said, and looked at the houngan.

"Why you whispering?" he said in a completely normal tone, startling us all and breaking the tension. "Okay. Me go back now. You stay. Wait Polo signal."

We assumed Polo would contact us when he had found a way to let us in, by doing something with the yarn. Morse code or whatever. But we assumed we'd be waiting in some less frightening place. Of course, it made sense to camp out right by the gate. But it was freezing. And there was no shelter. And daylight wasn't coming any time soon.

"Motel," said the houngan. "Go on, *vit, vit.*" He started to shoo us out of the hearse.

The *Motel 666* sign blinked. It would have made fizzy sounds if it was a real-world sign. But it was silent. It might as well have said *Bates Motel.*

"We don't have any money," I said.

"Yes, we do," said Red Polo.

"Shut up," Donut said. "You're a zombie."

All at once, I realized why we had had to bring a zombie with us. A *particular* zombie. There was a reason for everything. The universe *is* one humungous eleven-dimensional Rubik's cube after all. There is a plan, I thought.

"I may be dead," said Red Polo, "but daddy's credit card still works … in every dimension."

30

A Night in Motel 666

Kim

From the outside, the hotel had the creepy atmosphere, complete with blinking, fizzling, sputtering neon sign, of the Bates Motel. But inside it was more like, say, a Holiday Inn ... a lot of green faux leather in the lobby.

We managed to prop up Red Polo long enough for him to wave his dad's magic card. It wasn't that hard since the guy behind the counter was a zombie as well, the real kind, not the brain-eating movie kind. He had glazed eyes and moved about robotically.

"Can we have a room?"

The zombie didn't speak.

"Room," Zombie Polo growled.

Suddenly, I realized that the "man" behind the counter had an astonishing similarity to Sister Euphemia. In our last adventure, Sister Euphemia popped up in weird places, too. Perhaps she was part of some kind of cloning experiment. Maybe the zombie version was some kind of aborted experiment.

"Room!" Red Polo said again. Euphemia-zombie was jolted into action, bringing out a tray of keys and rooting through them, keys of all shapes and sizes.

One key ... a crystal key.

"That one!" I said.

Because it matched our other crystal key from last time, and so maybe it was like a matching square in a Rubik's, maybe I was supposed to choose it ... finding the connections in a chaotic cosmos.

It had a little label marked *Presidential Suite.*

"Can we afford it?" Donut said.

"Polo's Dad can afford anything," Danger said.

So we insisted on getting the Presidential Suite, and the card went through. That was amazing. The bellboy who came to take our luggage (we didn't have any!) was amazing too, as it was another Euphemia zombie, this one an adolescent.

We got into one of those elevators in old movies, you know, with metal grating, a clanging door, that creaks as it ascends.

The suite was on the thirteenth floor ... I thought hotels weren't supposed to have them. I mean, thirteenth floors. Our room *was* the thirteenth floor, with the elevator dumping us in the living room.

It was almost like a parody of Donald Trump's living room — everything was gold — but there weren't any fake Greek statues or anything like that. There were statues all right, but they were monsters.

The one in the middle of the room I knew at once, It was Pazuzu from *The Exorcist.* But you know, I wasn't scared. I know a movie from the real world, and I'd known we were in a kind of movie since we found ourselves in this Hollywood Haiti.

The others, now, they were weirded out. There were other statues, too. There was a mummy and a vampire, all in gold and marble. There was a "creature from the black lagoon" as well as a marble replica of *Alien,* drool and all, large as life and hovering over the grand —

"Piano!" Fluke said. And he sat down and launched into a spooky rendition of *Danse Macabre.*

There was one huge four-poster bed in the suite's main bedroom, and a smaller room with twin beds, and adjoining that was a sitting room stocked with a bar and fridge.

The fridge contained nothing but pomegranates.

"I could eat anything," Danger said. "Even fruit." He grabbed one, but Fluke said, not looking up from the piano, "Don't eat the pomegranates."

"Why not?" Danger said.

"Because we're kind of in the realm of death, and if you know anything about mythology, you know that if you eat the pomegranates you will be stuck here for all time. Six seeds and you'll have to live in the underworld six months a year. Twelve and you're a goner."

"Mythology," I said. "You don't believe it, do you?"

"The metaphors can speak the truth," Fluke said. "Haven't you noticed yet that we're actually *living* in a myth right now, with labyrinths and balls of yarn and statues of Babylonian gods looking down on us?"

Danger ruefully put back the fruit.

Fluke said, "We still have food with us that we packed. Nice crunchy, uncooked ramen and flavor packets. Yummy."

Lavender Danger dug them out, and even found another jar of brains.

"Speaking of time," said Donut, "how long *are* we stuck here?"

"Hard to say," Fluke said, diving into a Bach fugue without missing a beat. I did hate how he multitasked. "We're in some kind of perpetual night here. Is time at a standstill?"

I remembered how Cardinal Crank had stopped time at our school last term, and only us Club X members had been able to move about. If here, inside the *inside*, the same thing had happened, how could we know *when* to do anything?

That rosary-thing we were all wearing was what allowed more than one of us to inhabit the same universe. Was it also the thing that kept us all tethered to some deeper *time*, a kind of *time* that underlay all the different kinds of subjective time that we experience.

Were the rosaries like the crystal keys, a recurring pattern that anchored all of us in the same reality?

Whatever. The suite, as I said, was the whole floor. Behind the master bedroom was an ensuite marble bathroom, and in that bathroom was a doorway that looked really familiar ...

The closet door from Club X!

And guess what? We couldn't open it. Not even the two Dangers, pooling their powers. None of the keys we had on us — not many — even though they were made of crystal.

"That's gotta be the way home," Donut said. "Any door that opens easily around here is *never* where you *need* to go."

Then came the time for allocating the bedrooms. Red Polo wanted to sleep with the Dangers. "Now that I have the rosary," he said, "I won't leak any bodily fluids on you and you *are* my best friend, or friends, after all," he said.

"You're a corpse," Lavender said.

"Corpses don't sleep in beds," said Blue.

"And they certainly don't sleep in beds —"

"With *us*," Blue said, and it was a bit annoying, them finishing each other's sentences, but I suppose it made sense.

"Aw," said Red Polo. "You used my dad's credit card."

"He has a point," Donut said.

The Dangers said, "Let's give Kim and Fluke the royal bridal master bedroom," and then Lavender said, "But who will be master?" and Blue said, "and who will be mistress?"

"Fuck you all," I said.

Our Danger said, "We'll hang out in the living room on the couches." Lavender said, "You know how we love talking to statues." Blue said, "Even scary ones."

"Okay," Donut said. "I'll take one of the twin beds and, since there's no rotting corpse smell, I guess Red Polo can sleep in the other bed."

"I won't *actually* sleep," said Red, "but I think my tissue regenerates."

"It probably does," Fluke said. "You've leaked so much, you'd have nothing left if your body didn't create more of you. It would be fascinating to study how consuming brains is crucial to zombie metabolism."

Fluke didn't say anything about the whole "bridal master bedroom" joke thing. That *was* a joke, wasn't it? I often don't get jokes, although I'm handling my Asperger's a lot better than I used to.

I closed my eyes and tried to think of puzzles, multidimensional Rubik's cubes, and shapes clicking into place. Of the world being righted. By me.

Fluke and I used to sleep in the same bed all the time. But we were kids. And last year things had been weird.

Were our friends setting us up for something?

Then Donut asked the question we were all thinking, but didn't dare ask.

"If time is at a standstill, what about *our* Polo in the coffin? What if time doesn't pass, and he's in there forever?"

31

Cream Polo

Polo

... I think I am aware of motion....

I'm not sure. I'm trapped inside myself. In darkness. Yes. There is motion. Swaying. It's not like a ship. It's not like a car. It's ... a horse-drawn cart of some kind. I feel a ripple that runs through tensed haunches and makes the coffin walls vibrate. Am I scared? No. I'm really calm.

We rock, we sometimes seem to skip over an obstacle, a stone in the road maybe.

In the darkness, I hear a voice....

The guru.

Be who you are meant to be, my child.

I may be meant to be a lot of things, I'm thinking, but *dead* isn't one of them.

After a time, the motion stops. The starts again, but it's up, then down. The coffin is being lifted. And then something smooth, machinelike ... maybe a conveyor belt.

Hope it's not the kind they have at the crematorium.

But no. It just glides along, eerily noiseless, and finally it eases to a halt.

I'm wherever I am supposed to be.

Things are very, very still for a long time. My body is still paralyzed. But I ... I seem to have room to shift a little. It seems that ...

I'm thinning out, becoming lighter than air. The coffin has become porous. All I have to do is — *Nope!* I just banged by head on the lid.

There's a pallid light. The inside of the coffin is all gilt, and the light plays off the gold tones, glistening.

And when I turn to look down at where I've been lying I see that I'm still lying there.

I'm glued to the coffin lid looking down and I see my face. Eyes closed, seemingly frozen in time. The *coup poudre* is still working. So why am I able to see myself?

Then, suddenly, I feel myself being pulled right through the lid. And I'm standing beside this golden coffin, in a manysided room. I can't tell how many sides, because each time I start to count, it shifts.

There are other coffins in the room. All kinds of coffins. Wooden, plain ones. Glittering, gold and silver coffins. Egyptian sarcophagi. The white coffins you find at Thai cremations.

The room has as many walls as I want to see, the walls moving, gliding, sliding back and forth. The room is square, it's a pentagon, a hexagon, a decagon, and more, and more ...

Each wall is a mirror.

I see myself reflected back and forth a million times and the person I see is perfect Polo, in a different school uniform. The shorts are a tasteful cream color, not bright white like tennis, but subtle. My face isn't made up but it's naturally lit to enhance all my best bits. My hair is exactly halfway between boy and girl.

And I hear the voice of the guru from my dream of last year ... *Are you really yourself now, this time?*

I walk all the way up to the mirrors and they are also windows. So this room is a room of ever-changing one-way glass walls, but with one-way you can always still see a little bit. And I do.

The first mirror wall I go up to, I stick my face right against the glass but I don't see any breath marks. I'm not the same as the me that is still in the coffin. I'm a kind of *essence*. The houngan had told me that my soul would leave me body, that there are two souls in their belief system the *ti bon ange* and the *gros bon ange*, I didn't really catch that part but I know that my *ti bon ange* left my body before, when I was dancing and the drums were pounding and a snake-god took over my body.

So I am not a zombie yet.

And I'm not even really in *time*, I'm just floating around in some kind of *between*.

Pressed against the glass ...

It's the school. *Our* school. St Cecilia's in the mist of morning. A few boys wandered around in blue shorts, maybe on their way to breakfast. And I *am* able to slip through the solid glass, because my *ti bon ange* is so stretched out that it flows through the gaps between molecules. I wish Fluke was here to explain how it all works.

I'm flying above the school. Blending with the wind as it disperses the morning fog. Now I am dripping down a pipe, coiling along the edge of an electrical wire. I'm in the school chapel where Father Vichai is saying mass to a congregation of three, including the principal.

Nobody sees me at all.

I am a kind of ghost, I guess.

I get back into the mirror room just by concentrating hard. Once again, I'm standing next to my coffin. What do the other mirror-windows lead to? Other worlds?

I slip through the next window and it's chaos!

It's Red Polo's world. The front of the school is a battlefield. Zombies are shambling about. Barricades have been set up and priests and nuns are patrolling with rifles. Some students have weapons too, everything from baseball bats to kendo sticks. Father Vichai is running around trying to asperge the zombies with a censer. Now and then lightning bolts from the sky zap a kid and he immediately starts turning into a zombie.

I remember now. Red Polo said it started with a video game.

Red St Cecilia's is trapped inside a game. I see it now. Father Vichai is running in circles, a continuous loop. When the zombies run to a certain point they boomerang back to where they were before. Look! There's red versions of Pueng Pang and Tommy — charging around like demons on skateboards, wielding baseball bats and decapitating zombies, left right and center! Heads flew through the air and landed in shuddering piles. And after a minute, the heads flew back onto the zombies' shoulders and the they would regroup and attack again.

I start to see ... each character is on its own loop, so there are many interactions that don't duplicate exactly, but I'm guessing that there are mega-loops on top of the loops, and mega-mega-loops on top of the mega-loops ... this entire thing is a lifesized digital simulation ... overwhelmed, I squeeze myself back through my mirror-window.

I'm standing in the room next to my coffin again.

Now there's someone moving around. I see computer consoles, knobs, buttons, and a few zombies. There's also a human being. A nun.

Sister Euphemia?

But she's not wearing the St. Cecilia's habit. This time she is in purple. With a bit of gold trim. Kind of showbiz looking, honestly.

She looks right at me and doesn't see me.

Then she turns towards someone I can't see. I only see a long shadow that makes the room gloomier.

"This way, Your Eminence," she croaks.

What's Cardinal Crank doing here?

ZOMBIE IN THE FRIDGE

32

Conservation of Pomegranates

Kim

Even though we were supposedly stuck inside a single endless night with time standing still, our bodies still told us we were hungry. Maybe it was the fields cast around us by our rosaries-ARCs that kept our body clocks ticking to the beat of another universe.

"We're starving," said Lavender Danger.

"And running out of dry noodles," said Blue Danger.

"I don't know. Maybe I should go for a pomegranate," said Donut, but we stopped her.

And Fluke had told us not to eat the pomegranates in the fridge. Wisely, I assume.

Amazingly enough, there was room service.

We got on the phone and started ordering everything we could think of. Steaks and lobster thermidor and caviar and bottles of champagne. And even a plate of *crevelles* for Red Polo.

Eventually a dining table came up through the floor with silver platters and wine goblets. The food smelled amazing. But when we opened the dish covers ...

The steaks were chopped, shaped pomegranates. The caviar was mini-pomegranate seeds. The lobsters consisted of weirdly-shaped pomegranates stuck together with pins to form a lobster shape. Even the brains were just mashed up pomegranates in a thick pomegranate sauce.

Fluke said, "We can't eat any of this."

"You're gonna let us starve to death because of ... mythology?" Donut said.

"There's truth in mythology," Fluke said.

I knew he was right. It was one of the most important lessons we had learned from the mysterious Dr. Leopold Strange ... that every universe had its own truth, and more than one truth can be true at the same time.

"But we're Club X," I went on.

"Yeah," Fluke said. "That means we can see the cracks between worlds."

"Maybe there's a crack big enough for a few candy bars to sneak through?" Donut said.

Our Danger said, "Let's think. We might be able to pry something open."

"Red Polo came to us through a fridge," I said. "There's a fridge here."

We went to the fridge full of pomegranates and we started to empty it out. That's when we saw the back of the fridge. There wasn't a back. Just darkness. Tunnelling to forever.

"Check the map," I said.

Fluke unfurled it — it wasn't always an easy map to deal with, because it wasn't the same in every reality — and he said, "It's possible there could be some kind of space-time anomaly thing down there."

"You mean we could connect to some other reality?" I said.

"Maybe."

"I bet we can *pick* a reality," said the two Dangers. "We're hungry enough to try."

Fluke said, "You're always saying you can't control your powers. But maybe, just maybe, with the two Dangers feeding off each other, making some kind of transdimensional feedback effect —"

This was really way beyond any of our weirdness limits, but there was only one way to test this. First, we positioned the Dangers on either side of the refrigerator door. "Now," Fluke said, "concentrate as hard as possible on where the back of the fridge should be ... which just seems to be leading off into infinity and ..."

"Concentrate on what?" said Lavender.

"On our mother's cooking, of course," said Blue.

"Now, Donut," said Fluke, "poke your head in ... what do you see?"

"Um ... what am I supposed to see?"

"Another fridge?"

"No, just darkness."

"We're concentrating as hard as we can," said the Dangers.

The two of them stood there, eyes closed, their hands on the two sides of the fridge. Little blue sparks danced from the tips of their fingers.

"Her lemon tarts are amazing," said Blue.

"Her spaghetti with tom yam sauce," said Lavender.

I was salivating.

"I got an idea," Red Polo said.

"You don't get to have ideas," Donut said. "You're a zombie."

"No, I'm serious." Red picked up a pomegranate (they were lying all over the floor since we'd emptied out the fridge) and pitched it hard into the emptiness.

We heard it bounce, and bounce, fainter and fainter ...

"You know, maybe he's right," Fluke said. "Maybe there's some kind of law of conservation at work. The same reason there can't be a two-Polo paradox...."

"The law of conservation of pomegranates?" I said. "Ridiculous!"

A lemon tart came whooshing out of the darkness, landing with a squishy thunk on top of the pile of fruit.

"I may be a zombie," said Red Polo, "but do have brains."

"For breakfast, you mean," I said.

He threw another pomegramate and out came a calf's brain on a bed of lettuce. "Look's like Father Boucher is still visiting the school," Donut said.

We flung more fruit, and goodies came flying out — sticky rice with grilled pork — mango pudding — all of Danger's mother's top hits. We got into a frenzy, happy as hell to see familiar things to eat —

"Slow down!" said Lavender. "We're losing focus!"

The food got weird. The rice was purple. A live octopus wrapped around a cucumber.

"Stop, guys!"

It took a second but we did. We had used up most of the pomegranates.

"I think the octopus needs to go back," Donut said.

"I think we can do without the baby rats on skewers, too,' I said.

"But they are rather interesting," said Fluke. "That means we're getting transtemporal leakage as well as spatial displacement. The Romans used to eat baby rats dipped in honey. There must have been a brief slippage into ancient history."

"Interesting doesn't mean we need to eat it," Donut said, gingerly picking up the rat kebabs and throwing them as hard as she could down the tube.

A tub of chocolate ice cream came bouncing back out.

"That's more like it," she said.

"We can't hold the portal anymore," said Danger. "We forgot to get drinks," Fluke said.

A jumbo bottle of chilled champagne sailed through as the two Dangers kind of half-collapsed onto the floor.

The two Dangers staggered over to the coffee table which stood in the shadow of the big Pazuzu statue. They plopped down on a plush sofa. Donut, Fluke and I carried the huge haul of food. The champagne was, seriously, gigantic.

"That's called a Jeroboam," Fluke said. "Three liters."

It took two of us two to hold the bottle while Fluke deftly unwound the metal wire. The pop was startling; even Red Polo perked up.

We feasted. We probably got a bit drunk, because in the back of our minds there was this constant dread that we were trying to suppress. And the thought of our friend, in a closed coffin, perhaps conscious, but physically paralysed, was gnawing at us. So yeah, between us we did finish off that Jeroboam, and all the lemon tarts and sticky rice and mango we could care to eat.

We laughed and made stupid fart jokes and picked on Red Polo, who did have a kind of deadpan humor. If you see what I mean. But eventually we had to go to bed.

"Let's see Kim and Fluke off to the bridal suite first," Danger said. I don't even remember which one, the Dangers were starting to blur.

"Who's going to carry who over the threshold?" said the other Danger.

"We're not —" I began.

But then I thought about what Fluke had said in the confessional last year, when he thought I was Father Vichai. And there was the night ... what happened that night? Did I want to remember? All I know is, I was going to sleep with my best friend, something we'd done on and off since we were little kids, yet somehow, in the Presidential Suite of some phantasmagorical hotel with a fancy four-poster bed, I was getting flustered.

Was it that I didn't like being ribbed? Or was it because I was afraid something would happen? That we would cross a line and not be able to come back?

Finally Fluke said, "At least we won't get each other pregnant."

Everyone laughed but me.

33

Haunting Evangeline

Polo

I was staring Cardinal Crank right in the face. His neck was twitching; maybe he was getting ready to take off his head again.

I looked right into his eyes — my forehead was about level with his nose — but he couldn't see me.

Because I wasn't there.

No, Your Eminence, it's just my *ti bon ange* standing around in cream-colored shorts while the rest of me lies paralysed in a coffin. Are you going to send me off to fetch something from the fridge again, Your Eminence? A glass of ice-cold blood, maybe? Or a platter of human hearts, still fresh, still quivering?

Here, I'll shake my fist right in your —

The cardinal doesn't see me. I'm jumping up and down and all up in his face.

I'm invisible!

Now, I know the real reason I'm here. I have to use the time *before* I wake up as a zombie to learn everything I can. I have to set the sabotage in motion. I already found out how the red world works ... each character is an interlocking loop. I can't wait for Fluke to solve this.

Maybe I can figure out the lavender world as well, before they get me out of my coffin.

The Cardinal has moved away now and he is talking to a shadowy figure in a black cape. Dr. Strange! Or is it *Mr.* Strange? Or some third, even *stranger* Strange?

They spoke in murmurs. Me being a ghost didn't give me super-hearing. But I could see that Strange was leading the cardinal around and pointing at various mirror-walls, maybe showing him the features of the different versions of reality. They walked over to a very ornate marble coffin — with angels, bas-relief biblical scenes, and bunches of marble grapes and leaves.

It wasn't a coffin though.

Strange yanked on a grape and a kind of control panel opened up. There were flashing LEDs, a monitor, buttons, and a keyboard. I was peering over their shoulders — a curious trick since they are taller than me, but my invisibility also came with the ability to hover above the ground. I could see a kind of wheel of rainbow colors on the screen that could be spun with the tip of a finger. I could see a number of little windows that seemed to open out onto different views of our school. This computer was ground zero for whatever they were doing to all the St. Cecilias. The wheel was used to pick which universe to monitor.

They were whispering, but Cardinal Crank's idea of a whisper could be quite booming. So I could hear him even though I couldn't make out the other side of the conversation. I could hear odd phrases like "virtual reality cosmological construct" and "string-driven transdimensionality" — I thought I'd better try to remember this shit, in case Fluke could figure it out when I told him.

The Cardinal just kept saying, "Ah yes. I see. Fascinating." I don't think he quite understood any of it, although he always acts as though he is the supreme source of all knowledge.

The evil version of the Stranges led the Cardinal on a further tour of the zombie laboratory. The room widened and thinned to accommodate their walkabout. There was a coffin I recognized, too. It was the one that used to be in our school, the one Dr. Strange liked to be carried about in.

It was standing in a corner, with a big old chain and padlock around it. Double padlocked in fact. Someone inside the coffin was banging and I could hear some muffled curses.

The Cardinal said, "I see you're keeping your dark twin under wraps."

Strange merely chuckled. Was *our* Dr. Strange a prisoner? Was that where he had been the whole time?

There were a few more workstations, each one grafted onto a museum-quality sarcophagus. The Egyptian ones were the gaudiest.

There were zombies, typing on keyboards, but very, very slowly, one finger at a time. Just how you'd expect zombies to act.

I decided to see if I could squeeze into Lavender World just as I'd drifted into Red. The minute I *thought* it, I was funneling through another window that had become soft and porous.

I was drifting in the breeze. I was making the treetops rustle. It was dawn, and there was Sister Evangeline, sitting by her own grave. She wasn't crying, just watching over her other self, her face a mask. Was she sad?

"Don't be sad, sister," I whispered.

She didn't hear me. She only sighed.

I tried to put my arms around her but they went right through her, she slipped right through my fingers. Of course. I am not really there. I'm just a ghost. I sit down right next to her. We're on a little knoll that overlooks the burial place. She leans against a tree. She's singing a little lullaby to herself. How to reach her?

Eventually, Sister Evangeline closed her eyes. She was drifting into sleep. And I was thinking ... When you are asleep, your *ti bon ange* is still conscious. If I can enter her dream ... I can talk to her ... and she will *see* me!

Sister Evangeline is gradually fading from consciousness. I concentrate, the way I was taught in the meditation center last year, and I try to become one with her breathing ... in, out ... in, out ... I'm thinning out, flattening, shrinking to the size of a dust mote in the breeze ... Sister Evangeline is breathing in ... drawing me inside her head ... and I let her breath take me inside her mind....

Sister Evangeline stands on a mountaintop, looking at the sky.

"Sister," I say.

Now, at last, she sees me.

"Are you an angel?" she says. "You look like an angel."

"I'm Polo."

"But you're in cream. What happened to your uniform?"

"You can hear me!"

"Yes I can. Why wouldn't I be able to?"

"Because earlier ... when you were awake ... you couldn't even see me."

"I *am* awake."

"You're dreaming, Sister, and I'm just kind of a spirit in your dream."

"Dreaming? No, I'm not."

"Look around you."

She did. Where we stood overlooked a vista of the national park ... mountains, fog, valleys, forests ... St. Cecilia's in the distance.

"How did you get here?" I said. "I mean, all the way to the mountaintop."

"I drove."

"There's no road all the way to the top."

"I remember driving."

"Where did you park?"

She stood in thought for a while. At length, she said, "You have a point. Maybe this isn't ... completely real. But I'm a psychiatrist. I really should be more aware. This is a lucid dream, I guess." We could still see the spot where Lavender Evangeline, presumably, was buried, and the little church. But this wasn't any actual view from anywhere in the real world. And the color of the sky ... rose and gold with a brilliant light from on high but no sun ... this was a dream-sky.

And then the singing started ...

It was a single voice at first ... it was clearly Sister Evangeline's voice, floating, coming from high above. It had no words, or else the words were in some alien tongue, but it was the kind of music that you imagine only angels sing ... high, pure, and shimmering.

"Oh, listen," she said. "I'm with God." She smiled.

More Evangelines now. They came from different parts of the heavens, all blending perfectly. We couldn't see them at first ... they were up there, behind layers of golden cloud.

"Oh, my," said Sister Evangeline. "Thank you for guiding me to this dream," she said. "Can I go up there too? Can I go be with the other Evangelines? That's what I long for, you know."

"No, no, you can't go there yet." Now I understand why I need to appear in her dream. "We need you in the world. The Lavender world. You have to do what Lavender Sister couldn't do. You can't give up like she did."

She wouldn't listen at first. Her mind was on the music. I realized that she hears music the way Fluke does, on some completely different plane than us normal people. She seemed completely transported. I didn't think she'd want to go back to the real world, but I needed her to try.

"St. Cecilia's is all screwed up," I said. "You can fix it because you weren't born in that world, you *know* what's what."

"I know, I know," said Sister Evangeline. "But I still want to hear the music first."

As we watched the sky, a stairway formed. It was made of starlight. Not a stairway exactly, more like a shining escalator, only a mile wide, and at the foot of it, there was St. Cecilia, the one who stands in the lobby of our school. She had a harp and with each note she plucked, the heavens rang. And she kept beckoning us to go on up ... you know, like the girl in a uniform they have in Japanese department stores who bows to every customer and invites them to ascend the escalator.

Evangeline went on to the escalator up the sky, and I followed.

"These are the Evangelines who have already gone beyond," she said. "They're the Evangelines who already crossed over to be with God. I could stay here, I could join my sisters. Oh, that would be beautiful!"

The very air was shining and we could see the first Evangelines ... a rainbow of Evangelines ... winged Evangelines, each one singing her heart out, each voice melding perfectly with the others. The Evangelines wore robes of many colors ... blue Evangelines, red Evangelines, green, gold, silver, white ... the sky was crowded with Evangelines now, an angel choir so beautiful my heart ached ... and then I saw ...

"Sister," I whispered. "Sister, there's no *Lavender*."

"What?" she said, jolted from her reverie. "Of course there is."

"Look, Sister. There are hundreds of Evangelines from the hundreds of universes where Evangeline already died and went to heaven ... but *there is no Lavender Evangeline.*"

"What do you mean?"

"She's not dead," I said. "Sister, you have to get back to the world. Lavender Evangeline didn't cross over. She's alive somewhere ... which means we have to find her. She needs to be brought back into her proper world!" I understood now what the dream meant. "Lavender Evangeline is missing and the world can't be fixed until she returns to it!"

"But ... if that's true .... how was *I* in the Lavender world? And who is buried in my grave?"

34

Bridal Suite

Fluke

Okay, so Kim wasn't laughing. He just stood there looking like a
dork.   His face kind of fell when I made the joke about us getting
pregnant.

"We can't get pregnant," he said at last. "We're guys."

I said, "C'mon, Kim, you haven't had an Aspergers moment in
months."

"Oh. A joke." Then he finally laughed, but I have to say it was half-
hearted.

The others were still giggling as we opened the door to the Bridal
Suite. I looked at Kim and the others, then, with an awkward grin, put
my arms around him and hefted him over the threshold. And now he
really was laughing as we both landed in a heap on a silky carpet, and
I slammed the door with one hand and we lay in the half dark.

Kind of on top of each other. Well, me on top of him.

And then, without meaning to, we kissed.

Maybe the second time, though, we did mean to. I'm not sure we
were supposed to open our mouths but it just happened. The taste of
champagne lingered.   The feeling was wet and mushy and it tingled,
but not in the lips.   The tingling started lower down.   It's like the
subject in the *Art of Fugue*, starting on the low D and going upward in

thirds only to slither back down again. Was it stupid of me to compare it to music? But Bach is the most sublime thing in the universe.

There would have been a third time, but I guess the second time scared him too much. It was a bit intense. I wasn't scared. But I didn't want to go anywhere he didn't want to go.

"Let's get some sleep," I said.

I took both his hands and pulled him and we sat on the edge of the bed. There were two layers of drapes; the outside was velvet, the inside some kind of sheer material, soft and see-through.

"We don't have anything to wear in bed," Kim said.

"Who cares?" I said. I took off my shirt. So did Kim, but he folded his into a perfect square, very very carefully. I took off my school shorts and so did he. He folded, I didn't.

We lay back on the bed, facing opposite directions.

"Let's try to get some sleep," I said.

We weren't touching but I could feel a kind of puddle of heat emanating from where he was lying. The warmth seeped through the bedclothes and enveloped me. It felt good. I didn't fall asleep yet. I just let the good feeling flow over me, like a blanket.

I don't know if I drifted off or not but I became aware that the warm feeling had changed. It was physical now. I could feel skin against my skin. Kim had turned around and I had kind of backed into him. I felt his breath on the back of my neck. He had his arm around my waist.

He was making soft murmuring noises, the kind of rhythmic grunt he makes when he's intent on solving a Rubik's cube. Was he dreaming? Gently, he was moving against me. I suddenly realized we weren't wearing any underwear. When had that happened? I panicked for a moment. Maybe it's a dream, i thought. Then I sort of felt the melody of the *Art of Fugue* and I found myself moving in a kind of counterpoint. I don't know if it was arousing really, but it was kind of comforting. It didn't feel weird. At some point we both cried out and there was a big wave of sensation that swept over me. It was beautiful and awesome and frightening all at the same time and I gave into it, as into the resolution of a fugue.

I still don't know if I drifted off. I think I did. Then after a while I was conscious again and I really needed to pee, so I kind of wriggled free of his arms and felt my way to the ensuite bathroom behind the bed. I reached for the light but I couldn't find it. Still, there was a cold radiance in the bathroom … It was all white marble, and cool on my feet. A shadowy statue loomed over the toilet … an angel with outspread wings. It was an odd thing to be looking over you while you went to the toilet and I have to admit it was creepy.

So when Kim came in as well, and we were both doing it into the same toilet bowl, I felt almost relieved.

"Do you remember anything?" he said.

"What?"

"I think I had a dream about ..."

"Sex?"

"Or something. Not sure. It's fuzzy."

So maybe he hadn't been conscious. Maybe I was the only one who had experienced ... whatever it was I experienced.

"So," I said. "You weren't awake at all, just now? Not even a little bit?"

"I'm not sure. I just know I have to piss like crazy."

"Me too."

"Does it feel weird to you?"

"Why? We always pee together." It was true. It wasn't something that we'd ever been bothered with.

"I guess it's some kind of bonding," I said softly.

I'm not sure what happened next but we could make out the door, very clearly, in the half-light. The door that looked exactly like the closet door in Club X.

And, as finished, and we flushed, that door creaked open. A faint blue light played through the narrow opening.

We stood there, with nothing on, watching the doorway back to our home world open up. I reached out to touch the doorknob. It swung open and we could see the whole familiar room. We even saw Boom, sitting on the sofa, seemingly asleep. We saw the busts of composers, the refrigerator, everything. Just two steps and we'd be away from all this turmoil.

"Wow," Kim said. "We could go back."

"What made it open?"

But in my heart, I knew. Whatever had happened in our half-dreaming state, in the four-poster bed of a hotel in the underworld, had unlocked something deep inside ourselves.

"It makes no sense," Kim said.

"And yet, maybe it does," I said.

"Is it telling us we should go back, abandon this quest?"

"We're not going to do that," I said.

"No," he said, "we're not."

171

We were Club X. "We don't abandon our friends," I said. "This is some kind of test."

No matter how tempting it was to forget about our quest.

And, as we watched, the door slowly closed, and we were in the dark again. Had it been a test, and it so, had we passed? I don't know. We drifted off again, this time into a deep, dreamless sleep.

35

I was a Teenage Zombie

Polo

No sooner had I asked that question than I felt an irresistible *pull*. It seemed to be coming from ... *myself*.

I was calling myself back from the land between life and death. I knew my own voice, even though it was the soundless cry of a corpse. I found myself fading out of Sister Evangeline's dream. She was waking up. Just like that, I was back in school, and I was sitting beside Sister who had been dozen off in her own couch in her school psychiatrist's office. The whole vision overlooking the churchyard on the hill had been a dream, the images of angelic Evangelines all dreams within dreams.

"Sister!" I called out.

In the half-world between sleep and wakefulness, I think she heard me. "Polo?" she murmured.

"I can't stay," I said. "The minute you wake up, you won't see me anymore."

"You have to come back. And not as a dream. As you. Maybe we can find this world's Polo. Together we can bend this world back to the right path."

But I didn't have time to hear the rest of this because I was already kind of siphoning out of the world and reconstituting myself inside the dark center of the Crystal Pathway. I was standing next to my coffin and zombies were taking off the lid, and I was getting sucked, whoosh, right back into my own body.

Oh! It felt so confining! I could feel my blood now, sluggish, but starting to circulate. My heart was flopping, then, abruptly, jump-starting. My brain was whirring and the first thing I could actually *feel* again was pain, so much pain, pain in every limb, pain stabbing the base of my skull.

I screamed. And you know I can scream.

But you know what? The zombies didn't even blink. They apparently *couldn't*. That was one thing about them. They had this vacant stare. They moved about the room, pushing buttons, pulling levers, and turning knobs, while monitors showed various squiggly lines, maybe life signs. They all wore white uniforms. Now none of these were rotting corpses like Red Polo; they were the scientific Haitian variety, unable to think, drugged to the gills with datura.

I sat up. That was a major effort. I went on screaming.

Presently, that gold-and-purple version of Sister Euphemia came bounding into the room, her skirts flying. She had a couple of zombies with her and they were holding various tools that looked like a cross between medical tools and mediaeval instruments of torture, including a monstrous hypodermic, and enormous tweezers. I went on screaming.

Sister shut me up with a resounding slap in the face.

I wanted to slap back but I resisted. After all, I was supposedly a zombie. I was supposed to feel no pain. I tried not to blink, but Sister wasn't too observant. She didn't have any reason to think I was anything other than another candidate for living dead.

"You're a loud one," she said.

I started to answer but bit my lip.

"I am Sister Eudaemonia, our Houngan Macoute's chief lab assistant. You will be trained here before be sent out on assignment. Now you will take a pill. It will keep you from ... regaining your senses."

She had the nearest zombie force open my mouth and she popped in this monster of a pill.

I moved it to my cheek and pretended to swallow.

"There's a good boy," she said. "Or should I say, girl? I can hardly tell you young people apart!"

I stood there pretending to be dumb.

"Well, just stay here now, yes, just like that, perfectly still, for a few hours. The Houngan Macoute will deal with you after that. He's in a meeting right now. I've got a few more zombies to do, then I'm off to fetch him. But he'll be back and he'll train you for one of the top jobs! The specimens sent by Jacques Florissant are always special!"

With that, Sister Eudaemonia turned abruptly and stalked away, with her entourage. I was so startled I almost swallowed the pill. Luckily, I was able to spit it into my hand in time and I stuck it in my coffin, in a fold of the lining. I tried to be a bit secretive about it, but it occurred to me that none of the zombies working here actually paid any interest to me. Or anything else. They were just going about their tasks like ... well ... zombies.

I took a stroll. The room was as I'd seen it when I'd been away from my body, but this time I couldn't see it from all the angles, because I was stuck inside my fleshy cage. There were the windows into other dimensions, but I when I walked it to them I banged my nose ... I couldn't waft right through them like when I'd been a disembodied *ti bon ange*.

I could wander freely. No guards, nothing. Why would they need them? Nobody here but us zombies!

After a while I saw Sister Eudaemonia puttering about again, shoving another pill down someone's throat. I ducked behind a standing sarcophagus. Sister finished with one zombie and strode towards another coffin that was being opened. That was another screamer, and I heard another slap. Apparently a lot of them scream when they wake up. I guess it's pretty traumatic coming back from the grave.

Sister Eudaemonia eventually finished her rounds, and she went out through a door marked STAFF ONLY, which she did not bother to close.

I followed her and stepped out into a corridor.

A *crystal* corridor! The walls sparkled. There were doors set into the walls on both sides, all kinds of doors, so I knew that this was another section of the pathway that connected all the dimensions.

Sister abandoned her zombie attendants and started down the corridor. It kept forking. I followed a little way, but she walked really fast. I couldn't keep up. Shit! I tried to retrace my steps. That was not too hard, because soon I found the zombies standing right where Sister Eudaemonia had left them. They hadn't moved a muscle.

"Do you know the way out of here?" I asked them.

They didn't say anything. Just stood and stared.

I picked a likely one, snapped my fingers in its face. It blinked! So, they weren't a hundred percent brain-dead.

"Is there someone in there?" I said. "Blink once for yes, twice for no...."

The zombie blinked again, very, very slowly.

"Is there a way out of here?"

A long pause. Then ... *Two blinks.*

That couldn't be true! "Maybe there's no way out in *your* world," I said. "But I know there's ways. I'm from Club X. We see the cracks between the worlds!"

The zombie looked confused. It blinked. Then it blinked twice. Then once. Then twice. Presently it started blinking up a storm, and then it started spinning like a top. After a minute, the zombie collapsed in a heap.

These creatures were a lot easier to deal with that the brain-eating kind! You just had to get them with a paradox or two, and they became useless.

I had to find my friends. Then I remembered that bit of yarn that was attached to my wrist. I knew it reached through the worlds and was attached to Donut ... and through her, all the way back to Boom.

Carefully, I yanked at the yarn.

Nothing.

I tried again.

I felt a little tug now, coming from the right. I walked down the corridor. The tug was getting stronger. I went from door to door, standing in front of each one for a moment. After about a dozen doors there was one where the pull was strongest. It was a dirty old wooden door, like the one to the room of Uncle Sert, the school janitor.

The tugging was powerful now. My heart was pounding! This had to be the right door. And Sister Eudaemonia's zombies were still in sight, so I knew this had to be the way back to the control room. I reached out and turned the knob....

36

Double Danger

Danger

I never realized how interesting I was until I met myself. We sat together on the sofa, waiting for I don't know what to happen, while Donut went off to sleep with the zombie and Fluke and Kim went to sleep with each other.

"We really shouldn't rib them so much," I said to my other self. "Some day they're going to get pissed off and hurt us."

"Some day they're going to get so pissed off, they'll actually *do* it."

"Yeah, maybe right now."

"What, shall we go and listen at their door?" he said, smirking.

"You're different from me," I said. "You're a lot cruder, more physical."

"Why?" said Lavender. "Because I've had a little experience at trying out as the opposite sex? Or because, unlike you, I've actually *done* it, while you've only had fantasies?"

"How's that work in the Lavender world, anyway? And has it always been that way?"

"Not always. We were a lot more like your world, but then, this year, everything suddenly changed. New orders on identity awareness came down from the government. It was kind of fun for a month or so, but it got to be kind of ... a chore. Not being myself. Sucked."

"I've wondered about what it be like to be like Polo ... able to cross over whenever."

"He sure does," said Lavender Danger. "At the drop of a hat."

I realized that Lavender ... *knew* something about his Polo that I didn't know.

"So what are you saying? Did you switch off bottoming and topping?"

"Now who's being crude?"

"You can't blame me for being curious. *You* would be."

"Okay, I'll confess, it was more than just fumbling around a bit. And then our Polo went off somewhere and she's been missing. And *your* Polo isn't the same. Your Polo's a lot more self-assured. Cocky, even."

When I looked at Lavender Danger in the half-light, it was kind of like looking into a mirror, except for the slightly smudged lipstick. "Did you enjoy cross-dressing?" I asked him.

"Kind of. You and me ... we never got to try on our mother's lipstick while she was out ... because she was never out ..."

"... And because she doesn't use lipstick. But the Sriracha sauce kind of worked —"

"Holy shit! You did that too?"

I looked at Purple in amazement. He really *was* me, after all. "You're like a mirror," I said.

"Just what I was thinking."

"Only mirrors aren't reversed. Your left side is my right side. Like a camera."

"Yeah." He reached out and touched my cheek. Then, without warning, he kissed me.

"What the fuck?" I said.

"Hey! I'm *you*, remember? Didn't you kiss the mirror when you were seven, and wondered why it didn't kiss back?"

"Fuck! No one knows that except me."

"I *am* you. I told you." He kissed me again.

"I think this what Father Vichai calls the sin of self-abuse," I said.

"Good thing we're not Catholic."

"It's not 'self-'abuse if it's another person," I said.

"But it *is* if that person is yourself," he said, laughing.

"Dr. Strange would call that a paradox," I said.

"I don't care what Sister Strange thinks," he said.

"You haven't really told me what it was like, with Polo," I said.

"Words can't describe it. But ..."

He — *I* — held myself close. I looked into my eyes. In those eyes, a memory stirred, a memory that wasn't mine, yet *was*. In the memory, I was with Polo. I was in bed and Polo was rearing up over me, only

Polo was every teen idol, male *and* female, rolled into one, with a blonde wig flying in the wind, smiling mysteriously as his face descended on to mine. I could smell his breath and it was very pleasant, kind of like mint and roses.

"No!" I said.

"Yes," the other I said.

"Maybe," said Polo in my memory, laughing softly. I was living this. It looked like the Dangers all shared this vision thing, so we could all look into each other's memories. I wondered about all the other Dangers. Was there a zombie Danger in the red world and could we access his brain-dead thoughts? In Lavender's memory, Polo's lips were hovering over mine, now.

At that exact moment, Donut came bursting into the room, along with Red Polo, who wasn't the Polo in the memory my Lavender counterpart was sharing with me.

"My yarn!" Donut said. "It's yanking like shit!"

And it was. Donut was being hurled around the room by an unseen force. She was being flung in the air. She held on the edge of a sofa and the sofa got dragged along with her. Lavender and I held onto Donut and we got dragged around too.

I got slammed against the door of the bridal suite so I started banging on it.

"No more screwing around!" I screamed. "Code red!"

The door to the bridal suite burst open and it was Kim and Fluke, who didn't have any clothes on.

Kim said, "We weren't screwing around."

Fluke said, "Were we? If we did, I slept through the whole thing."

"What happened to your pants?" I said.

"If you're implying some kind of coitus interruptus —" Fluke began.

"What's all the noise?" said Kim.

"Ha! The bridal suite!" said Lavender. "We predicted it! You guys wouldn't be able to resist getting it on, finally."

"So crude," I said. Meanwhile, Donut slingshotted across the room and got plastered to the far wall.

"Shut up," Kim said, grabbing a tablecloth from the coffee table and draping it discreetly. Fluke didn't bother. Meanwhile, Donut was levitating to the ceiling.

"The Exorcist!" Kim said. "Cool!" He started quoting some old movie. *"The power of Christ compels you!"*

Oddly enough, it worked.

Donut came crashing to the floor. The ceiling kind of opened up, and Polo landed on top of Donut.

"You look a bit pale," Kim said, turning on the light.

"Get your clothes," Polo said. "We only have a couple of hours to save the universe."

When Kim and Fluke hesitated for a moment, Polo went on, "Not just *this* universe. Every other universe, too. The multiverse."

"Yes, but when you came through the ceiling, the opening closed up," Fluke said.

Polo said, "Danger will open it up again."

"You know I suck at opening doors," I said.

Kim said, "But now, there's Double Danger."

37

Zombie Command Center

Kim

"So, what have you learned?" Fluke said.

"Okay," Polo said.   "First — the boss monster of this whole operation is Mr. Strange, and our own Dr. Strange is being kept a prisoner in a coffin in the control room.   Second, they're doing some kind of experiment with our school, fooling around to make different versions of the universe just for the fun of it."

"As evil villains do," Fluke said. "In the end, evil is its own reward."

"In proper storytelling," I said, "this would mean that the fate of the universe boils down to one man."

"Or woman," Donut said.

"Or non-binary," Polo said.   "But in this case it really is one *man*.   Or boy, I suppose. It's Fluke. Because I heard a lot of shit that I think only you can understand."

"Tell me," Fluke said.

"There's some kind of force-wall around the Red School," said Polo. "Beyond the wall, the world is probably pretty much normal.   There might be one around Lavender as well."

"So our schools are kind of like Petri dishes," Fluke said.   "They're breeding different strains of St. Cecilians … as if we were some kind of bacteria!"

Polo said, "The zombie problem in the Red School is to do with a computer game that had a virus that let it leak out into the real world."

I said, "So Fluke can program a counter-virus."

"That might be too hard even for me," Fluke said. "But not if Kim helps. He's the one who solves riddles."

"But what about me?" Red Polo said. "If you fix the problem *now,* what about people like me who have already become zombies?"

Fluke said, "We've already established that the Crystal Pathyway links spaces *and* times. We'll have to go back to a time *before* the zombie virus infected the world."

"Does this mean that that whole universe is just some kind of programmable video game?" Donut said.

"Yes," Fluke said. "It's the hologram theory of the universe. The simultaneity of past and future is possible because of quantum entanglement — particles and their twin opposites being linked in an instantaneous dance that ignores space and time."

He'd lost me. Not to mention the rest of us.

I said, "Dude, bottom line. What are you talking about?"

"Everything is connected to everything else."

"Oh, you mean like the Force."

"Yeah. So Kim, you're gonna find where the connections are, and me, I'm gonna connect them."

"I learned something else," Polo said. "You know that Lavender Polo is missing. I thought he'd committed suicide or something. I mean, I would, if I wasn't free to go back and forth between genders. That's how I was able to enter their world without popping out of existence before. Lavender Polo is walking between the worlds. But, it turns out, so is Lavender Evangeline."

I said, "We need everyone back in their own world to make things completely right." Yes! The universes make up a mega-Rubik's cube and every square needs to be put back.

We pushed the sofa to the middle of the room and put the coffee table on it, then a little chair on of that. We'd *just* be able to touch the ceiling that way.

"This is what we'll do," I said. "The two Dangers are going to concentrate like motherfuckers and just keep that portal open no matter what."

Our Danger climbed up on the sofa, stepped onto the coffee table and ended precariously standing on the chair. Lavender Danger stood at the best, holding the chair steady. The two Dangers looked at each other, and their eyes locked in a way that was more intimate even than lovers.

I could almost see the energy flowing between them —

Not almost … there *was* an energy there. A jagged bolt of blue lightning was shooting back and forth between their eyes, gathering strength. When it was unbearably bright, the two Dangers pointed up at the ceiling and the lightning redirected upwards. It was burning through the ceiling. There was hole circled with blue flame and it was widening!

"Quick!" said Lavender. "Go through and hold it open!"

Danger stood on tiptoe and held on to the edge of the opening. He pulled himself up. I could see his head above the whole and he stretched out his hand. "Come on through!" he shouted. First Donut, then Polo sprang onto the stool and were helped up.

"Come up, Red Polo," Polo said.

"I'll only be in the way."

Fluke clambered up and so did I.

We were all clustered around a hole in a floor; around us everything was dark and we couldn't really tell where we were. We looked down and there was Red Polo, looking quite forlorn; I guess that's normal for a rotting corpse.

"You don't need me," he said. "I'll be shambling around stupidly while you guys battle boss monsters and reprogram the universe."

"Don't be silly," Polo said. "You've come this far. And technically, I'm a zombie too, now. Come on!"

We all reached down at once. The hole in the ceiling must have resembled an octopus with all our dangling arms. The two Dangers stood at the twin poles of the circle, holding it open with their minds, but I could see that they were struggling.

Finally Red Polo started to climb up. He was standing the stool. He reached up and Fluke and I each caught a hand and started yanking … but the portal was closing. We yanked as hard as we could.

The whole closed up, sheering Red Polo in half. The energy of the blue lightning seemed to cauterize him, so his torso was sealed off.

"Fuck, Red, I'm so sorry —" I said.

"No hard feelings, dude." Red's torso looked up at me. "You can stick me together later. Hey, I'm a zombie. I don't feel pain." He put his hands on the floor and pulled himself forward a bit. "Always wanted to try walking on my hands." A small piece of intestine emerged from what remained of his rear end, and it flopped about like a monkey's tail.

"Look," he said. "It's prehensile!" The intestine started crawling up my leg.

"That's disgusting," I said.

The two Dangers laughed.

"Where are we?" Donut said.

The darkness around us started to resolve into a bright, garishly lit scene. We were in some kind of lab, a huge room lined with windows, each window looking out at a parallel vista of St. Cecilia's School, each vista subtly different. This was clearly the control center for whatever was happening to our worlds.

Polo said, "Okay, I better get back in my coffin before the people show up." There were a few zombies walking around, working at various computer consoles, but they seemed to be doing the kind of repetitive tasks that zombies do, I suppose. "Kim and Fluke, pick a workstation and start fixing the universe. I think we've got about an hour before they come back."

"I'll keep watch," Donut said. "Along with Red Polo."

"She can watch the door," Red said, "I'll watch the floor in case any more portals open up." He scurried along on his hands, his lone, loose entrail curling up behind him."

Fluke sat down at the nearest computer console. A photo of Cardinal Crank adorned the desk. I pulled up another chair.

"Here goes nothing," he said, "It'll probably take an hour even to hack the password."

38

Quantum Disentanglement

Fluke

Actually, the password turned out to be 0123456789.

"Told you it would be easy for you," Kim said.

So much for advanced security measures. Or maybe security was the least of their concerns? We're here, I was thinking, in a kind of protected enclave of a space that's in the cracks of other universes, and the only people who work here are zombies anyway, so who's to hack?

Me?

But I had to try.

"Look," Kim said. "There's a couple of thumb drives here. We might need to download something fast so ..." He scooped them up and put them next to the keyboard. "I'll stick one in in case."

But as soon as it was inserted, patterns started dancing on the screen. A title page came up with the logo of St. Cecilia's ... and the words *The Project*.

Kim leaned forward against my shoulder. I felt less afraid. I had guessed the password in one try. Maybe there was no password at all. Maybe I could penetrate through to the heart of the problem. I typed a few random keys. The words *The Project* dissolved in a cascade of colors and it seemed that the screen projected itself outwards, transforming into a holographic display that took up the whole desk. At first it was just random designs and color patterns.

Then the computer *spoke*.

Well, fancy seeing you here at last! You are the first of the Club Xs to penetrate this far!

I jumped out of my skin, especially when a holographic face formed in the computer screen. It was the face of Cardinal Crank.

"Fuck," said Kim softly.

I had wised up since last year. Now, I knew now that Cardinal Crank wasn't some creepy sexual predator. But maybe he was something far worse.

"You lured us here," I said. "You set up all of this!"

Young man, young man ... the sharpness of a sword is tested in the swiftness of the slicing. Well! I shan't intrude again, except perhaps ... when this all ends. And he did one of those hideous smirks.

"But why?" I said. "Why do you have to keep meddling with us? We're teenagers. Our lives are fucked up enough as it is."

Then the image of the cardinal faded slowly.

A menu came up on the screen.

Quantum Entanglements — Disentanglements

There followed a clickable list of colors:

Blue

Red

Purple

Green

... and then the colours started getting fancier ...

Cerulean

Fuchsia

Primrose

Burnt Umber

... and then they were names and numbers ...

Pantone X126351723

... and mathematical formulae ...

$x-3x\sqrt{(7x-2)}y/y+2$

"Those are universes," Kim said. "See ... they just run out of color names. Blue is us, and we're the prime world anyway, so they say."

I clicked on Blue first, and the first screen was a schematic of Club X. We were all there, the five of us plus Boom. We were all icons, a bit like anime, but the resemblance was striking. I clicked on myself and there were several ways visualizing myself ... as a dot moving through a 3-dimensional matrix where I could switch between dimensions ... as a timeline snaking through future or past ... as a puzzle with a million pieces. I could zoom out from myself and see the whole school.

"But can you change *us?* Can you change our world?" Kim said. "The prime world?"

"It's locked," I said. "And I'd never do that. I wouldn't want to wake up tomorrow, and everyone has two heads."

"Better than one," Kim said, laughing.

I fiddled with the other buttons. "Red and Purple aren't locked," I said. Kim moved his chair and put one arm over my shoulder. He squeezed a little. I clicked on Red.

I saw the same icons at first, centering on Club X. But Polo's icon had a big X on his head. So did mine. "Looks like Red Fluke's a zombie too, now," I said. I selected my icon and followed my timeline back into the past. I saw it right away, a big smudge in the timeline. "This is where it changed," I said. It was about three months ago. I could see the infection that had been introduced into the program. "Red," I said. Red Polo skittered up to me. When he reared himself up, he reached about my knee. "Kim, pick him up and put him on your lap. Oh, don't mind the bodily fluids, we'll take a nice long shower when we're done."

"Together?" Red Polo said, giggling.

"At least being sliced in two hasn't taken away your sense of humor," Kim said.

"The video game that everyone started to play," I said. "Where was it exactly?"

"I think ... Sister Edward's computer ... reception, school lobby."

"I'm going to make a virus killer," I said. "And then we're going to go in there and plug it in before it has a chance to —"

"Can't you fix it from here?" I said.

"Sure," I said. "I can do it remotely. Unless ..."

I started typing furiously. I used the puzzle as the graphic metaphor because it went much more quickly when Kim told me where to go, which pieces to move.

I dove into the virtual world. With Kim holding on to me, I was bold. I used the combined power of our imaginations ... my wild imagination and Kim's literal-mindedness keeping me grounded. I expanded the holographic field until it engulfed the three of us.

We were swimming in puzzle pieces. Jigsaw bits, cubes and polyhedrons from Rubik-style puzzles, crossword fragments, riddles, even Scrabble tiles. They were coming at us. But Kim just stood there calmly, saying "This one ... that one." He took the pieces literally. He wasn't confused by the metaphor at all. Because to him, it was all literal. I reached out with my hand — a virtual hand, because it was really my mind — and started building my weapon to end all weapons. It was simple actually. In a way. I just had to use the virus against itself.

Kim told me what pieces to use but I was the one who saw what they meant. It was amazing when we worked together like this. He knew without understanding, and I understood without knowing.

There was a single algorithm that pushed the video game virus into something much more sinister ... something that converted virtual reality into actuality ... and it was all to do with entanglement ... particles that were waves that were strings, stretching across the dimensions and needing just a little ripple in the multiverse to slingshot reality into another reality. Setting the Red World back to rights would require tiny reverse engineering in the coding. It was like one of the Bach fugues that could be be played upside and backwards and still sound like music. I almost had it, and yet — "This is too much," I said. "It's too difficult. I'm a genius, I'm not God."

"You're the closest thing we got," Red Polo said.

"I can't create something from nothing."

"God can," Red Polo said, sounding strangely like Father Vichai in my catechism class.

"Be quiet, Red," Kim said. "How much more time do you need, Fluke?"

"Maybe fifteen minutes."

"Wait, what about *this* piece?" Kim said, pointing to something that didn't even look like a puzzle piece. It was just a black spot. A little round blob of emptiness.

"Shit," I said. "That *is* a puzzle piece. It's a piece of *nothing.* It's *nothing* that's also *everything,* because nothing and everything are opposites. It's a black hole that might be a portal to —"

Kim had seen the solution. All I had to do was incorporate a piece of *nothing* into just the right segment of the code and —

"We're fucked," said Red Polo. "Someone's coming."

"I just need a minute or two," I said.

"Someone *is* coming!" Kim said. "Duck!"

Polo

So, I'm lying in the coffin, and the Dangers are sort of crouching beneath, and Kim, Fluke and Red Polo are working on one of the workstations. And I hear someone coming in. Nothing I could do. I was supposed to be in some kind of datura-induced trance and I couldn't give myself away yet.

"I left you standing in the corner." came a creepy, witchlike voice. "Who put you back in the box?"

A few zombies grunted. Stupid of me! I had forgotten where I was supposed to be.

"Idiots," she said. "If only we could leave your intelligence when we remove your free will!"

And then Eudaemonia, Sister Euphemia's evil twin, was gazing down at me. "Something isn't quite right," she said. "You look a little bit too ... *alive.*" She summoned an assistant, who produced a handful of pills. "Perhaps you've even been walking around *on your own!* Maybe I underestimated the datura dose. Go on, dear, down the hatch!"

Eudaemonia leaned over me and was about to stuff half a dozen zombie pills into my mouth. A zombie stuck its finger in my mouth and started to pry it open. I wanted to scream but that would give it away.

Sister Eudaemonia lunged for my mouth. I bit down hard. I spat out a finger.

"Sorry," I said.

The zombie started screaming. Sister was distracted for a moment, but came at me again. Just then, though, the two Dangers dragged her off me. Sister Eudaemonia was going to scream and get someone to show up, I was sure. I got out of the coffin. The zombie was howling, and jumping up and down, loose finger in hand. "There there," I told it. "We'll get your finger sewn back on in a jiffy." I looked around. Another zombie was standing with a basket of what looked like medical supplies.

The two Dangers had a hand over Sister's mouth and dragged her toward an open, standing sarcophagus. She was struggling. "We need her hands tied," said Lavender. "Hey, Red Polo! Help us!"

My zombie double jumped off Kim's lap and crawled towards us. He shot out his intestinal tail and started winding it round and round Sister's hands. I grabbed some surgical tape from the zombie's basket and started to wind it around Sister's mouth. "Hold her mouth for me, damn it!" I shouted at the nearest zombie.

To my amazement, the zombie shambled up and held Sister's mouth tight shut.

"These creatures will obey any human," I said. "Not one in particular. It's also the reason I was able to wander in and out of here

... and fetch my friends. You guys are so arrogant, it never occurred to you that someone from outside could ever show up here."

Sister Eudaemonia struggled and looked daggers at me and the Dangers. But the zombie had her mouth taped pretty well. They do have superhuman strength, I guess.

Danger said, "Should be shut her up in King Tut's sarcophagus over here?"

"I don't know if she'll be able to breathe," I said. "We're not killers."

Then I turned to the zombie who had taped up Sister's mouth. "I bet you can suture real good," I said. "Stick that finger back on your friend, huh? There's a good zombie."

39

Science versus Magic

Polo

So, I'm lying in the coffin, and the Dangers are sort of crouching beneath, and Kim, Fluke and Red Polo are working on one of the workstations. And I hear someone coming in. Nothing I could do. I was supposed to be in some kind of datura-induced trance and I couldn't give myself away.

"I left you standing in the corner." came a creepy, witchlike voice. "Who put you back in the box?"

A few zombies grunted. Stupid of me! I had forgotten where I was supposed to be.

"Idiots," she said. "If only we could leave your intelligence when we remove your free will!" Of course. It was the zombies' fault. What a relief.

And then Eudaemonia, Sister Euphemia's evil twin, was gazing down at me. "Something isn't quite right," she said. "You look a little bit too ... *lively.* Not quite pale enough." She summoned an assistant, who produced a handful of pills. "Perhaps you've even been walking around *on your own!* Maybe I underestimated the datura dose. Go on, dear, down the hatch!"

Eudaemonia leaned over me and was about to stuff half a dozen zombie pills into my mouth. A zombie stuck its finger in my mouth and started to pry it open. I wanted to scream but that would give it away.

Sister Eudaemonia lunged for my mouth. I bit down hard. I spat out a finger. There was no blood, just a sticky kind of thick foul-smelling sauce.

"Sorry," I said.

The zombie started screaming. They weren't supposed to feel pain!

Sister was distracted for a moment, but came at me again. Just then, though, the two Dangers dragged her off me. Sister Eudaemonia was going to scream and get someone to show up, I was sure. I got out of the coffin. The zombie was howling, and jumping up and down, loose finger in hand. "There there," I told it. "We'll get your finger sewn back on in a jiffy." I looked around. Another zombie was standing with a basket of what looked like medical supplies.

The two Dangers had a hand over Sister's mouth and dragged her toward an open, standing sarcophagus. She was struggling. "We need her hands tied," said Lavender. "Hey, Red Polo! Help us!"

My zombie double jumped off Kim's lap and crawled towards us. He shot out his intestinal tail and started winding it round and round Sister's hands. I grabbed some surgical tape from the zombie's basket and started to wind it around Sister's mouth. "Hold her mouth for me, damn it!" I shouted at the nearest zombie.

To my amazement, the zombie shambled up and held Sister's mouth tight shut.

"These creatures will obey any human," I said. "Not one in particular. It's also the reason I was able to wander in and out of here … and fetch my friends. You guys are so arrogant, it never occurred to you that someone from outside could ever show up here."

Sister Eudaemonia struggled and looked daggers at me and the Dangers. But the zombie had her mouth taped pretty well. They do have superhuman strength, I guess.

Danger said, "Should be shut her up in King Tut's sarcophagus over here?"

"I don't know if she'll be able to breathe," I said. "We're not killers."

Then I turned to the zombie who had taped up Sister's mouth. "I bet you can suture real good," I said. "Stick that finger back on your friend, huh? There's a good zombie."

The two zombies waddled off and what do you know, a big scary needle was produced and one of the them started to sew the other one's finger back on.

I turned to Kim and Fluke. "Hurry," I said.

"I'm working as fast as I can."

It was amazing to watch them actually. Kim would point and Fluke would click. They were totally in sync. It was true love.

I heard Donut who had been watching the door. "Someone's coming!" she said, and scampered into the room.

Just then, Mr. Strange marched into the room and was looming above them.

Shit!

Kim

"Watch out!" Donut shouted from the door.

I felt a heavy hand on my shoulder.

"Stop what you're doing right this minute, young man!"

I whipped around. "Dr. Strange!"

"*Mister,*" he said. "Don't confuse me with my idiot twin." He had one hand on each of our shoulders and he was powerful. I squirmed.

Fluke turned, wriggled free. "Grab the thumb drive," he whispered to me. "We can't fix it from in here."

We both wriggled free of Mr. Strange and pushed him back. He wrestled me to the floor. Fluke leaped on top of Mr. Strange. I threw the thumb drive to Polo. Polo caught it. Mr. Strange jumped up and bore down on Polo. Red Polo flung himself on Mr. Strange, using his loose intestine as a slingshot. Sister's hands came lose and she started to tear at the tape around her mouth.

The two Dangers

Polo threw the drive back to me.

"Get that thumb drive!" Mr. Strange screamed at a zombie.

The zombie wrenched the drive from my hand and shambled toward Mr. Strange.

"Get that thumb drive!" Polo yelled at another zombie.

"Swallow it!" Mr. Strange shouted at the first zombie.

Not missing a beat, the zombie popped the thumb drive in its mouth. Polo repeated to the other zombie, "Get it, get it!"

The second zombie grabbed a pair of scissors from the medical basket, tackled the first zombie, and started to cut a hole in its belly.

Fluke said, "We need help. We need *our* Dr. Strange."

Polo said, "He's in that coffin over there." He pointed to a standing coffin in one corner, with a double padlock.

"C'mon," Fluke said. We left Mr. Strange trying to pull scissors zombie off thumb drive zombie. We could hear someone banging inside the coffin.

"Help us, Dr. Strange," I said. That's who it had to be. "Fluke, what about the padlock?"

"I can't unlock anything that isn't virtual," he said.

"The Dangers," I said. "Guys, use your superpowers and unlock this thing."

"We can't let go of Sister," they both said.

Then Red Polo came hopping towards us. He jumped into my arms. "Turn me around," he said. When I did that, his prehensile intestine shot out from his ass and began fiddling with the keyhole of the first padlock. It came off in a jiffy, and so did the second.

"Never send a boy to do a man's job," Red Polo said. The coffin door opened with a creak and me and Fluke fell on the floor. It was Dr. Strange all right.

"About time!" he said. "Thank you for liberating me, but it's not a moment too soon!" He spied his twin across the room. "Desist from tampering with the delicate fabric of the universe!"

"Do you think you can stop me? You, with your pseudo-science?" Mr. Strange shouted.

"Science will always trump magic," said Dr. Strange.

"Rubbish. You will always be hidebound by logic."

"You may think you're some kind of supernatural being," Dr. Strange said, "but you still need a computer program to upset the balance of the universe."

Mr. Strange reached into the guts of the now disembowelled zombie and pulled out the thumb drive. Blackish fluid oozed down his arm. He held it up, triumphant. "A computer program! A metaphor, nothing more."

Dr. Strange rushed him and tackled him. The drive flew up in the air. "Catch, Kim! I'll distract him while you infiltrate the Red World!" I caught it in one hand.

"How do we get in?"

Dr. Strange pulled a crystal key from his pocket and threw it to Fluke. "Through the mirror! Quick!"

"Which mirror?"

"I know which one," Polo said. Fluke and I went to the mirror-window she pointed at.

The nun broke loose now. I chased after her.

"Take that, you overweight neutrino," Mr. Strange said, flinging a bolt of lightning at Dr. Strange. Dr. Strange writhed and howled.

The Dangers flung their own lightning back. The nun was trying to subdue Polo, but Red Polo had climbed up onto her shoulder and was poking at her eyes with his intestine. Kim and I stood at the window. We held the key to the glass, but there was no keyhole.

Dr. Strange hobbled over to where Mr. Strange was cackling in full movie monster mode. "Magic, eh, Theodore? Here's a bit of science for you — force equals mass times acceleration!" He yanked a computer off a workstation and brought it crashing down on Mr. Strange's head. "Take that, you diminutive demon!"

Mr. Theodore Strange clawed at the air.

Dr. Leopold Strange sat down at the terminal and typed a few commands. "Quick! I'll hold off my idiot brother and hold the portal open!"

A door appeared on the surface of the window. Fluke unlocked it with the crystal key.

A wind whistled through the room. The window vanished. We stood on some kind of ledge on a cliff. Clouds were streaming past. We were looking over the school from way up in the air. I was starting to get vertigo. I gripped the key with one hand and Fluke's hand with the other.

"Just you and me?" he said.

"We'd better jump," I said, closing my eyes.

"Yeah," he said. "Here goes nothing."

Squeezing my hand hard, he took the leap, and me along with him.

40

Nuns with Guns

Kim

We didn't plummet to the ground. Instead we were riding the wind. It was just before sunrise. We made a soft landing right at the lobby entrance of St. Cecilia's. It was uncannily like going back to home base.

Still, we're not really allowed in this part of school until the wakeup bell.

"It's just you and me, then?" I said.

"Sorry to ruin your all-boys party," came a voice from above. It was Donut. She fluttered down to the ground. "Figured you might need my expertise, especially if we have to sneak into the nuns' quarters."

"But Red Polo said it started in Sister Edward's computer — that's in reception," I said. "Just quick in and out, pop in the drive, a few clicks and we're out."

"No, no, I'm glad you came, Donut," Fluke said.

"Yeah, whatever."

We entered the lobby.

"It's dead quiet," Fluke whispered.

"That's morbid," Donut said.

"Shut up, guys."

The lobby ... the same but so different. There was St. Cecilia, the old carved wooden saint just as out of place here as back in our school, her paint peeling, her eyes gazing on some inner world.

Sister Edward's station was in the far corner of the lobby. There was her computer, and there was the drawer where she kept her keys and papers. Kim and Fluke went over to the computer and I rummaged in the drawer. Lot of use that was — the drawer was empty.

Fluke put the drive in a USB slot, but yanked it out after a minute or two.

"Shit," Fluke said, "there's nothing on this 'puter that we can use. It's all being run remotely from ... looks like ... a laptop in ... where is this?"

He zoomed in on the GPS coordinates. I glanced up at the screen.

"There's a reason I needed to come," I said. "That laptop is in the nuns' sitting room ... over in the Convent."

"But we're guys. We're not allowed ..." I said.

"Unless you know the secret way. And by the way, you'll have to go in drag."

"Not the nun outfits!" I said, remembering Polo last year, popping through the closet door in one of those robes.

"Yes," Donut said. "Nun outfits. Ha, ha."

"I don't know if should dress as a nun," Fluke said. "I mean . . I *am* Catholic. I think cross-dressing's a sin. Probably just a venal sin, but still —"

"Just go to confession," I said.

"So you'll eavesdrop again?"

Donut took us through the woods to an open basement window and got us to climb in. "The nuns have to be awake for the dawn service," she said. "But we have a little time. Breakfast is after the dawn service and during that service they're all in the nuns' chapel. We'll hear them coming and get away in time."

There were a lot of habits on hangers, and other folded ones, and a laundry hamper filled with habits for the laundry, I guess.

"Surely we don't need to dress as nuns?" I said. "We're not like Polo. We're not good at passing as female."

"Well ... to be safe ... if we happen to encounter one in the corridor, and keep our eyes demurely downcast, we won't be noticed."

Following Donut's terse instructions, we slipped the habits on over our school uniforms. I had trouble with the headgear, but we ended up just putting it on loosely; I'd have to hope it wouldn't slip off.

"By the way," Donut said, "there's also a short cut to Cub X here ...

if we push our way through to the back of the closet."

Fluke said, "It may come in useful for a quick escape."

We went into a corridor and took some back stairs. We were in a corridor, like a T-shape, and ahead, at the T junction, we could see a whole bevy of nuns of different sizes and shapes moving from left to right. "They're going to the chapel," Donut whispered. "In a moment they'll be there and we'll be able to take a left to the sitting room."

When the last of the nuns had gone through, we crept into the sitting room. It was a comfy room with a coffee bar and books and a mini-altar with an antique silver cross, a couple of pretty statues of the Virgin Mary and a portrait of the Pope. Behind the coffee bar there was a refrigerator.

There was a laptop on the table and Kim opened it. He inserted the thumb drive and easily got into Sister's account. "I already hacked her last year," he said. "She never changed her password."

Fluke was clicking away. "I can't seem to get the antivirus to work. This is designed to stop the virus in its tracks, but it seems to have already taken hold of the system"

That was when I noticed the time in the menu bar. "Fluke," I said, "we're too late."

"Fuck," he said. "I didn't allow for temporal lag."

"Not you. You didn't make the portal. It's Dr. Strange," I said. "He's always off by —"

"Two minutes!" Donut gasped.

"Two fucking minutes!" I said. "Just like his classroom schedule!"

Suddenly, the screen dissolved into a swirl of colors and an apocalyptic voice intoned: "WELCOME TO ZOMBIE HIGH." And we were in an overhead view of the school. Zombies were shown as little red zombie icons moving around. Students were blue, nuns and other adults were gray. We could zoom in closer. "PREPARE TO UNDIE!" said the computer. Dramatic video game music played — full orchestra horror movie style music — very dramatic, as if John Williams had composed the theme to *Halloween*.

"Shit," Fluke said. "It's taken over the system."

Zooming down to the convent area, we could see the gray dots that were nuns, all gathered in one little room. It was the morning prayer. We could see ourselves. Little blue dots, just down the hall.

Fluke said, "Let me see if I can reboot." He flicked a button on the laptop and we heard the *ping* of it trying to restart. But it didn't! The video game wouldn't let Fluke log off! A big ERROR message came up: "Zombie High has canceled reboot. Try again?"

Before he could try again, the screen once again zoomed back in on an overhead view of the room we were in. "Uh oh," I said. "There's a red dot in the room."

"Where?" Fluke said. We looked warily around. "I don't see anyone but us."

"Put it on maximum zoom," I said.

He did. The dot was behind the bar. "It's in the fridge," Donut said.

"Okay," Fluke whispered. "Maybe it will just stay in there."

We heard someone at the door. We rushed to hide. Donut tried to dive behind an armchair. She didn't quite make it in time. So she just sat down in the chair; after all, these nuns all look alike, right? Kim and I decided to tough it out, too. It was pretty dark — if whoever it was wouldn't turn on the light —

Too late. It was Sister Edward, and she flipped the switch. *We're never going to get away with this,* I thought. But Sister Edward seemed … distracted.

"Oh," she mumbled. "You got here quickly, I thought I was first out."

We nodded and mumbled and tried to look away.

She said, "The weapons are under the altar. You'd better get some."

Guns? I thought. Surely nuns and guns don't mix. Still, we got up and lifted up the tablecloth over the little altar. I saw rifles and pistols. At least when we were getting weapons, our backs were to Sister. I took a pistol. I think Fluke got a rifle, and so did Donut.

"We've locked all the entrances to the convent," said Sister Edward. "Father Vichai's guarding the main door. None of those *things* have breached the building yet."

We nodded and mumbled again. Sister looked at her laptop. "Hmm, I wonder what this is," she said, pulling out the thumb drive. She put it on the table.

Then Sister Edward said, "I surely could use a drink," and walked over to the refrigerator.

"No!" the three of us shouted at the same time. It was too late. She had opened the fridge. She turned to look at us.

"Are you new?" she said.

Something crawled out of the fridge. That something was rearing up behind her. It stood in the shadows. She didn't notice. Of course, it wasn't breathing down her neck. The undead don't breathe!

"If there's anything you need, Sisters," Sister Edward said, "please don't hesitate to ask me." She chuckled. "Funny, I didn't know any new novitiates were coming this week. Euphemia is so absent-minded, she never —"

The *thing* bit down hard on her shoulder and put both hands on Sister's head. I fired with the pistol. Fluke fired. Donut ran up and got the creature point-blank in the forehead. As the zombie sank to the floor, I realized it was *me*.

Too late for Sister. Her head had been twisted completely around, *Exorcist*-style.

She was dead ... but she was changing. Sister Edward let out a series of screams, as though she were giving birth. She was, in a way ... giving birth to a zombie version of herself! Her eyes became hollow.

"Donut! Grab the drive!" Fluke shouted, since she was closest to the laptop. "We have to get out of here."

"The way we came?" said Donut, as she picked up the drive.

Sister Edward's eyes were terrifying. Her head was still on backward. Like Red Polo, she wasn't a shambler. She loped towards us at top speed. "Brains!" she shrieked. My pistol was out of bullets. I grabbed a Virgin Mary and smashed the statue down on Sister's head. I tossed the pistol, took a rifle, and some boxes of ammo.

We ran from the room. In the corridor, nuns were hysterically running this way and that, and Sister Edward, soon ignored us and started terrifying her fellow nuns. We fired a few shots to keep her at bay and fled down the corridor to the stairs into the basement.

"The portal — outside the main lobby — can we make it?" I said.

"Doubt it," said Fluke. Because when we got into the vestry, it was swarming with zombies. When the nuns blocked all the entries, they must have forgotten the basement window. More were climbing in. I recognized Polo ... in one piece ... once more confirming that we had traveled back in time ... just not quite far enough!

The zombies hadn't noticed us yet, but any minute now —

"This way!" Donut said, taking my hand. We pushed through the hanging vestments and habits. "The Pathway ... it's through here!"

41

Disentangling Dr. Strange

Polo

So, the Strange twins were chucking objects and casting spells at each other, while the Dangers were trying to restrain Sister Eudaemonia.

Donut and Kim and Fluke had jumped out of the window and been whisked off to another universe. Red Polo was hobbling about on his hands.

And me?

I was standing around panicking.

The Stranges were rolling around on the floor now. The Dangers were still trying to gag the struggling Sister with their hands. She broke free, with Red Polo's intestine still twining around her legs, and half ran, half limped over to the Stranges, trying to land a kick here and there. I had to do something, so I went over there and punched Sister Eudaemonia in the chest.

"I'm not a zombie!" I screamed. The medical zombies were done with sewing on the finger. "Bring datura," I yelled, "and shove it in the nun's mouth!"

The zombie approached with a fistful of pills. Idiots indeed! They obeyed the nearest human. "Make sure she can't open her mouth wide enough to order any zombies around," I said to the Dangers. "If she does order one to do something, contradict it with another order. They get confused easily."

The Stranges were fighting ever more energetically. It would have been comical if the fate of our world hadn't depended on it. Dr. Strange was swinging a mouse on its cord like a slingshot. Mr. Strange was waving his hands and muttering spells, most of which didn't seem to work.

The zombie was shoving pills down Sister Eudaemonia's throat. She started to zone out and soon the Dangers could let go of her. She was shambling around in a daze.

At that moment, Kim, Fluke and Donut came charging in — not through window, but through the door to the Crystal Pathway.

"Dr. Strange!" Kim gasped. "You were two minutes off! We gotta get back in there, it's going crazy!"

"I'm a bit occupied," Dr. Strange said, as he hurled a computer keyboard at his brother. It missed but knocked out Sister Eudaemonia, who tumbled into my empty coffin.

"You nefarious nincompoop!" Mr. Strange said, cackling hideously. "Keyboards can't harm me. Throwing mice isn't going to work."

"Guys," Fluke said. "The rosaries!"

All of us clutched the rosaries that weren't rosaries and held them in the air, Jesus end pointing outward. We started to converge on the duelling Stranges. We formed a circle of outstretched crucifixes. Boldly, we moved toward Mr. Strange.

Mr. Strange appeared confused at first. Then he started shrieking, "Ah! Ah! It burns!" Smoke fumes escaped his face.

Dr. Strange stood straight and brushed himself off with a hand. "You superstitious old sod," he said.

Mr. Strange continued to writhe. We got closer and closer as Dr. Strange stepped out of the way. Our crosses made a crown around Mr. Strange's scalp and he screamed.

Then the screaming turned into a hideous cackle and he whirled about, transformed into a bat, and started flying erratically around the room, squeaking! He hit the ceiling, and, more like a hawk than a bat, swooped down on Dr. Strange, a streak of shiny black. I pushed Dr. Strange out of the way. "Daylight!" Dr. Strange whispered.

Kim said, "He's right. We have to make daylight."

"Yeah. Daylight," Fluke said. "We can make daylight."

As the Stranges battled, as the nun struggled, and as the zombies shambled around confusedly, we members of Club X made a circle in the center of the room. We held hands. We concentrated.

Fluke said, "Dangers, you have the most power. We'll all help. We'll bring down the sun on this vampire."

We closed our eyes. The imaging came from the two Dangers, a ball of heat and warmth high above us. We could all feel it.

"Imagine," Fluke said, "the Aten ... the Egyptian god, shown as a sun-disk stretching a hundred arms down to earth, touching us all with life-giving light."

Fluke was so good at finding the metaphor ... while Kim often didn't even notice when something *was* a metaphor. But I kept my eyes tight shut and tried to imagine an infinite pool of warmth in the sky, reaching down to touch me ... like the Guru in my meditation vision who had told me how to find myself. At first I couldn't feel anything until I started to imagine the Guru himself, the gentle smile, the eyes that were full of warmth. Maybe if I imagined the sunlight shining out of his eyes ...

It was working. His face filled my inner video screen. I was zeroing in on his right eye. The eye was the world. Now it was expanding so much this black pupil was filling my entire inner vision. I was being sucked into the great sea of black. And there was a yellow gleam in the pupil. The sun!

The warmth of it hit me all at once. This must have been the moment that my focus linked to the Dangers'. I could feel them first, reaching up toward the sun, drawing it down. There was a hand touching my forehead ... it was so hot, but I didn't burn ... it was a conduit for the life force. It was like an outpouring of endless love.

Now I could feel Kim and Fluke chiming in with their minds. Even Donut, with a little fledgling energy, was carried along by the others. It was beautiful. Club X, focusing as one, could nudge the universe in a new direction....

I could feel the sun like the Aten-disk in Fluke's imagination. I could feel the sun's arms reach out and touch each one of us. "Now!" Fluke whispered. Each one of us grasped one of the arms and started to pull.

We had been standing in darkness, but the dark ceiling split and sunlight was pouring in.

We heard a scream — like a wounded animal, kind of shrieking and yelping all mixed together. I opened my eyes — we all did. Mr. Strange was writhing around like a pole dancer, and literally giving off smoke. His eyes were bulging.

"Help me get him in a coffin," Dr. Strange said.

"Just use the one I came in," I said.

We lifted up Mr. Strange, tossed him in my coffin, and for good measure, added the padlock from Dr. Strange's coffin. "We can nail the lid in later," said Dr. Strange. "He won't come up as long as the sunlight holds."

"Why can't we just let him die in the sun?" Donut said.

"First, because it's sunlight from another universe, so after you let go of your focus, it might fade and he won't die. Second, he *is* my brother. I am not entirely devoid of family feeling, you know!'

We took a breath. The ceiling had been ripped right off and sunlight was streaming in. The whole room, with all that light, seemed fake, like a stage set without the moody lighting. The computers looked like they were made of cardboard. The zombies looked like extras in a school play. They just stood around blinking.

"Help us, Dr. Strange," I said.

"I – will have to get in a coffin myself, soon," he said. "I can't be in sunlight long, either. I have porphyria. Remember?"

"What should we do?" Kim said.

"Can we try the intervention one more time?" Fluke said. "But go back two minutes earlier?"

"I'm weakening," Dr. Strange said. "I can open the portal ... but I don't know if I can hold it open ... it's up to you, my children. It has *always* been up to you. You are Club X. There's no mystery you cannot solve."

But I suddenly knew what to do.

"Jacques Florrisant," I said.

"Jacques Florrisant?" said the others.

"Remember?" I said "You say name, me come?"

"He didn't say that," said Kim. He said, "Me *try* come."

"Yeah, but what do we have to lose?" said Lavender Danger.

And then, all at once, we were hollering the shaman's name at the top of our lungs, not knowing if it would work: *"Jacques Florissant! Jacques Florissant!"*

42

Jacques Florissant

Kim

We all picked up Polo's chant. Louder and louder. The pounding rhythm infected the zombies and they started to sway.

But how the hell was a voodoo priest going to just pop into being here. in the heart of Strangeworld?

And if Dr. Strange was just going to fade away from his porphyria …

But no. As we chanted the name of the shaman over and over, something was happening to Dr. Strange. His whole body was shaking … fibrillating … then vibrating so fast he was like a blur. And then he was there again.

Well … not quite there.

He was standing in front of us, and he *looked* like Dr. Strange — kind of. His features had morphed a little in the direction of a native Haitian. His eyes kept changing color.

Then his eyes rolled up in their sockets. There were only whites.

"Bonswa zanmi m yo!" he said in a kind of James Earl Jones-Darth Vader voice. *"ki koté mwen?"*

"Huh!" said Polo. *"You're* Jacques Florissant?"

"As a matter of fact," said Dr. Strange, "we're both in here. In fact, it's a good thing the *houngan* has taken over. Or I'd be fried to a crisp, I'm afraid. All that bloody light!"

"You! You go back inside!" Dr. Strange said in the voice of the shaman. "Or you burn up!"

"Righty-ho," said Dr. Strange. "Over and out."

Great. Our English teacher not-vampire had been possessed by a witch doctor.

Fluke said, "He's in there. We have to get him to speak through Jacques."

I said, "Danger … reach him."

The Dangers both said, "Me?"

Fluke said, "Yes. That's why there are two of you. Your power is logarithmic. It's not doubled but squared."

Whatever that meant.

The Dangers stood on either side of Strange-Florissant. They reached out and put both hands on his face. "It's like when those dudes are being possessed by their gods and they dance around."

Lavender Danger said, "They're both in there, and both of them have very dominant personalities!"

I said, "Dr. Strange, we need to get back into the Red World again. In time to stop zombie virus from infecting the game."

"Open the portal!" Fluke said urgently.

Dr. Strange staggered over to a computer terminal and starting typing. He didn't seem well at all. His fingers moved erratically and it looked like he was still trying to log in.

"Me no have password," said the voice of Jacques Florissant.

"Danger, both Dangers, probe his mind! Ferret out that password!"

"That's disgusting," Fluke said. "When Cardinal Crank did that to me, I was traumatized for a year."

That was true. It came back to me all at once. Me and Fluke, holding all those secrets deep down, unable to talk to each other for so long. "But we have to save the world," I said. "Saving the world has a price."

"Dr. Strange's sanity?" Fluke said. "What kind of price is that?"

The Dangers nodded at each other. "Worth it," they said.

But before they could probe deeper into Dr. Strange's mind, he started to speak again. "Timeline … contaminated … leaking … butterfly effect …"

"What's he talking about?" I said.

"He's saying that the last time we went in, we disturbed something," Fluke said. "And now we can't get back to the exact spot."

"The password's probably something really stupid," said Polo, "like his birthday."

"On it," Fluke said, and dashed off to the next terminal. His fingers flew, just like he was dashing off a Bach fugue. "Holy shit ... Christmas ... 1827. Can't be right."

"Ha! Me more old than him!" said the *houngan*.

I pushed Dr. Strange's fingers off the keys and typed it in myself. It worked. "Dumb luck, Polo," I said, "plus Fluke's great hacking skills."

"Still," Fluke said, "I'm not sure I can puzzle my way through Dr. Strange's *stuff* fast enough to get us in."

Polo thought of something. He took a sheaf of papers lying around the terminal, fanned them out and held them above Dr. Strange's head like a parasol. "Help me," Polo said. "Dangers, Donut ... block the sunlight. It will revive him a bit."

Our Danger said, "We can also do this...." The two Dangers concentrated. A gaudy sunshade, the kind you might see at a beachside cafe, suddenly appeared over Dr. Strange's head. Dr. Strange plunged into shadow.

Dr. Strange spoke, sounding a little better. "I must solve this. And the shaman must solve this. Magic and science must work together." Then came the voice of the shaman. "*Dokté Étranj*, him make vaccine. *Mwan*, make antidote. Need both."

"You'll have to get into the main school computer," Fluke said. "With these shifting algorithms, you'll need to be writing the code on the fly. I can stay here and keep the portal open ...."

"The portal," Dr. Strange said. "It keeps fluctuating. You probably won't arrive together. It won't be *the moment*. It'll be a bit before, a bit after. This means some of you will be staving off an infection, and others will fighting off zombies, and I don't know who will have to do what. But I think *you'd* better do that coding, Fluke. I shall keep the portal open as long as I can."

With one hand he was at the keyboard. With his other arm, seemingly operating entirely independently, he was reaching into drawers, pulling out reagents, pounding ingredients with a mortar and pestle. He actually *was* two people inside one skin.

"*Mwen* making antidote," came the voice of the shaman. Here's the thing. When he was the shaman, Dr. Strange only spoke out of the left side of his face. When he was himself again, he spoke out of his right side. What would it be like if they tried to speak at once?

They did. It was cacophony!

"One at a time!" I said at last.

"Time's the problem," said Lavender Danger.

"Yeah. We're running out of time," Polo said.

"Not really," Fluke said. "Every moment is a speck forever in the ocean of spacetime."

"Tan an se yon rivyè," said Jacques Florissant, *"men larivyè a ka koule dèyè."*

"True," said Fluke. "He says that time is a river, but the river can flow backwards."

"Quiet!" said Dr. Strange. "The portal is opening!"

A golden door was materializing in the middle of the room. It was opening and behind it we could see other doors, all unmarked.

"The doors on the left are before the anomaly," said Dr. Strange. "The doors on the right are after it. Left to prevent, right to fix."

"Both directions better," said the voice of Jacques Florissant.

As usual, I ended up making the plan. "So … Polo and Donut … you'll appear *after* the virus hits and shower every zombie you see with the antidote. Dangers, you'll stay and keep the parasol going so Dr. Strange doesn't drop dead. I'll go with Fluke to the school computer and try to get into the system to vaccinate it before the virus pops up. We'll approach the anomaly from both sides of the timeline."

"All zombies they go with Polo," said the *houngan.* "Me command. They sprinkle antidote. Twenty minutes, cover whole school." Dr. Strange-Jacques barked some orders at the zombies and all of them got in line as the shaman handed out little bags of the powder he had just created. It looked kind of like cocaine. Not that I ever tried it, mind you. "Take extra bags," he said.

There seemed to be an unending supply of bags of antidote. "You've only been making it for five minutes," I said. "How come there's so much of it?" Because the entire desk was piled high with little plastic bags.

"Se yon mirak," said the houngan. "Miracle. Big Jesus miracle. Like loaves and fishes."

"What about me?" said Red Polo, forlornly wagging an intestine.

"Um," I said, "guard the door."

"Yeah," Polo said. "Like you're going to be so useful with half your body in another dimension."

"If we don't screw this up, we'll only be gone a second," Fluke said, "because no matter which door we exit and enter from, we'll always come back to this moment. As long as the portal stays open."

"That doesn't make sense," I said. "If it only needs to be open for this one moment and we will be back immediately —"

"To quote the Red Queen in *Through the Looking Glass,*" Fluke said, "'Now, here, you see, it takes all the running you can do, to keep in the same place.' Dr. Fluke has to impose a temporal stasis field on the—"

"Forget I ever asked," I said.

The door opened wider. Mysterious, angelic music issued from it. A fragrance wafted out, kind of like incense in the school chapel. Polo and Donut, and a dozen zombies, all stood there with bags of white powder. But the perilous journey into the moments *before* the infection happened … that would be just me and Fluke.

"Dr. Strange! Hold the gate open no matter what!"

"Aye, aye, captain," said Dr. Strange.

Even Dr. Strange knew who was boss.

43

Zombie High

Donut

So, me and Polo were thrust into Red World like a couple of cannon balls, spinning as we vaulted over the school building. Luckily our fall was broken by a huge heap of laundry that was piled up outside the convent.

"This laundry's been piling up," Polo said. "And it stinks."

"Blood."

"The nuns were all having their periods?"

"It's not that kind of blood," I said. "But I guess *you* wouldn't know the difference, since you don't have a —. This blood is pretty fresh. It's ..."

"Zombie blood?" Polo said.

It would be getting dark soon. We crawled out of the heaped up habits, brushed ourselves off a bit, and looked around.

"Maybe this is the wrong time period," I said. "Maybe the zombies have all been taken care of."

"Yeah. We got propelled a few centuries into the future, the zombies have all eaten each other and the planet is ruins, and these filthy clothes are all that remains of human civilization," Polo said.

"Blood's too fresh."

We stepped out into the pathway. It was the way from the convent back to the Old Building where our rooms — and Club X HQ — were.

The convent was sheltered from the rest of the school by a small wooded area. The pathway curved, so if you didn't know there was a clearing with the old convent building, you'd think that the woods went on and on.

The trees thinned out and from this point on, the path was lined with flowers and led to the

There was a rustling noise. We popped behind the nearest tree. Someone was walking up the pathway from the main school. Not walking exactly. Shambling.

It was Sister Edward! "If she's a zombie," I said, "we've arrived *after* the last visit."

Polo said ... "That means Kim's already ..."

As we peered from behind the tree, the sight was chilling.

Sister Edward had something cradled in her arms ... and she was hunched over it, snacking on ... the oozing brains of the President of Club X!

"I thought Kim already *was* a zombie in his world," I said.

"I guess they eat each other's brains, when they're *really* hungry."

"I can't look," I said.

"You have to. Come on," Polo said, "It's worse for me. I saw *myself* with dangling entrails."

"I know. It was disgusting."

"More than disgusting. Bad hair, too."

"Okay. I think we'd better both try to access our inner machismo now," I said.

"You sound like you're channeling Sister Evangeline," Polo said.

"Shut up," I said.

The zombie nun was approaching. We could hear the lip-smacking gurgle that you only hear when a zombie is snacking on brains. It's not the kind of a sound you forget. She wasn't one of those *fast* zombies. It took her a while, shuffling, shambling, grunting, and slurping. We readied our little bags.

She was there! We leaped out and sprinkled her from both sides! Sister Edward fell writhing to the pavement. Kim's head rolled from her bosom. She foamed at the mouth and dribbled green froth and bits of brain. Was it working? "This is for your own good," I said, echoing what she so often said to us kids.

Sister Edward was morphing! Her bloodshot eyes were starting to look healthy, she was drooling, and she getting up on her hands and knees. She wounds were closing up. She looked around, terrified. She began crossing herself and reciting *Hail Marys* over and over, barely even noticing us.

Then Kim's head started jumping up and down, bouncing like a basketball, and with every bounce it seemed to grow a bit, a neck, now a bit of shoulder, now he was hopping about on one arm....

"Kim!" I said.

"Leave me alone," Kim said, "I hurt all over and I can't stop moving and this pavement isn't exactly a trampoline, you know, it's — ow! ow!"

Sister Edward could talk, too, now. "Children! What is going on?" she said. "I feel as if ... I've actually been in hell! How could I have been? I mean, I hardly ever sin. Hiding Sister Euphemia's candy doesn't really count, it's for her own protection...."

Polo went to hold Kim steady. "Where's the rest of me?" he was saying. Polo steadied him. Across the universes, they still had a relationship. It was a little bittersweet, I have to say.

Kim stopped hopping and held onto Polo rightly while his torso rebuilt itself, then his waist, and then ... below the waist . . I couldn't help staring.

"It's not my fault," Kim said, "my head wasn't wearing any clothes."

He was manifesting the rest of him right before our eyes, and he was very, you know, naked, and very, well, male. "Stop staring," Polo said to me. "Kim, put on my school shorts, I have boxers on underneath."

"Your shorts are the wrong color," Kim said. "And ..." looking at me ... "Who are you?"

"She's the principal's daughter, Kim," Polo said, very patiently. There were a lot of different things about this universe, including me not being in this school.

I said, "Sister, you gotta help us. We're from another universe and we're here to help fix your zombie problem."

"I don't know about that," said Sister Edward. "If you don't go to this school, you'll need to get Dr. Prachaya to sign a visitor's permit."

"Are you joking, Sister?" I grabbed her shoulders. "Take a bag of this white stuff."

"Good Heavens!" said Sister Edward. "Are they drugs?"

"Don't you remember anything from before you changed?" It looked like coming back from hell also included a memory wipe. Just as well. If I were a zombie, I wouldn't want to remember it.

"Not really," she said.

Polo said, "It's going to come back to you real soon."

Because at the moment, Donut's old nemesis, Pueng Pang, came running out of the school — pursued by his best friend, Tommy — who was now a zombie. "Watch, Kim," Polo said. "Watch carefully."

"Help!" Pueng Pang screamed.

Tommy had leaped up on Pueng Pang's shoulders and it looked like he was going to rip off his head. Polo dumped a bag over them both. Tommy screamed. It was heartrending in a way, a tiny, pinched sound like a squalling baby.

As Tommy became human again, Pueng Pang got mean again, too. "Who are you?" he said to me. "Isn't Polo girl enough for the school already?"

"Shut up," Polo said, "she's the principal's daughter."

"And we're from another universe, and we're here with the antidote," I said, "and you're going to help us, Pueng Pang."

"How do you know my name?" he said.

"I don't have time for this," I said. I handed Sister Edward a bag of powder. "Just do what we do, Sister." I gave one to Pueng Pang. "You weren't a zombie," I told him. "You remember it all. Now, you're a bully, and all bullies are cowards, but try to man up. As soon as they attack, sprinkle them." Pueng Pang was just staring at me, openmouthed, still trying to figure how a *girl* could know so much personal information about him. Still gaping, he took the bad. "Give Tommy one," I said.

Tommy was walking in circles, in the throes of post-zombie amnesia.

Sister screamed.

A bunch of zombies was now traipsing out of the woods at a good lick. But these were clearly Haitian-type zombies, not oozy, slurpy shamblers, just very singleminded and robotic. They had bags of antidote, too.

"Don't worry about them," I said. "Those zombies are on our team."

Kim said … "I'm starting to remember." He turned to Sister Edward. "Wait a minute!" he said. "You ripped off my head!"

"That's all over now, dear," Sister Edward said.

Pueng Pang said, "Look, I came this way to escape the zombies. Why should we go back? If we just sneak out of the gate behind the convent, I can call a Grab."

"You don't get it," said Polo. "This whole school is encased in a force field. There's no way out. Just shut the fuck up and do what we tell you."

"You tell him, Kim. You're our leader," I said, although this Kim didn't know me from Adam. Or Eve, for that matter.

"Right." Kim said. I could see him process all the bits of the puzzle. He was the wrong Kim, but he was *our* Kim as well. I wondered how they would be if they met. "Most of the kids and teachers who haven't been *turned* are holed up behind behind some stacked bookcases at the front entrance of the lobby. We need to plan this like a military strategy. We need to trap the zombies in the front courtyard."

"Can't Fluke help us think this through?" I said.

"Fluke? He's in New Zealand," Kim said.

The temporal lag between their universe and hours was more than days. It was *months*. "I get it now," I said. "I'm not *at* this school yet. Fluke hasn't come home yet. The two of you still aren't talking."

"What are you talking about?" he said. I could see the flash of anger … and sorrow.

"Listen," I said to Kim, "you don't know who I am, but I know things. He's coming back, Kim. You'll be friends again."

"I don't even *want* to be," said Red Kim.

"Yes, you do," said Blue Polo — *our* Polo. "Trust me, Kim."

"I guess I have to," Kim said. "I'm wearing your shorts." Gaining confidence as the piece of the puzzle came together for him, he said, "The zombies will probably come en masse around nightfall. Right now they're encamped in the front lawn. Polo, you send *your* zombies — the docile zombies — into the parking lot — take the long way round. Give them some of your powder. The zombies will make for the main entrance, because they can smell the most brains. We'll climb in through the kitchen window and hand out bags to our friends. I'll try to gloss over the whole 'telepaths from another universe' part. Maybe not. They all know I don't lie. After all, I have Asperger's. I *can't* lie."

Kim always takes charge and he always has a plan.

I was sad for him though. The Red Kim had no Fluke. He didn't have the spark to set him free from his literal-mindedness. I knew Fluke would come back.

"Okay. I can't explain *too* many things or they will go crazy, so Donut, you lead the zombie battalion. Take Tommy and Pueng Pang — so seem to have figured out how to wrangle them better than any of us. I'll sneak to the kitchen with Polo."

"What about me?" said Sister Edward. "Shall I just go to the chapel and say a few Hail Marys?"

"Not at all," Kim said. "You used to be a zombie. You ate part of my brain, you know! I don't know if I've got it all back yet. Thing is, the zombies won't know you became human again. I can hardly believe it myself. So your job will be …"

"I get it!" I said. "Once the trap is laid, Sister Edward will lure them out!"

Sister Edward looked at me … then at Kim. "You mean, I'm … the bait?"

44

Lost in the Web

Kim

We materialized right where we'd materialized before, in front of the big door that leads to the front of the school. But it was earlier. Before dawn, I think. A good time to break into the school computer and snuff out the virus before it sucked up everyone we knew.

The door wasn't locked and we crept right in, crossed the big hall where the statue of St. Cecilia stood, through the library and into Sister Edward's little cubicle. It was. literarily, *déjà vu*, because we'd just done all this. It better work this time, I thought.

"I'll break in quickly," Fluke said. "Sister Edward's not the kind of nun who would think too hard about a password. In our world it was 1234567." And so it was here.

"Last time we were here you made a big fuss about how you had cleverly remembered Sister Edward's password from when you hacked her last year."

"Yeah, but I was showing off in front of Donut. I don't have to, to you."

"Yeah, I already know you're brilliant, and I have no imagination, anyway, so you can't impress me."

"It's almost an insult to have to apply my super-intelligence," he said.

"You don't have to use your whole brain for *every* task," I said.

"Did you bring the thumb drive?" he said.

I fumbled in my shorts. "Yeah," I said. Hadn't Sister Edward grabbed it, though? No. That was a different future, a different timeline. We were going to prevent all that. I stuck the drive into the slot. "It might not work," Fluke said.

"But when we broke the timeline," I said, "it was further up."

"Yes, but we could have some quantum pre-echo. You know, causality breaks down in the nano-world. You would go crazy."

"I am already," I said.

"Quick. Let me work," Fluke said.

I watched him.

I rested my hand on his shoulder and stared past his face at the shifting lines of figures, patterns, formulae, and the odd random image — Egyptian gods — shopping malls — concentration camps. This isn't the kind of thing I'm good at watching. I reached out with my other hand, the right hand, and lightly touched his wrist as he moved the mouse.

"We're saving the universe," he said, "you and me, like we were always meant to. But right now ... I have to find the node ... the place where the virus started to enter. Help me."

"How?" I said.

"Not sure yet," Fluke said.

We had maybe half an hour till dawn. The wakeup bell would ring soon, and the school would burst into a frenzy. "I think we got sent back to the wrong day," Fluke said. "According to Sister Edward's calendar, this isn't just moments before the virus attack, it's a full day."

"There's usually a reason things like this happen," I said.

"Sure. It must be a causality nexus or something."

We heard footsteps. They sounded really familiar.

"Someone's coming."

"Shit!"

It wasn't easy to hide in Sister's little space, but Fluke managed to crouch under the desk and I found a bookshelf I could squeeze behind. It was tight. Someone was tiptoeing. And I *knew* those footsteps. I knew the sound of those bedroom slippers! Looking across the cramped little cubicle, I saw that Fluke recognized it too.

I watched myself walk into the room.

The last time I'd seen myself, it had barely registered before my alter ego got a bullet in the head — and anyway, he wasn't *really* me — he was just another zombie climbing out of a fridge. But now, he was *totally* me. Except for the red shorts.

He was in a hurry. He sat down at Sister Edward's computer. He didn't seem at surprised that Fluke had already accessed the account. In fact, he seemed to expect it. "Your signature's all over the system," Red Kim said softly. His eyes were sad and I wished I could reach out. Though we'd be paradoxing the past even more if I talked to him.

He was concentrating hard. He hit a few keys. I knew his mannerisms perfectly. But what was he searching for? You know me. The soul of discretion. I found myself inadvertently lurching forward and leaning over him. He murmured something and I peered over his shoulder. I knew even before he did it that he would turn around and that he would look at me *just like that*, because I was piece of a puzzle that didn't fit.

"I'm not imagining this," he said —

"Because I've got no imagination," I said.

We stared at each other.

"What happened to your shorts?" he said.

"I'm another you," I said. "I'm from a world like this, and we're just two of millions of Kims, side by side. But most of us will never know another Kim."

"Don't tell me. You're here to save me."

"Not just you, Kim. I'm here to save everyone."

Red Kim looked down and saw Fluke, staring up at him from under the desk.

"What the fuck?" Red Kim said. "You're in New Zealand."

"And you're not talking, are you?" I said. "Not after what happened."

"You *know* about that?" he said.

"We're not just from another world." Fluke said. "You can call us the Blue World because in *our* St. Cecilia's the school shorts are blue. We're also from the a different point in time."

"You sent me a message. To come *here*," said Red Kim. "But you and me, we're not even talking right now. We don't talk I was glad you left. So we wouldn't have to talk about it."

Fluke said, "We're talking, aren't we?"

"What was the message? What am I doing down here in the middle of the night?"

"How should I know?" said Fluke.

"*You're* the one who messaged."

"I'm not the Fluke who ran off to New Zealand," Fluke said. "I'm the Fluke who came back."

Suddenly I realized why we were here. "Kim, what year is it?"

"Are you joking?"

I looked at the computer, where the date was showing in the upper right-hand corner. "I knew it, Fluke," I said. "This isn't just a few minutes before the zombie invasion. It's *last year*. We've been brought here because it's the nexus."

"*Nexus?*" said Red Kim.

"Yeah, nexus, node, what ever Fluke wants to call it," I said.

"Oh! I think I get it." Fluke said. "Can I come out now?"

"Red Fluke is the key."

"And we're the *key* to the key," Fluke said.

"As long as the key's not in the toilet again," I said, laughing, while Red Kim looked at the two of us like we were crazy.

"Who do you mean, Red Fluke?" said Red Kim.

I said, "That's what we call you guys. So far, every universe we've ever visited has different colored shorts."

"And why is he the key? The key to *what*? I told you, you're — he's — in New Zealand."

"And he shouldn't be," I said. "That's the source of the anomaly. You guys should have kissed and made up already."

Had I said the wrong thing? Red Kim looked away, embarrassed. It was the word *kissed*. They weren't the same Kim and Fluke. Maybe ... I remembered what Fluke had told me in the confessional last year. Maybe there were things about the Reds that were different. In the relationship. It always came down to that in the end. The relationship. The things unspoken.

"This is definitely the moment," I said. "The place where it changes. The source of the virus."

Red Kim said. "Why? What do me and Fluke have to do with a virus anyway?"

Fluke said, "Kim always gets the answer. He sees the one place where everything aligns, and he goes for it."

"Answer?" said Red Kim. "What's the question?"

"Answer this question, first," Fluke said. "Have you ever heard of Club X?"

"Sure, I'm the president."

"Have you ever heard of the Crystal Pathway?" I asked him.

"Hmm. Something in a novel, maybe? Or a TV series? Rings a bell."

"And is there a closet in the club room?" said Fluke.

"Yeah, but it's locked," said Red Kim.

"That's the first thing about your world that we're gonna fix," I said, and Fluke and I just grabbed Red Kim, one arm each, and pretty much shoved him out the back door.

45

The Battle of St. Cecilia's

Polo

It wasn't hard for the two of us to sneak over to the kitchen window. We took the short passage past the refectory to the school lobby and we saw a few dozen kids clustered at the partly open front door, peering anxiously out into the school grounds. Behind the kids there were a few nuns. They had makeshift weapons — mostly stuff from the sports department like baseball bats, hockey sticks and stuff. Someone even wielded a cricket bat.

St. Cecilia's very inclusive about sports. They have sports from every country, and they're not good at any of them; any urban soccer team would eat us for lunch. Lots of equipment, though. Good endowment. A lot of it from my dad.

I think he was hoping it would help me not turn out the way I did.

Yeah. Today I envied how Kim managed to take charge, no matter what. I mean, five minutes ago, he was a zombie. As we emerged from the corridor he was already charging on ahead.

Our friends all had their backs to us. They were all paying attention to the courtyard, not to the lobby.

At that moment, though, a door opened begin the statue of the saint — near us. The first aid room! A sister was peering out, first left ... then right.

It was Sister Evangeline. Well, that was a relief. After all, she was my secret sister. Though maybe not in this universe.

"This way!" I said. "C'mon, Sister!"

"We're here to help," Kim said.

But Sister Evangeline grabbed the baseball bat from inside the first aid room and bore down on us, brandishing it heroically, like a nun version of Wonder Woman. "Get away from us!" she screamed. "Zombies! Zombies have made it through!"

"I'm not a zombie," Kim said.

"You were seeing coming out of a fridge—attacking Sister Edward!"

"Yeah, I know, but I'm all better now. Swear to God."

"What happened to your shorts?"

"I had to borrow Polo's."

"Yes, but they're blue ... and Polo is wearing ... cutesey boxers that are three sizes too tight! Nothing says 'dress code violation' like floral boxers, my dear!"

"He's telling you," I said. "There's a red world and a blue world and we've come back through space time to save you from the zombies."

"I see," said Sister, not sounding that convinced. "Well, Kim, you're not drooling or hocking up green phlegm, and ... you're disobeying the school code with the shorts, and you rarely tell lies — and it's just about weird enough that it might be true. But you'll have to have more proof." She stood there waving the bat, but I have to admit it was kind of comic. I mean, this was Sister Evangeline, our very own nun with a dark secret that *I* held over her.

"Sister, we don't have time to convince you!" I said. "You need our help."

"We came from the Crystal Pathway!" Kim blurted out.

"The ... *pathway?*" she said. "It exists?"

This world was a lot different from our own — I mean in my world, she had told *me* about it. Kim said, "Look, we loaded up on the zombie antidote. It obviously works, doesn't it? I mean, Sister Edward ripped off my head and was eating my brains, and now I'm just fine."

"Not *that* fine," Sister said. She pointed behind us. I screamed.

There was another Kim, with the right shorts, but with no head, and he was walking around in circles, his arms flailing.

"Use the antidote," I said to Kim.

"But what about *me?*" he said.

"I'm the only one around here who's allowed to have an identity crisis," I said, running up to my headless schoolmate and sprinkling him with the powder.

Well ... he stopped flailing around. A new head started to sprout, but it didn't look real. It looked like a balloon with a smiley-face painted on it. Then, the ex-zombie dropped to the floor and fell still.

"Only one Kim per universe," Kim said, "law of conservation of Kims. I guess the powder doesn't work without a seat of consciousness."

Sister Evangeline said, "All right. At least it immobilizes them."

We followed Sister across the fall, past our school saint. We both bowed to St. Cecilia's statue as we passed her; force of habit. The kids were gathered by the door, being very quiet. It was tense.

"Kim has something to tell us," Sister Evangeline said.

"Ew, you're a zombie," someone said.

"No, no, I'm fine now," he said. "Honest."

We started giving out the bags. Since Kim was the only one making any kind of authoritative statements, everyone fell into line pretty quickly. I think that Red Kim was even bossier than Blue Kim. "In just about two minutes," Kim said, "Sister Edward is going to come running towards us. She's going to be pursued by zombies. Now ..." he looked around. "You guys — form a tight line at the door, two thick. On my first signal, let Sister Edward through — and no one else. The rest of you — you run over to Sister's cubicle, to the nurses' office, to anywhere where there's a chair. Bring chairs. Set them up behind the doors. You're going to climb up on them, lean over the doors and on my *second* signal, you're going to fling the white dust on the zombie brigade. Now, behind the first zombie wave, there is a wave of *good* zombies. They have the powder too. If I explain where the good zombies came from, I'll still be telling tales when the zombie apocalypse comes. The point is — we are making a sandwich, and the filling is going to a pile of juicy, rotting human steak. Any of you get bitten or mauled, the others will sprinkle you with the powder before you can turn too far. Got it? We gotta be totally in sync, like, you know, a Roman phalanx or something."

It looked like they were going to break out babbling, but Sister Edward came sprinting across the courtyard at that very minute, pursued by lurching, stumbling, shambling, putrefying schoolboys slipping and sliding through oil-slick-like puddles of bodily fluids.

"Let her through!" Kim shouted.

The wall of boys opened and Sister came staggering through, gasping for air.

"The stench!" she screamed. "I've been in hell all over again!"

The boys joined ranks again just as the zombies got there.

"Now!" Kim cried out.

White powder rained down from above! Zombies collapsed, writhing! The ground was a mass of arms and legs and shrieking heads.

Across from the sea of flesh, the Haitian zombies stood, shaking their bags over the pile of kids. And then here's what happened —

Limbs were straightening. Wounds were closing up. Our school friends from another were sitting up, rubbing themselves, looking around bewildered, scratching their heads. When then turned around, the Haitian zombies were still sprinking them with the powder. Donut and the two school bullies were haranguing them, trying to get them to stop.

Our guys in the red shorts were all trying to talk at once. The post-dezombification amnesia had set in. They had no idea what was going on. They looked in terror at the Haitians looming behind who were still strewing white dust.

Kim said, "Don't mind them. They're harmless. They cured you guys from being zombies."

"But ... *they're* zombies!" said Mando, a nerd we hardly knew even in our real school.

"They're good zombies. You guys are ... *were* ..." I explained, "*bad* zombies." I sounded like an idiot. I didn't have Kim's knack for making the weirdest things sound true. "Kim, convince them," I said.

Donut was still trying to get the Haitian zombies to stop sprinkling. "Stop! Stop!" she was shouting at them.

"Maybe they only speak Haitian creole," Kim said. "If only Fluke were here."

I said, "It's kind of like French, isn't it? Who speaks French around here?"

Sister Evangeline sang out, in a glass-shattering soprano, "*Arrêtez!*"

The zombies not only stopped sprinkling, they stopped, as in *stopped*. They froze as if someone had pushed an off switch. They stood there just staring stupidly.

"That's the Haitian kind for you," Kim said. "They program them to be like, mindless slaves. They're not even really dead, just drugged with datura."

"Fluke must be rubbing off on you," I said.

Kim turned to me. "Since he's been away," he said, "I keep checking his google history. I know a lot of the stuff he researches."

"He was researching zombies?"

"Yeah. Fixated. Don't ask me why."

227

Sister Evangeline said, "Well, children, maybe it's time we all went back to class. Perhaps we should all sing something?" When she was in her "let's all sing a jolly song together" mode, Sister Evangeline was unstoppable. Still, maybe it would get all our bewildered kids focused.

"We shall perform ..." she cleared her throat. *"Heigh-ho, heigh-ho, it's off to work we go*, from the immortal cartoon classic *Snow White."*

"Um, Sister ..." Pueng Pang said, "were *you* even born then?"

There was no stopping her. She gave the pitch and started to conduct. Everyone joined in, even though no one knew the words. It was kind of a feel-good moment. A good singalong is good for your stress level, when you've been fighting off a horde of zombies.

Then — suddenly, we heard a *bang*. The floor was shaking. And I mean, *shaking*.

Sister Edward let out a scream.

There was a thundering, earthquaky kind of a sound. The singing stopped in mid-phrase.

The lobby floor was splitting open.

"They're coming up from the basement," said Sister Edward, awed.

Rotting arms were reaching up. Creatures were clawing up out of the cracks. Heads were peering up.

"All right, everyone," Kim said. "Bags ready. On my signal, we rush them."

"Fat chance," Tommy said.

"Yeah," said Pueng Pang. "The bags are all empty."

"Damn zombies!" Kim said.

... and they were clambering up now.

"Run!" Kim said. "Into the parking lot!"

46

The Dark Past

Fluke

I took the two Kims to Club X. Club X in this world wasn't that different from ours. The same paintings on the walls, including the fake Mona Lisa, the busts of Mozart and Tchaikovsky and Brahms ... no Bach here, either. The piano was in a different corner. Actually it was blocking the closet door.

"Help me move the piano," I said, and the two Kims pushed it to one side.

"So," said the other Kim, "what's *in* the closet?"

"If the timeline hadn't broken in your world," I said, "you'd know."

"But how do we get in? There's no key."

"Feel a shit coming on?"

Kim and I laughed. The other Kim looked really confused.

"No time to explain," I said. "But in our *blue* world, I made a movie about our adventures. There's a whole section about shit and keys."

Red Kim said: "*Oh.*"

Blue Kim said, "Now you know why Dr. Strange had the lesson about false friends."

"It was a piece of your reality that didn't match the shifting timeline," I said. "Causality always follows the path of least resistance. If a change doesn't *have* to happen, it won't ... even if doesn't quite make sense. You know, like ... human beings' vestigial tails. Or the appendix."

"I don't know what you're talking about," said Red Kim.

"You know Fluke," said my Kim. "Always a know-it-all."

"I don't need a key" I said. I was with my Kim. Over time, we'd learned that the door will open for us. Many doors will open. Just from the power of us being together, balancing each other exactly, electron and positron.

When we're together, we fit, like a lock and a key. The Crystal Pathway makes way for us. Together we're like Moses parting the Red Sea, and apart, we can't even part hair.

The *other* Kim made it almost overload. It's like his psychic connection with the absent Fluke was heightened by the fact that their timeline had been so bent out of shape. And I knew where the point of divergence had to be.

The private concert.

When I thought the man in black wanted to do something bad to me. He did, but it wasn't about sex. I guess, I'm a teenager, I probably think about sex too much, especially since I'm not sure I've really done it, unless you count....

We stood at the door of the hotel room again, in that Mediaeval German town.

Last time, it was me and Kim looking at our former selves in the hotel room. He was straightening my bowtie ... always looking for order and symmetry, so Kim.

Now there were three of us looking in, and two of us from the past, in the room, and Kim was adjusting "my" bowtie.

"Watch carefully," our Kim said to their Kim. "Fluke's going to go and play the concert now, and then, when the concert ends, something bad will happen. And he's going to call for help."

"I know," said Red Kim. "But I ... I couldn't find him."

Blue Kim and I looked at each other.

We didn't have to say anything. Kim is supposed to find me at the bridge. He gets all riled up because he can't stand to see me get hurt. He interrupts the man in black and then he pushes him and then — that terrible thing happens — and we can't talk to each other for a year — but I came back.

In this world, I didn't come back. Because Kim wasn't there to save me.

"Shut the door!" I said. I grabbed the handle and slammed it myself.

The three of us stood inside the club room once again with the door closed.

"You're supposed to find him," I said to Red Kim. "You don't know ... how much I hurt. If you hadn't found me I'd never have gotten over it."

"What do you mean?" my Kim said. "You didn't talk to me for a year after that."

"But I came back," I said. "Here, in this world, we should be together by now. Not waiting for zombies to infest the school. Not waiting for ... Red Kim to be shot in the head by Donut!"

Red Kim looked me Blue Kim, then at me. "I got a phone call," he said. "Kim said he was being threatened by someone. He told me to come and rescue him. I left the hotel. I looked for him all night, all through the streets of Oldenburg."

I said, "I'll show you."

I concentrated. I took Kim's hand — my Kim's — in mine. Together we touched the door again and it opened. A few hours had passed.

The room was empty.

Fluke ... *their* Fluke ... staggered into the room. He was disheveled. His clothes were torn. There were burn marks on his jacket. His face was bleeding, too. "What's wrong?" Blue Kim whispered. "Did someone ... rape him?"

"It's worse, in its way," I said, remembering. "He got into my mind. He reached inside with his slimy tentacles and looked at the places where I hurt the most. I'm still not over it, but if Kim hadn't shown up ... what happened to your Fluke would have made him completely lose his ... sense of self ... his mind."

"Worse?" Red Kim said.

"He would have siphoned out everything that makes me a human being. He would made me like a thing of synapses and circuits. A machine."

Red Kim said, "God ... a zombie."

Blue Kim said, "Shit! *That's* what happened! That's why *all* of it happened!"

Red Fluke was bawling into his pillow. And Kim wasn't there. Fluke was alone. I *knew* what he was feeling. My Kim went on, "Only Fluke would be clever enough to create the zombie virus and hack into the school's computer all the way from New Zealand."

"No," I said. "Even I'm not *that* much of a genius. Sure, I can introduce a virus into a school computer, maybe even a national defense system. That's a piece of cake. But this isn't just a computer virus. It's a virus that leaks into the real world, that changes the fabric of reality. It's gotta work on quantum entanglement theory. And there's only one place that comes from … Listen, Kim … and other Kim … Fluke had help. He had higher technology. *Alien* technology."

I could see Red Kim getting more and more confused.

We watched Red Fluke crying for a long time. At length he seemed to calm down a little.

He sat up. His face was set, his eyes hard. He looked, it seemed, straight at us.

"He can't see you," I whispered to Red Kim, who was kind of in shock.

"Or hear you," my Kim reminded me.

In the hotel room, my other self — I could almost see the gears grinding in his mind — after all, he thinks the way I think. "He's mad at the whole world," Red Kim said.

"He's thinking, if he's been turned into a zombie, everyone else should too," I said. "Believe me! I know him like I know myself."

Red Fluke got up. Methodically, he changed out of his concert clothes. The way they were torn … it wasn't like someone had clawed at them. The marks were angled, like they'd been made by a machine. He reached for his cellphone and dialled a number.

"Monsignor," he whispered. "I'm coming back. Teach me."

47

The Final Conflict

Polo

So yeah, we trooped out of the lobby, armed with a few pathetic weapons like baseball bats, pencils, and our fists. In front of us stretched the school grounds, with parking lot and trees before we could reach the school gates. But wasn't it true that the school was just part of some kind of bubble of reality that the Cardinal was using for experiments? It didn't look like it from here.

We'd won the first round by trapping zombies in a sandwich, but a new lot were on their way and we had to find a way to fight them off.

In front of us there was a kind of hillock of dead and dying zombies. Behind *them* were the friendly zombies that had come with us from inside the Cardinal's lair, along with Donut and Pueng Pang. We refugees from the Blue World looked at each other across the wall of writhing half-zombies.

We had to climb over the shuddering undead to reach the friendly undead. That couldn't be helped, but it was *disgusting*, like swimming through a sea of egg yolks.

Intestines, glop, severed limbs were still jerking around. But my friends and I managed to get over it, and we stood with our much duller group of friendly zombies that kind of stood in a frozen line, still holding their empty bags of antidote over our zombie-friends.

So here's the thing ... the pile of corpses was quickly regenerating. Arms were reattaching themselves. A head flew through the air and landed on someone's neck. They were all babbling, too, with no idea how they had ended up in a heap in the parking lot.

And they were even harder to deal with than when they were zombies, because they all had amnesia, more or less. That's what happened to Red Kim, before, and even now he was disoriented.

Donut, Pueng Pang and Tommy had been leading the friendlies, but they'd gotten all tangled up with the ex-unfriendlies while trying to stop the friendlies from sprinkling the powder, and now they were trying to explain what was going on to the recovering zombies.

"Let me have a go," I said. "Guys, you were all zombies until a few minutes ago, and unless we fight back, you might become zombies again —"

"C'mon, Polo," said one of the kids from Sister Evangeline's singing class. "You were a girl yesterday, and you might become one again —"

"He's right," said another. "It's coming back to me and —" The kid started shrieking in horror. Probably had a memory flash. "No! No! Let go!"

It became a chorus.

"Shut up, children," Sister Edward screamed. "Just listen to her! Or you'll all get detention!"

That worked.

"Everyone listen up!" I said, before realizing I didn't actually have a plan. I looked imploringly at Kim.

Kim said, "We'll run toward the school gate. There's some parked cars there and we can use them as a kind of barrier."

Sister Evangeline began singing some kind of Valkyrie warcry and we all ran. At the edge of the parking lot, next to the trees, near the entrance to the school grounds, had half a dozen cars and a van or two, and a decrepit looking school bus.

"We'll use the cars and the bus as a barricade," said Kim. Everyone get behind them.

Our group got into position, and the zombies from the Pathway sort of shambled into a line in front of the cars. "They're so slow," I said.

"We'll have to use them as human shields," Kim said, "if you know what I mean."

We crouched down behind the cars. The rumbling came louder and louder. Suddenly, the front door of the school lobby came flying off its hinges and crashed down the steps to the pavement. Zombies started to stream out. There's this kind of grunting sound that a herd of zombies makes. They don't breathe — they're not alive — but there's a wheezy, gasping sound of air being pushed past their vocal chords.

You never forget what a zombie army sounds like. The way they move — no kind of order, randomly shambling about but somehow managing to go in the same general direction — the rhythmless pounding of their feet, you don't forget that either. Or the smell. The smell! We were all choking as we watched the crowd move towards us.

We had two layers of protection — a group of amnesiac ex-zombie stragglers who were still a bit out of it — and the line of Haitian zombies from the lab.

But we were outnumbered, two or three to one, it looked like.

Even at shambing speed, they reached our first line of defence in a minute. But then something extraordinary happened —

When they reached where we'd emptied the bags of antidote, they started transforming back! The front line of the zombie phalanx was writhing as zombies morphed back into humans!

"I thought we ran out of antidote," Kim said.

Suddenly I remembered what Jacques Florissant had said when we asked him how come the bags of powder kept multiplying. *"Se yon mirak!* Big Jesus miracle! Like loaves and fishes!" I realized that the white powder was reproducing itself.

Yes! The powder that we had scattered on the first batch of zombies was reappearing! "Check your bags!" I said.

Kim said, "Cool. It's not just an inanimate powder. It's a living thing! Every speck of white dust can make little baby white dust specks!"

"Fascinating," said Sister Evangeline. "I wonder if it's sexual or asexual reproduction."

"Who cares, Sister?" I said. "No one asks if you've got a penis."

She let out a hideous roar and I realized that in the Red universe, Sister and I had not had our "little talk" … she didn't know I knew. Too late to worry about that now.

The zombie attack was only delayed.

As soon as the front of zombies became human again, they were being attacked by the second line and pushed towards us, transforming back into zombies at the same time that their attackers were being turned human by the residual powder. We watched the spectacle awestruck. It was hypnotic. Boys into zombies and zombies into boys in a kind of weird spiral, but even though this was slowing down the attack, they would eventually reach us.

"Are we getting any more powder in our bags?"

"No," said Kim. "If you totally empty the bag, the microorganism can't reproduce."

"We're fucked!" Sister Evangeline screamed, making the other nuns cover their ears and causing a ripple of nervous laughter.

"Into the bus," Kim said.

We all stampeded into the bus and shut the doors. That bus was crammed. It was probably over its weight limit, but at least the doors were closed … and the gross zombie stench was shut out, too.

The zombie tsunami was getting closer and closer.

"Who's gonna drive?" I said.

Sister Edward said, "I will. Where's the key?"

The zombies were getting closer.

Kim said, "Even if there *was* a key, you wouldn't be able to start the bus. We're trapped in a horror story. The bus never starts."

They were at the doors now. They were climbing on the roof. They were jumping up and down. They were dribbling on the windows.

Sister Evangeline went to the front and shoved Sister Edward out of the way. "I'll hot-wire it," she said.

"Hot-wire?" said Sister Edward. "Heavens!"

Sister Edward stood tall. She ripped off her wimple, revealing a punk haircut with a bald spot — and a gang tattoo. "Polo already spilled the beans," she said in a decidedly huskier voice. "But before you defrock me for having a dick, I'm gonna save your asses."

She winked at me. "Sister!" I said softly.

"I know how to do this shit," she said. "Before I became a nun, I was in a motorcycle gang. We used to steal cars."

48

Really, the Final Conflict

Kim

"We're going back in," I said. "Fluke, let's wind the timeline back a few hours and try again."

We opened the closet door again and this time we had stepped into the back of some kind of private concert hall. The three of us stood in the back. I stopped Red Kim from stepping all the way in, because if he did, he might cause an anomaly, and one of the Red Kims would have to disappear. We had to save that for later.

I was afraid to make a noise, even to shut the door ... so, behind us, we could still see a little piece of Club X.

I had never seen this part of our past before because I was really in the hotel room, fidgeting, waiting for Fluke to come back. And now I realize how special that concert must have been. Those clerics and nuns and high-society critics sitting there in such a silence, the kind of silence that maybe only exists in outer space.

What an audience! The Pope was there, it seemed. And of course, the Man in Black, who we knew to be Cardinal Crank — before he became a cardinal.

Fluke was playing the Goldberg Variations. Every now and then he sits randomly at a piano somewhere and polishes off one of the variations, but now, hearing it all in one, unbroken skein, I could feel how unified he and I were, in our minds; we had a totally different way of getting there but our destination was the same. Every note Bach wrote was a piece of a cosmic Rubik's cube and every note Fluke played was flawlessly sequencing those pieces into an image of the cosmos.

The whole audience could feel it. Fluke's "superpower" if he had one was that when he played, people were transfixed. They were hypnotized. They could touch the still center of the universe.

I could feel my Fluke's hand on my shoulder now, pulling me back.

When the door closed, when the music cut off, I could feel a terrible grief, a sense of loss. "I wanted to hear it all," I said. "I never got to hear you play the Goldberg Variations."

"I'll do it again," he whispered, "after this is over. And it will be over. Concentrate. We have to find the exact moment in time. I need you now. I can paint the picture but you have to break it down to the exact pixel."

We stood at the door again with Red Kim right behind us. Fluke and I put our open palms against the door and we both concentrated.

In our minds we entered a kind of dream state, I guess. I saw puzzles, shapes, jigsaws. I'm thinking what he experienced was more aural … maybe he heard snatches of music, weaving in and out, like strands of DNA.

We had to find the exact point where the door should open. We had be about right twice now, and we could use those points to kind of triangulate. And we had to find the balance between Fluke's *feelings* and my *literalness.*

So, I don't know how Fluke saw the inner world. But we were working together. We came to a place where our pathways met. In our minds, in the club room, in the crystal world, the points were converging.

"Now!" we whispered at the same time.

We both opened the door.

I started to step over the threshold but Fluke said, "Wait. I can't go with you."

"You have to!" I said.

"There are three of us here," he said, "and we only have two of the alternate-reality-generating rosaries. The minute we all go in, there'll only be *one* Red Kim. And he's likely to follow the same path again, because when the path changes, it becomes the path of least resistance."

I thought about this. We had dragged Red Kim to Club X, but it was in his own universe and timeline. We had opened the door and allowed Red to *look* at himself in another part of his own timeline, but he hadn't *stepped through*. If he had, it would be a paradox; he couldn't be in two places at the same temporal coordinates. What Fluke was saying made sense.

Yet Fluke seemed positively *eager* not to step back into this other version of our past. He was scared.

"There's something else, too, isn't there?" I said.

"Yeah. I don't want to relive it — not that, not the Man in Black."

"But *I* have to," I said. "Because I'm the only one who can be my own guide."

Polo

If you want the *definition* of stark terror, it's this:

You're crammed into a rickety bus with a hundred terrified high school boys, and zombies are swarming all over the roof and banging on the windows, and a nun who just turned out to be a Hell's Angel is trying to hot-wire the bus...

Everyone was screaming. My throat was raw. "Guys!" I shrieked! "Let me do the screaming!"

Pueng Pang shushed everyone. "Polo's earned the right to scream," he said. "You guys toughen up now."

They quieted down, making the pounding of zombie fists get louder and more menacing.

The windshield was cracking in two places.

One face leered hideously. I realized it was Uncle Sert, the janitor.

"Not you, Uncle Sert," I said. Uncle Sert rolled off the hood.

And then the bus kind of started. Well, it lurched and squealed and puffed.

"Let's get out of here," said Sister Edward.

Sister Evangeline said, "The trouble us, I can't drive. I can hot-wire, but I only know how to deal with Harleys."

"Very well," said Sister Edward. "You steer, and I'll —"

"It's not even an automatic!" Sister Evangeline said.

Red Kim said, "Sisters, move out of the way —"

He elbowed them to one side and, with an air of supreme confidence, sat down in the driver's seat.

"I didn't know you could drive," I said.

"I've read a few manuals," he said as the bus lurched again, and started moving in reverse. Zombies started flying off the roof. "I'll have to turn around," he said. "Hold onto anything you can, I have to pop the clutch."

The bus swiveled and squealed.

And he ground along, mowing down a few zombies. Noisy *splats* and flying gore and intestines everywhere.

"Hopefully this'll get fixed down the timeline," he said. "For now, *we* gotta get through this in one piece."

A torso plopped onto the windshield, followed by a head and a hand.

"As opposed to more than one piece," Red Kim said.

"How can you joke about this?" Sister Evangeline said.

"He's not joking," I said. "He has Asperger's."

Kim gunned the accelerator. We were on the driveway and the school gate was ahead.

"You're gonna crash it!" I said.

"So, you're gonna get out and open the gate?" Kim said. We went faster.

"Kids!" Sister Evangeline called out. "Brace position!" We'd all seen that on airplane safety demos. Quickly, we all tucked ourselves in.

We were going to crash the front gate! "Brace, brace, brace!" the two nuns scream at us. But you know how I am. I peeked. I knew this was going to be a spectacle.

But before we hit the gate, the bus shifted. It was moving upwards, on an incline, defying gravity! Everyone started screaming again.

I looked out the window.

Zombies were raining off the roof!

The bus was climbing up into the air!

"I just figured it out!" Red Kim said, as I snuck over and squatted beside him. "We're inside a kind of energy bubble and the whole school is contained in a force-field."

"Yeah. Red Polo told me back in our universe. He said there's a wall around the school and when we run into it, we end up back in the middle of the school ..."

"But *if* we can hit the forcefield with sufficient velocity —"

No need to explain. We were already accelerating up the wall and an impossible angle, with zombies flying past and any moment now we'd probably be upside down and then what'd we do?

Above the screams, reading my mind, Red Kim said, "We'll worry about it when we get there."

... which was in about five seconds ...

241

49

Really, I Mean it, the Final Conflict

Kim

Me and my twin, we left the hotel through the front door. Maybe the hotel clerk did a double take, or at least he thought he was seeing double. I pushed Red Kim out the door as quickly as I could. He made a left. So far, so good. We knew the concert location was somewhere near Oldenburg's historic church. We were there earlier today, with the school tour group.

It was already late and on Sunday, Germans don't go out much, especially in these provincial mediaeval towns. The narrow streets were already pretty much empty. There were no cars. The center of this town is a no-driving zone and it's all cobblestones. I remembered every turn, every corner from the last time, and from the nightmares. The alleys. Even the coffee shop where an old woman shooed me away. The streets were completely dark. A few shops were dimly lit. We turned into the town square.

We passed a piano store — I remember Fluke looked in the same window earlier today. I looked at Red. He remembered, too. So far, so good. The Lamberti Church loomed ahead, looking more like a mediaeval castle than a church. Red Kim went up the steps.

"You're gonna pound on the door" I said. "But it's too late. He's already run into town. She can't dawdle or we'll miss him."

That saved us thirty seconds.

We heard footsteps.

"He's over there," I said.

A corner. Our shoes clattered on the cobblestones. Other footsteps, more deliberate. "The Man in Black," I said. "We have to duck into this alley —"

"But the footsteps came from that way!" Red said.

"It's a short cut."

A nun stood blocking our path.

"Sister Euphemia!" I said.

"I don't know who that is," she said. "Go back to your hotel. There's nothing for you here!"

We turned a corner. "I think this is another short cut," I said.

Another Sister Euphemia. "Go back!" she hissed. She marched toward us, gesticulating. "This is not your business!"

"They *planned* this!" I gasped.

"We should get back," Red Kim said. He looked despairing.

"Out of our way!" I shouted at the nun. My voice echoed in the empty street. A light came on in an upper story.

"You think *two* of you can resist me?"

Another Euphemia emerged from the shadows.

And another. "Try *three* of us," said Euphemia Three. They weren't quite identical, though. And they wore different habits. They waved their arms at us as though to cast a spell. Their robes rustled and flapped.

"What's this, *The Clone Wars?*" said Red Kim.

I shoved the nearest Euphemia out of the way. "Impertinence!" she said.

I grabbed Red Kim's hand. "Do you love him?" I said urgently.

"I don't know," he said.

"It's time for you to know," I said. I yanked him toward the nearest alley. Then down another. We heard the nuns, squabbling amongst themselves. "They didn't expect two of us," I said. "They brought on more Euphemias. Come on."

The Euphemias tried to head us off at the next corner. We doubled back, cut through someone's garden. More Euphemias greeted us at the next corner.

We heard the voice of the Man in Black. We coudn't make out the words yet but they seemed to have a hypnotic effect on the nuns, who suddenly shut down and just stood there, like pushing a switch.

I knew what this meant. "He's stopped time," I said. "He can do that. But *we're* immune. Trust me. We went through this last year."

Red Kim poked at one of the frozen nuns. She didn't move.

We looked away from the nuns. First we heard the sound of the river.

Then we saw *them* on the bridge.

Fluke in the clutches of the Man in Black.

In this world, it was even scarier than what I'd gone through. "Are we too late?" Red Kim said.

The Man's eyes burned and he was speaking in a deep voice, both terrifying and seductive. "You're special," he was saying. "You have no idea. We've searched the world … this world and many others … for someone like you. You hold the key! And you *will* share it with me!"

"No," Fluke said. His voice was weak. I knew why my Fluke didn't want to relive this. I was getting weak, too. I wanted to run.

"I've had nightmares about that bridge," Red Kim said.

"Nothing like the nightmares you'll have afterwards," I said, "especially if you don't get this right." I let go of his hand. "It's Fluke. You'd *never* let anyone hurt Fluke. I'm you. I know. Go now."

I think it was *almost* too late.

The Man in Black held Fluke in a vampiric embrace. Blue flames were spurting from his eyes and a net of blue light was wrapping itself around Fluke. The Man in Black held Fluke tight. Their eyes locked. Fluke's eyes were going dead. His soul was getting drained away.

So then Red Kim rushes to the bridge. He starts pummeling the Man in Black with his fists. "Let go of him, you fucker!" The Man in Black leaned back and laughed the laughter of all movie villains. The cackling filled the night. I wanted to help. I charged at the bridge myself. Surely the two Kims could take him if one of us couldn't.

"I can handle this!" yelled Red. "He's *my* Fluke, not yours. *I'll* save him."

What followed was different than in my past. Red Kim managed to reach over and cover the man's eyes, blocking the blinding light. The light must have hurt because he immediately snatched his hand away, yelping from the pain, but those few seconds interrupted the old man's spell. Fluke twisted free and they both shoved the Man in Black against the stone side of the bridge, right in the neck, and —

His head came clean off his shoulders, vaulted over the bridge, crashed into the river!

Red Fluke and Red Kim looked at each other in horror.

You could still hear the head cackling and gurgling. They moved toward each other. I could have sworn they were going to kiss. Well, that wasn't what happened in *my* timeline! I felt a twinge of envy.

Their lips touched briefly. Then Fluke pulled away. He looked at the river. Fluke whispered, "He's dead, isn't he?"

"We killed him," Red Kim said.

"We have to tell someone."

"No."

They were going to say nothing. This traumatic moment was going to come between them for a whole year because they thought they had killed the Man in Black. Their lives were going to be miserable.

I started to shout at them: "It's okay! You didn't kill him! He's just an alien with a detachable head!" but before I even start speaking, I could feel reality whirling all around me. Everything was swimming. What was happening? Red Kim and Red Fluke were dissolving, and the only sound was the roar of the river and the cackling of the Man in Black whose head was bobbing up and down....

Polo

Just as we reached the upside-down moment —

I think Red Kim must have slammed the accelerator with both feet. Everyone was shrieking in horror. Kids were sliding down the aisle of the bus. The two nuns were hugging each other and sobbing. Pueng Pang was bawling like a baby in Tommy's arms.

For just a split second the bus was actually suspended from the ceiling of the forcefield, just like in one of those 360° roller coasters, and then —

"*Kim!*" I screamed.

Kim was dissolving. Into thin air.

My friends were dissolving. Into wisps of smoke.

The sky was shifting from day to night and back again, time running in reverse at super-speed.

The entire bus was disintegrating and — I was engulfed in shimmering blue dust. I was up in the sky, and around me, everyone was blinking out of existence.

I collapsed onto the hard floor of Mr. Strange's laboratory.

50

Cardinal in Blue

Polo

When I came to, the half of Red Polo that I had left behind was already starting to shimmer and fade.

"I guess I'm going to rejoin my other half," he said, "back in the other world."

He vanished.

Then Donut came crashing down from the ceiling. She hit the floor and was out cold.

"Leave her," said a voice. Dr. Strange, masquerading as the Haitian shaman. "Me do some magic, she come back from dream land."

I heard a banging noise. A few zombies had been put to work nailing up Mr. Strange's coffin. Dr. Strange watched, approving.

The daylight was fading into a sourceless pale glow, the normal light inside the world of the Crystal Pathway. Overhead, the ceiling was knitting itself back together, blocking out the sunlight from another world. Simultaneously, the parasol that followed Dr. Strange melted into thin air. The two Dangers heaved sighs of relief. "It was tough to maintain that for so long," Lavender Danger said.

"Long?" said *our* Danger. "They've been gone for all of five seconds."

The voice of the *houngan* came from the lips of Dr. Strange: "Me leave now. Zombies go home."

Dr. Strange's face began to whirlpool around over his skin and finally was a blur … and then the blur started to resolve into Dr. Strange again…

And slowly, our English teacher's face became more natural looking, not that Dr. Leopold Strange *ever* looked natural. "Well!" he said at last, speaking from both sides of his mouth, "I'm glad he's gone."

"Were you tired of having to say things like 'me leave now?'" Danger asked him.

"Not really," said Dr. Strange. "The way he speaks has a European vocabulary but its grammar is akin to certain African languages. Zero copula. A single pronominal form for both subject and object. From his point of view, it's *our* grammar that's weird."

"There you go again" came a familiar voice.

"Kim!" I said. They were materializing out of a blue mist.

Fluke wasn't far behind. "Dr. Strange, you know you shouldn't talk about these things in class. It only confuses the kids."

"Except you, you mean," I said. "Fucking showoff."

"Yeah," Kim said. "But now we have to ask Dr. Strange the question that's on *all* our minds."

We shouted in unison: "So, did we save the universe?"

Dr. Strange said, "Well, let's check the list. You restored the Red Timeline. If Red Kim hadn't intervened, Fluke would have been somewhat brainwashed, and he would have fallen into Crank's scheme, to use a video game as a virus to alter the reality of his universe...."

"Did that," Kim said.

"So, you saved *one* universe." He looked at us, one at a time, his eye finally settling on me. "But there are others."

I knew there had to be a catch.

"And now," Dr. Strange, "let's get to personal growth. You, Polo, have advanced a great deal   in compassion by interacting with different concepts of selfhood — from zombiehood to gender compulsion. You, Danger — both of you — have learned from each other than you are not alone in the universe. Donut, it would seem, has learned ..."

"To sleep through anything?" I said.

Donut snored.

"And Fluke?" said Kim. "And *me?*"

Kim

"I'll answer that one," came a monstrous, booming voice. It made Fluke tremble and I held him steady.

'We toppled you before," I said. "We're not afraid."

"First sign of progress, Kim!" Dr. Strange interjected.   "You've learned how to lie."

"Could be useful," I said.

Fluke and I looked up at the source of the voice, and found Dr. Strange was already bending the knee and kissing the ring. Crank was every inch the cardinal, though for some reason, he was in blue instead of red. "Like it?" he said. "His Holiness is experimenting with new colours for the clergy. The curia are very much into it, and this also keeps our newly acquired fabric and dye holdings solvent...."

"Give me a break," I said. Maybe I was getting over that stark terror that stabs me whenever I think of him. But I was kidding myself. When Cardinal Crank joked, universes tumbled.

"I'm in blue to celebrate your victory, Kim, actually. Learning how to dissemble is a major leap for one such as you."

"So what did Fluke learn, then? How to have his mind sucked out?"

Cardinal Crank laughed. "You are all creatures of primordial slime," he said, "but you amuse me. I can't wait for the next experiment."

"You're an arrogant fuck," I said.

Dr. Strange said, "Arrogant fuck, *Your Eminence*, Kim. When insulting sometime, do it with *style.*"

"Yeah, what he said," I said.

"I'll tell you what I learned," Fluke said. "I learned that you come from somewhere else, whether it's just another world, another dimension, I don't know. That you're so advanced in technology that we look like rats to you. But I also learned that you have a *need* to figure us out. We have something you don't have. Maybe it's intuition. Maybe it's foolhardiness. We leap before we think. You guys are so busy weighing all the options and calculating the moves that puny little beings like us — we can overtake you. You *need* us, Cardinal Crank, Your so-called Eminence, Sir. What's more, you *envy* us. Don't you realize that while you were trying to siphon off my mind, you were vulnerable, and I could also siphon yours? We could give a shit about your super-intellect. You're ahead of us, but you're not *better* than us. We'll get there too, one day. And when we do, we're going to use it for more than playing stupid power games with rats."

I don't think he'd ever said this much in his life, not all in one go. Well, maybe in the confessional. That was a whole 'nother story. He'd actually ranted himself into breathlessness. He looked like he'd just played a concerto.

And you know what? Cardinal Crank actually shut up.

It was Dr. Strange who spoke up. "Jolly good of you, Fluke," he said, and clapped my friend on the shoulder, which confused him a good deal. "Most of us work for him, you know; we daren't call him names."

Cardinal Crank glared at us.

His robes changed from blue to green to purple and finally settled into red, which, I knew now, was their real color. Everything else was illusion.

Finally, he grunted, "I catch you next time." And he toddled off down the hall.

"So, Dr. Strange," I said at last, "are we going to stake your brother now?"

"Well done!" said Dr. Strange.

"Come on," Fluke said. "Kim doesn't do puns."

"And I don't do fratricide," said Dr. Strange. "But there's a nice little island in the Seine where we could leave his coffin."

"Of course!" I said. "They don't cross running water."

"Full marks!" said Dr. Strange.

He beckoned to the few remaining zombies, and they lifted up Mr. Strange's coffin. They formed a strange kind of procession as they left the laboratory.

So here we were, two Dangers, unconscious Donut, traumatized Polo, infuriated Fluke, and me.

"I guess we can go home now," Fluke said.

"Yeah," said the two Dangers.

"And her?" Polo said, pointing to Donut. "We take turns carrying her?"

"Is your Dad's credit card still good?" our Danger said.

"Probably."

"That settles it," I said. "We'll spend a nice, restful night in Motel 666 and we'll all sleep off this adventure, and in the morning we'll get back to the real world."

"Real world?" Polo looked away. His eyes were distant.

"You don't want to go home?" I asked him.

"Maybe not," he said.

51

Superpowers

Danger

We carried Donut to Motel 666. Didn't have to go through the floor this time. There was a door in the back of the lab that opened up into the fridge of the Presidental Suite at the 666. We stepped out of the fridge into the luxurious room Polo's dad's credit card had paid for.

That suite hadn't changed since we left; it was like the set of one of Kim's movies, if he'd had ever made one with a real budget. Cthulus and vampires statues and a big *Exorcist* demon rearing up. But we weren't scared. We'd faced down real monsters.

We laid Donut down on the sofa.

We sat on either end of her. We knew we'd have to split up soon, the two of us Dangers, each to his own world. That was tough. I'd never met anyone quite like myself before ... until I met myself. I wanted to know so much more about my other Danger. Was his mother as superstitious as mine? Did he ever get used to wearing makeup to class?

Polo was spending a long time in the bathroom. We heard the water running. Well, he'd been fighting zombies, getting down and dirty. He still hadn't told us what happened, why Donut was unconscious, anything about the epic zombie war that was supposed to have occurred.

Our suite was as I remembered, with all the gothic movie decor.

Kim and Fluke were squashed into one armchair. They were just looking at each other, ignoring everyone else.

"I think," Lavender said, "that she probably couldn't handle the dimensional overload."

It's probably true, I was thinking. Having Donut in our world was a major difference with the other universes. She had not been in Dr. Strange's mad plan when he set up Club X in the first place. We all loved having her, and she had proved many times that she was essential to the club. But did she have a "superpower"?

"How would I know?" Donut whispered.

"Wait! You read my mind!" I said.

"She's coming to," said Lavender Danger.

She wasn't moving, and her eyes were still closed. "You don't get it," I said, "I was thinking a question, and she answered out loud."

"No," Lavender said, "it was me she talked to."

"She hasn't moved her lips," Fluke said from across the room. "But she talked to me, too."

"Hey, Lavender," I said, "we need to do one last thing together, before we split up and close the door between our worlds."

"Yeah," he said. "Sure, I'll help."

We reached out, touched hands over Donut's midriff as she lay there on her back. Her flesh was warm. She was breathing. When Lavender and I touched hands we expanded our ability to see into the ocean of consciousness.

"Are you there?" I called with my mind. I used Lavender's mind as an echo chamber.

Here, came a tiny voice in our heads. *Can you get me out?*

It's like we were at the top of a bottomless well and Donut's voice was coming from really far down. *Lower the bucket,* she said.

Lavender and I immediately saw the bucket, as though our minds had put it in place the minute she spoke about it. And we started to unreel it.

It caught on something and slowly, agonizingly, we started to wind the bucket — and Donut's soul — back up.

Kim

"What are they doing?" Fluke said. We saw the two Dangers kind of crouched over Donut, gazing into each other's eyes. "Are they doing what we're doing?"

Which was nothing, except gazing into each other's eyes. Like us. I wonder if when they looked at each other, they felt the same confusion I felt.

Then I heard a voice in my mind … and I think Fluke heard it too.

Don't be silly. They're just pulling my ti bon ange *out of the well.*

"It's Donut!" I said to Fluke. "But she's speaking a foreign language."

"Oh, well actually, *ti bon ange* is Haitian créole for one of the two types of human soul," Fluke said with his usual smugness.

"I know you know everything, you fucker," I said.

"I didn't know Donut was a telepath," he said.

"She has a superpower after all," I said.

"We didn't know that," Fluke said.

"Thank God," I said. "I hate that she sometimes felt like a fifth wheel."

"And Boom? Sixth wheel? He didn't even get to come on this adventure."

Donut started to shake. We went over to the sofa, sitting on the two arms, me behind Lavender, Fluke behind Blue. The Dangers were still concentrating on something. We leaned over and we joined our hands to theirs, I guess trying to add our energy to the Dangers' although we couldn't do a fraction of what they did.

And then, just like that, Donut sat up.

"The bus!" she said. She looked around. "It was raining zombies."

"It' okay," Fluke said, "You're home."

She was in a state. She was terrified.

Fluke went to the piano, knowing he could play and she would calm down. He played a few notes but here's the odd thing … he kind of froze up a bit,

"I can't find the right piece of music," he said softly.

"Try singing," I said to him.

Fluke sang, a wordless melody that seemed to escape his lips like a bird from a cage. And then, he fingers began to move as well, as he improvised an accompaniment, and the song he sang soared above the stream of notes, and we all started to feel what you feel when he makes music: mystery, light, love.

Donut sighed. She sat up straight. She seemed more at piece.

"So what am I thinking?" Fluke said.

"I don't know," Donut said.

"So … you have a new superpower … and it only works when you're out cold," Fluke said. "To unlock your unconscious, you have to switch of your consciousness."

Our Danger said, "Hey, if we need her to read someone's mind —"

"We'll just hit her on the head with a hammer," said Lavender Danger.

"I don't know what you guys are talking about," Donut said.

Fluke said, "I think there's gonna be a process. We have to slowly ease her into her new telepathic ability. Or she'll go crazy."

"I can't read minds. Don't wanna read them," Donut said. "Imagine how filthy you guys' minds are. But ... I have a lot of other stuff to tell you."

"Tell us," I said. "Because you know, since Fluke and I fixed the timeline, none of it really happened."

"That's not what my memories are telling me," she said. Donut told us all of it. The Zombie battle, the miraculously multiplying anti-virus powder, Red Kim being zombified and dezombified and leading the school to victory — and Sister Evangeline turning out to be a biker.

"Holy shit," I said. "Last year, we won the Rome student film award. This year, our movie's getting the Oscar!"

"Not so fast," said a voice, stepping in from the bedroom with the ensuite bathroom.

Polo was good at being a girl, but this was *convincing*. He was wearing a white negligée, just a hint of makeup, and he'd managed to reassemble his hair with a couple of braided extensions. He looked like a souped up version of Princess Leia.

"Amazed?" Polo said.

"We're always amazed," I said. "But mostly at where you got the makeup and clothes from."

"Rummaging in closets is a useful skill," Polo said. "I always go where I shouldn't. You know that."

"You're just in time," I said. "I am gonna make the greatest movie since ... since my last movie! I could even start tonight — I'll get some footage with my phone, it's 4K, better than Blu-Ray quality."

Polo said. "Nah. Zombie armies ... Crystal Pathways ... dozens of alternate universes ... the special effects would bankrupt even *my* dad, let alone yours."

"Money?" I said. "I have my friends. We just saved the universe. We have to tell the story! We need a big budget-sequel to the award-winning *Vampire in the Closet.*"

"Actually," Polo said, "You might not have me for a while. I have some unfinished business."

52

The Greatest Story Never Told

Polo

You see, when Kim said, "You mean you don't want to go home?" and I answered him "Maybe not," I became more and more sure of this.

Lavender Polo had gone missing in Lavender World and Sister Evangeline was dead there. That's how I was able to be in that world, I guess, and how Evangeline was there, disguised. And Lavender Polo and Lavender Danger had had a *thing*. I really wanted to explore that. But the main thing is, I had an adventure to come that was largely about *me*, that impacted my identity, that was to do with how I see myself and how the world sees me. This new adventure was calling to me. I wasn't ready to back to Blue yet.

So I said to the others, "I am going to spend some time in Lavender world," and I went over to Lavender Danger and gave him a peck on the cheek.

"No fair," said Blue Danger.

"It's only until I figure out where the Lavender me has gone, or whether he's actually dead, like the Lavender Evangeline. And while I'm at it, I might lead a revolution and overthrow the gender police."

"Awesome!" said Lavender Danger. "I hate the taste of lipstick in the morning."

"So ... you might have to delay filming a bit," I said.

Kim said, "Well, I can afford real actors, now. Imagine, say, Michelle Yeoh as Sister Edward. And special effects. I'll have my agent call

ILM."

The two Dangers said, "Bullshit."

Kim said, "No, no! Remember when we were like five years old, Fluke, and my parents gave you a violin, and they only gave a stupid piece of paper, and I *cried* and my jealousy crushed me for ages? That piece of paper was a fucking *bitcoin!* We're millionaires!"

Everyone started laughing at him. Even Donut.

"We *were* millionaires," Fluke said. "Bitcoin crashed."

"Bullshit," Kim said. He pulled his phone out of his shorts. He got Siri to quote crypto prices. His eyes widened.

I guess he had been so focused on the gazillion solutions to the twenty-sided Rubik that he didn't see the news, even though every high school kid in Asia has a hundred baht in crypto — it's a wilder roller coaster than any video game.

Kim said, "This doesn't mean anything. I mean, okay, they have wifi here, but it's probably wifi from an alternate universe. Doesn't mean anything *here.*"

"Yeah," I said.

"I mean like, not the real universe. Everything's an illusion," he said.

We all sort of tried to make agreeing noises. But Kim always manages to to the chase. "So no movie," he said. "And no Polo for a shit knows how long. A zombie war in another universe — that's been erased from the timeline anyway. And a telepath who can only function when she's out cold. We saved the multiverse and this is all the bragging rights we get?"

"Let's make the best of it," said Danger. "Let's raid the fridge and have a wild night of exotic food."

"Yeah, our fridge is a secret gateway to the cuisine of a million worlds," Donut said.

"Drink, too," I said. "We're not making a movie now, so no one will ever know."

"Yeah," said Lavender, "a wild, decadent teenage party full of sex and booze, just like you see on those foreign TV series."

Fluke said, "We don't do wild teenage parties, guys. Remember? We're nerds."

"Sometimes," I said, "with all the cool things we've done, it's easy to forget that."

We still managed a kind of party. It wasn't that wild. Considering all we'd done in the last twenty-four hours, it was maybe even a bit of a downer. They say nerds don't know how to be cool, but maybe being cool is overrated.

I watched while my friends took turns taking the refrigerator gateway, bringing back everything from champagne and oysters to iguana enchiladas. We probably shouldn't have been drinking, but then again, everything in this place comes out of our collective imaginations — arguably, it's all an illusion anyway.

I knew I had another journey to take, one where the outcome rested on my shoulders alone. Something I had to do. In my mind's eye I saw the guru who had visited me during my meditation vision last year, telling me to become more and more myself.

Everyone kept saying they'd miss me, and Lavender Danger kept leering and blowing kisses. I told them that I'd be back in no time. Which might be true, if I can figure out how to have the whole adventure and return to the exact moment I left.

Fluke

Everyone was passed out in that massive living room except me and Kim. It wasn't much of a party; people had been in a strange mood. I mean, we'd triumphed over evil and all.

But something was still missing.

We took off our shirts and staggered to the huge bed, turned off the lights, got comfortable. We had our backs to each other. We both stared into our own private darkness. I couldn't sleep, and I knew Kim couldn't either. He doesn't breathe the same when he's asleep. His mind was probably racing. Mine was, I know.

"You know," I said, "with all this zombie fighting and leaping from world to world, and being in the same clothes forever, I probably smell like shit."

"You do. So I guess I do too."

"We should have showered."

"Nah. Too tired."

"Yeah." Then why couldn't we fall asleep?

"Is that why you're way over on the edge of the bed, turning your nose the other way?"

"Well … you stink."

"But you're my best friend."

"Prove it."

We both turned at the same time, and that's how I found myself kissing him. I mean, for real. A hint of tongue, even. He did kind of stink, but he also smelled of our childhood, that comforting scent of a place so lived in that you don't know it's there unless you've been away from it. He held onto me really tight.

He does love me, I thought. Even though he never had a moment where he really told me so. Well, I didn't either, except that time in the confessional, when I pretended not to know that he was pretending to be Father Vichai.

Maybe this was the moment I'd been waiting for, dreaming of, longing for, all our lives. I was thinking, *I hope he doesn't include this scene in his movie. Or at least, if he does, he'll do a closeup of my ecstatic face and then tastefully fade out.*

I clung to him. He wrapped his legs around me. It was the best feeling in the universe, just knowing he needed me as much as I needed him. It was the thing that had been missing from our adventure. I could barely contain my feelings. So much was welling up inside me, ready to burst.

The moment of truth was upon us.

"I love you, Kim," I said.

"No shit," he said.

"What kind of response is that?"

"What do you want me to say? I'm non-verbal."

"I guess I'll take my shorts off now," I whispered.

"What for?"

"Let's find out."

Thank you for reading this book and for sharing my quirky visions. If you want to read more of what I've done, feel free to visit www.somtow.com, where you can even sign up for a newsletter.

If you read this on Amazon, feel free, if you are so inclined, to leave a review. You can do so by clicking right here:

https://www.amazon.com/Club-Zombie-Fridge-S-P-Somtow-ebook/dp/B03R697NZ4/

— S.P. Somtow

www.ingramcontent.com/pod-product-compliance
Lightning Source LLC
Chambersburg PA
CBHW010805250626
47156CB00010B/3001